THE BIG GUY

JASON PALMER

THE
BIG GUY

A Novel

 J P F

The Big Guy
Copyright © 2018 by Jason Palmer

This book is a work of fiction. Names, characters, places, and incidents are the product of the author's imagination or are used fictitiously. Any resemblance to actual events, locales, or persons, living or dead, is coincidental.

ISBN: 978-1-7340780-1-5

Part I
The Rook

1

Newfish used to come in on a train that ran through the yard in the old days, until a group of cons tried using it to escape. There used to be a stone wall, too, but only sections of it are still standing. I imagine how it was over a century ago when Seamax was built, when military prisoners from Fort Lew marched six miles each way for a decade to work all day building an even bigger prison. Now a chainlink fence joins the widely spaced chunks of the wall, the stone formations monuments of a time when men had physical courage. Except for a few old timers, the gun bulls today are men who have never been to war or shot at anyone who was shooting back. Everything is cheap to look good on some accountant's spreadsheet, and the hardest part of prison is the crumminess of everything, not the cold steel bars. But maybe the prisons are made to fit the prisoners. The incompetent fools and overgrown children who keep the place full today never would have tried that train. They mope around and talk about how there's no God in The Max.

I stop in a spot where the tower hack shot a convict through the neck, last year, ten feet from the fence. It's a cold morning, but I stand still and wait two minutes. At exactly seven thirty, I look up at Tower 2. There he goes: the hack steps back from the glass. He'll sit and listen to Rick Ivory talk about the fights. I went up and down the radio dial in the library to figure out what his program is, and Rick Ivory's the only thing on at seven thirty unless he's into girl talk. Rick doesn't go to commercial for at least seven minutes.

I move a few paces across the stubble near the inner fence, pretending I'm not interested. I look along the angle across the yard to the inmate door and glance back at the tower. Then I keep moving. I wind up my shoulder a little as I go – my upper arm, the size of a Christmas ham, is sore from a tetanus shot. I push around the sore spot with my fingers.

Those old-time cons who took down the train were clever, coordinated, and bloody minded. They'd attacked a well-guarded transport with caveman weapons. When the fighting started, neither side gave a quarter. Bootleggers and gangsters from New York, Chicago, and Kansas City fought pipe and knuckle with guards who'd charged across the No Man's Land into the teeth of the Kaiser's machine guns. I don't know that I've met anybody during my time here who could conceive of that. I would rather have come in on a train and been kept in by a wall, but all I've got is the shabbiness and a release date that's getting pretty tolerable. I shouldn't complain, this place is full of guys who'd give a kidney to get out of here next July.

I look around the yard and see a lot of guys playing checkers and handball, playing Mexican train with dominoes. Most of them are unfocused people who turned to crime for no real reason and who have no qualities, good or bad. Instead of figuring out how to escape, they spend their time trying to figure out how they got here. They're a lot of unfortunate souls.

The unfortunate souls step out of my way. I pass through two rows of concrete tables, the ones where I'd seen the fight that left three bodies behind when the throng scattered. That was two years ago. I stand back with my spine against the wall of the prison and look out over the yard between Industries and Tower 2, noting the locations of the lights.

Later, back in my cell, my mind will fly over the fence. Not to tropical sunsets or pretty cocktail waitresses but to white linen tablecloths and brass rails, dark coffee, well dressed strangers ignoring each other in a hotel lounge, city rain sliding off a Morse jacket with a burgundy lining, snow in my headlights on a county two-lane. In my imagination my knees touch the bottom of the steering wheel and the car rides low to the ground because I'm so big. I don't like big cars, those are for kids and hillbillies.

There's an obvious problem with this new habit of mine: you don't start planning an escape with sixteen months to go on a nickel. But there's a reason for this. There's a guy missing from the yard, this morning. They call him the Rook. And if I'm the biggest guy around today, it's only because Rook is in the hole, and I may have had something to do with that. I tear my gaze from the double fence and the open field beyond to look at a group of men to my right - Rook's guys.

They look a little lost without him, but they won't have to wait long.

He'll be back on the yard again soon.

Castles get the drugs on Tuesdays. Praxlatan to shrink my muscles, Defenerin to prevent water retention. The normals - decks, in prison - spot my small testicles in the showers and see that the hacks are scared enough to drug me.

I look at the barbell as it bends into a frown between thick stacks of Weider plates, my knuckles full of white half moons from hefting the four hundred fifty pounds off my chest. Two sets of fifteen. I can feel the sore spot on my upper arm from the tetanus shot but it doesn't interfere with the movement. My deck stands around the weight bench with hands on their hips, regular cons straining to belong with me. A lot of guys are in the weight pile today, their wet and hollow odor filling the large space. It's April. Cold outside.

I set the barbell back on the rack slowly so it doesn't sheer through the screws and come down on my face. This cheap equipment isn't built for a castle like me. I sit up and tilt my head around, moving lazy between sets like a boa constrictor. After three and a half years of this weight pile (and not much else), I am musclebound. When I pass, the gun bulls look between me and their rifles, wondering if they shouldn't have more firepower, just in case.

On the outside, I mostly think about staying fit and trim, and I'm practically a vegetarian.

Just as I'm laying down for another set, a guy from Rook's deck walks past and says in this sing-song voice, "Rook's outta the hole in three weeks, Croft." He holds three fingers over my face and a guy in my own deck slaps his hand away like I needed his help. Another one bumps shoulders with him when he's trying to leave, looks are exchanged, tattoos twist on their necks as they follow each other with their eyes.

If I was some deck shotcaller they'd ask me if I'm going to put up with that, but they know better than to try putting me on the spot.

I pass fifteen reps and then twenty. From somewhere around me comes a low whistle.

I rack the weight again and sit up. I turn my left fist so the veins of my wrist face the floor and flex my arm, looking along it. All that muscle looks like it ought to be of some use, but the Rook...I can still hear the thunder of the whole block chanting his name the time he broke Figueroa's back over a railing and then pounded his own chest so hard I swear it rippled the water in my toilet. And Figueroa was a bad castle. The Rook's so bad that his deck is safe even with him in the hole, at least for a while. The guy who flashed his fingers in my face goes to stand with the others, all sporting tats of the rook chess piece on their shoulders, laughing and taking it easy.

Rook is that bad.

And I'm the one who got him sent to the hole. It will be a week tomorrow.

After six a.m. count, we go to chow. It involves a lot of standing and waiting. Civilian supervisors don't come in till eight, so there's extra time to kill after breakfast. I hit the weight pile for an hour and a half before work call, then head to my job in Industries. The building sits in the southwest corner of the yard and looks like any other industrial building anywhere, fitted with smokestacks that look like filter cigarettes. The morning sky looks like it came out of the smokestacks. There's a fence around the building, but the hacks don't bother with the metal detector at the gate as I go in to work. That's for the way out. Other cons come off the line outside the fence and head to the furniture factory, the motor pool, or the sweatshop where they stitch together uniforms.

"Popeye" McNeeley is the civilian shift supervisor in the furniture factory, and I head to his office. I'm a Quality Assurance monitor. I get the clipboard – something which always inspires awe and mistrust in other cons, no matter what it's for – and start looking over the machines. I have eight hours to do a job that takes about forty-five focused minutes, but since I'm not focused today, it takes longer. As I move along the floor making sure there are no materials inside the lines of yellow tape around the machines, I consider the reasons why I don't have more of an escape plan. Some of them are good reasons. I've kept to myself, kept my nose clean: no hacks on a roll, no business, no gangs, no connections to squeeze. That doesn't trouble me. But there's another difference between me and the decks. They turn into animals, on the Inside, wound tight as human mousetraps, but the opposite can happen to a castle: some of his lights go out. The thought brings a suspicious squint to my eyes. I point my way along the factory machines with a pencil, checking cables and connections and looking for oil leaks or smoke.

When I've finished my job, I do McNeeley's reports because the man doesn't understand percentages or division. Even with a calculator the size of a dinner tray to do it for him, he would have to understand what he's dividing. This also takes me longer than usual, today. The furniture factory grinds out about ninety thousand wholesale dollars' worth of finished products each month, about three grand a day: it's not going to take over Wall Street anytime soon. Around noon, Popeye pokes his head into his – my – office (he knows to keep out while I drink his coffee and do the reports, and usually some sketching of my own), to ask if I'm almost finished. His buzz cut makes him look like an overinflated ten-year-old.

"Almost finished," I say.

He hesitates in the open door. "You okay, Croft?"

I'm distracted but say I'm fine. The more I'm thinking, the less I'm talking. There's a good yardstick to measure by.

I almost forget to take a metal ruler out of my pocket before getting in line for the detector on the way out. I cross the yard back to the main complex at quitting time, thinking about that ruler (stupid fish mistake) with a clenched jaw and fists, thinking of where it could have sent me and who would have been waiting for me there.

My head isn't right. I'm not in the game. That's how bad things happen.

I'm at the commissary later that afternoon, buying paper and nub pencils and mouthwash and a magazine, and I've calculated the $8.37 before the old timer behind the register can punch it in with his index fingers. Cons are allowed only thirty dollars in cash each month, to prevent extortion, and my pay from the furniture factory goes directly to my commissary account. It's pennies on the hour, but I have few needs here. I notice the con behind me checking out my purchases, and I turn to eye him. I know from his bright-eyed look he's about to get cute.

"You might as well burn the rest of those clams, big dog, or else you could give 'em to some righteous brother like yours truly, if there's nothin' else you got to have in here." He puts a little extra twang in his accent, which is neither South nor West but Yard.

He's saying I'm going to be killed, but it's his rat-slang that bothers me. I settle my flat look on him.

"I have no idea what you just said."

He flushes with anger, but what's his anger to me? His lover - a small Latino with that wet-eyed look - is there behind him, tugging on his arm and hustling him out of the store. I hear them fighting outside because of the stupid risk he just took with me. I'm not dead yet.

I gather my purchases and spend a few seconds just standing in the doorway while they fade down the corridor. It's only going to get worse. Hell of a situation to come along with barely over a year to go. The question now is whether there's a way to stay and deal with it or whether it's time to write off the three and a half years I've stacked and try to bust out.

After dinner, I'm back at the weight pile doing curls with a dumbbell like a pair of wrecking balls. With each movement the sore spot on the outside of my arm tells me it's still there. My deck stands around with their arms folded on their chests, observing my muscles and staring down everybody who passes by. This pattern is repeated all over the room: castles on a weight machine surrounded by six or eight guys circled up like hardhat crews.

I watch my arm and the dumbbell moving up and down in its arc. Technically, some deck iron freaks might curl this much, but I didn't have to eat six steaks a day for a year to get it, just three squares of sloppy prison chow. And that was with the Praxlatan slowing me down. I'm not a freakshow like the Rook, but I'm definitely a case. It's strange looking at all this weight, the decks probably thinking how massive it is, and how it still won't matter.

Shivs aside, some other weapons that wouldn't work on the Rook: rat tail (books twisted into a sheet); slock: soap, batteries, or padlocks in a sock. For Rook I'd need a barbell or a ten-pound wrench. Or a lot of other things way too big to conceal that would get me sent up to the Disciplinary Officer, who could send me to the hole and take away my good time.

Nick Karoulas, one of the guys in my deck, finishes a conversation across the room and gets my attention. He waits for me to finish a set of curls, says, "Croft, I have to tell you something."

I say nothing, just wait for him to talk.

"There's this new guy asking a lot of questions about you."

I don't want to hear this, now. How could it be anything good?

"Who."

He tilts his chin at a group of cons talking around an inclined bench, and I can't tell which one of them he means and don't bother asking. "This guy Bread. Transfer from Chesworth. He's asking what you'd do to change your situation."

Sounds like a setup or a scam. I ask, "He a snitch?"

Chesworth is a state prison. A lot of convicts are transferred from state prisons for their own protection. He probably is a snitch or a pedophile. The rare third alternative is that he's a boatload of trouble.

Nick shakes his head. "No. He's in the Book."

So it's something I couldn't guess about or he's a boatload of trouble.

"Tell him to get lost," I say.

I start another set of curls, focus on breathing, and I think about Rook. I should be working the larger muscle groups, doing squats and bench press, building some explosive speed. Maybe then I could do a double-leg takedown with a little hip hoist and put him on his back. Doubt it, but you never know.

When I move to get a drink of water, the decks clear out of the way. A new guy isn't paying attention and the older con next to him smacks him in the arm and tilts his chin at me. The young guy has to pile into him to get out of the way, and the old con has a good time telling him what could have happened, low enough so I don't hear.

The odds on Rook making jelly out of me when he's out of the hole three weeks from tomorrow are about fifty to one and getting worse.

Fucking decks. Never any peace with them around.

C Block is taller, narrower, and longer than the other cell blocks, built years later with a cathedral ceiling and an extra tier. The windows look out on B and D blocks only a few feet away. The narrow east wall of C Block is one of the few places in Seamax where the wall of the building is also the wall of the prison. If it had a window, you'd see the prairie grass bending in a cold breeze. Prisons and slaughterhouses get built in the middle of nowhere.

Hours after lockdown, I'm in my bunk listening to the thunder outside. I feel the latent power of all the sleeping castles in C Block, where we make up almost a third of the population. Story is the hacks wanted all the castles in one block so there'd be at least one quiet no-bullshit place in the prison. Because of our physical dimensions, we don't have cellmates.

A guard walks past my cell, never bothering to look inside. The graveyard shift is a skeleton crew of newjacks, hacks that need extra cash, and some that just melt in the sun. The hack who passed my cell looked like a six-foot pile of ashes. At some lonely hour, a third-shift hack will stroke his prematurely white stubble and tell you with a greenish smile

how he's finally adjusted to the schedule. How he's a real
night owl, now.

I can't sleep, and I turn under the sheets. Outside it
would be a good night to go down to the lounge for a
nightcap, listen to the piano player and keep company with
the other insomniacs. Instead I sit the dark and calculate like
a big roach.

Twenty-two months total minus six months good time
and work credit. Sixteen more months left, then out - free
and clear. Last year, my first parole board basically told me to
forget parole because of my high-profile crime, which made a
lot of newspapers at the time. There's a sensitivity about
getting on the news and crimes that shake people up where
they live. Not a whole lot of paroling going on, anyway.
Seamax is an end of the line, throw-away-the-key kind of
joint. So far I haven't had to do anything that would add to
my sentence or get me a new conviction, but that comfort is
coming to an end.

Midnight is the last time of day with a name. What's that
tell you? There is no light, outside; my window is completely
black except for the strobes of the passing storm. I sit on the
edge of my bunk flexing my useless biceps, and the silent
shocks of lightning show me veins like Canadian
nightcrawlers. Sure I'm big, but Rook, he's on a whole
different scale. Early each morning, when he pounds the walls
in solitary, I can hear it up here. It's probably just the
bulldozers wrecking down the old sawmill, but lately guys I
don't know like to walk past me when the ground is
trembling and say, "Hear that, Croft? Rook don't sound too
happy." They like the idea that they just talked some shit to a
castle.

I can see the cells on Tiers 2 and 3, animal cages for
uninteresting beasts. I feel more separate from it all than

usual. I don't know whether that's because I've been thinking about the outside or because I'm marked. I didn't snitch, exactly, but some hardline cons might think what I did was the next thing to it. Rook was found guilty of an administrative violation – a prison rule that's not exactly a law – and sent to the hole. At some point along the line, I was involved. A deck probably wouldn't get the benefit of the doubt, but then a deck you can kill with a toothbrush.

Rook...he's the reason a paranoid screw like Hurley keeps a pump twelve gauge taped under the desk in the lieutenant's office. When I think about that, I know it's hopeless.

I feel around the bottom of my mattress for a tiny bulge where red muscle-shrinking Praxlatan and yellow diuretic Defenerin pills are hidden in case I need to pass a random test. They can drug us enough to kill and stuff into an oversized coffin, but they can't turn a case into a deck. Sooner or later they'll notice I'm getting bigger, and they'll use that metal nozzle to *shoot* the pills down my throat, leaving behind this cold little white cloud and the metallic smell from the CO_2 cartridge. I'm just hoping they don't notice right away.

Maybe I'm imagining another few pounds of muscle will make some kind of difference. Still, it's something to do other than wait while I come up with a better plan. I lift up a corner of my mattress and drop it again like a dead thing. My bed looks like a wrestling ring and feels like a frying pan.

I lay back down on my side and tell myself the distant thunder isn't the pounding of Rook's fists against the walls down solitary. Then I fall asleep and dream I'm trying to strangle a dog that's biting me, but its neck is like a bundle of anchor ropes

.

2

The "Book" is a photo album containing mugshots of convicts who have attacked guards, attempted escape, and murdered other convicts in prison. It's kept up to date so that guards new to the prison will know who to watch out for, know them by sight. Being in the Book is a status symbol for mainline cons – anyone in it has proven he is unafraid of punishment. Turns out Bread is in the Book.

He's there the next day watching me work out, and I keep an eye on him. I realize I've seen him in my vicinity a lot, lately, and maybe that is no coincidence. I just hadn't noticed him until Nick pointed him out to me. I can see why they call him Bread: his head and hairline are shaped like one end of a sugar loaf, a sort of heart shape above a smart, flat face. My mind is on my own problems, though, and Bread and his questions about me are like fine hairs in a filmstrip. I see him in snippets, pacing back and forth with one finger on his lower lip while the others just wait around in case I need a spot. In over three years I haven't needed one, but that doesn't discourage them.

I'm staring at 1500 pounds of metal plates pistoning up and down on the leg press and wondering at how I can be so strong and still afraid of someone so much stronger. It's like a nightmare. The decks get to be spectators, no points to be gained smashing them up because it's so easy. I pump my legs so hard that I can feel my pulse in my sinuses and experience a partial blackout of my vision with each beat of my heart. If I was to go violently crazy in this moment, I would see a series of bloody strobes featuring broken limbs and running guards. The feeling in my head is just like being on a train passing close by another train.

My deck, I don't even know all their names. They recruit among themselves and then bring the new guy around to see what I'll do. I'm sure they scare the shit out of him first, talk about how I tore a guy in half for hooking his thumbs through his belt when he talked to me, or something else that sounds just stupid enough to be true. Fact is, all the recruits do is get messed with and go around talking about everything their castle's going to do when he finds out. But when Bread finally opens up *his* trap, he comes right out and says,

"Croft. Look at me."

I'm just getting ready to lean back on the military press and do the whole stack of ten-pound plates one arm at a time, but now I stop and look up through the tops of my eyes, sort of like a tiger.

"I should tell you, I've been telling people you have a big loot stashed in a lot off the Interstate."

I'm floored. My deck usually knows enough to leave me alone, and they damn sure know about making things up. I don't like them talking about me when it's true, much less made up. They all go quiet and dim.

Bread smiles. "I thought it was better you heard it from me."

I just look at him. He looks ordinary except for his unusual hairline. His clothes and shoes are mainline. The first thing any con with means will do is get a pair of babyshoes to walk around in, so Bread either has no money or doesn't go for the usual thing.

"Because this way, we might get some guards on your roll. Know what I mean? Could get Rook a little extra time in the hole. If he was to mouth off to a guard or threaten to kill the warden, for example."

I realize the guy is so deep in my business that I'm actually a little unnerved by him. I didn't see this coming: too ballsy. Crazy, even.

I'm staring at Bread, waiting for him to look away. I wonder what I'll do to him with a distant curiosity. It doesn't come up too often.

"Don't tell me you never thought of that? I heard you were a pretty decent crook."

Now, I do appreciate when people acknowledge I'm a crook and not just some neck popper. So instead of really trying to scare the guy, I blow air through my nostrils and start to lean back into the military press again.

"Tell you what," he says.

I stop again.

At this point, the men around us and several people passing by are looking at Bread like he just exposed himself to a female hack. Certain castles are a little more casual with the decks. I'm not one of them.

"You let me mention your name to some people, and I'll go right down to solitary and take a piss all over the Rook. Right now. Then we'll talk some more."

I look away for a minute, then say, "You'll piss on the Rook. You."

"Right through the chuck hole."

I give a dry little chuckle with no humor in it. The rest of the deck are looking back and forth between me and Bread like we're a tennis match. They seem to be nothing but eyes. "How are you going to do that?"

"First tell me whether I can use your name. Percy Croft, the crook with the buried loot."

He wouldn't do it even if he was willing to get himself sent there. Bread doesn't strike me as a suicide. I say, "Why do I want you to piss on the Rook?"

"To see if I will."

I take my time, like for a minute I forgot he was there. Then I say to him, "It's you, not me."

"Right."

And with that he picks up a ten-pound dumbbell, walks straight over to Rook's deck still smiling at each other near the chin-up bars, and whacks the hell out of the man who'd waved his fingers in my face. Hits him right over the ear with a clang I can hear thirty feet away.

They all jump him then, elbows and heels pistoning in that ineffectual way decks have, until the hack on duty hits the panic button on his radio and goes in swinging his sap. A minute later, they drag Bread's limp form out of the room.

For now, that seems to wrap it up. I towel off and don't think much more about Bread, except to feel a subtle new tremor of disturbance in an already bad situation.

I shower and find myself standing directly across from an old con with distended balls, like a pair of eggs over easy in a greasy paper bag. I let the hot water strike the knots tightening at the base of my skull and close my eyes. I try to measure the nineteen days left of Rook's segregation against the sixteen months I have left in prison, like there's some way of thinking about it that will make me realize it's too close to call and nineteen days practically *is* sixteen months. I'm sure it will feel that way to the Rook.

At least the heat and water pressure is good in the new showers, even if it looks like a brand new killing floor for hogs. Before Rook went to the hole, this place hadn't felt so much like a prison as it had a shabby dentist's waiting room. I wonder whether this is what prison is like for the decks all the time, but decide this is probably worse.

What gets me is that, massive as he is, the Rook wouldn't stand a chance against me on the outside. A lot of the scariest guys in Seamax would just shrivel up out in the real world. It makes me angry when I think of it that way. They don't *deserve* to beat someone who can make it. In a sane environment, they wouldn't even exist.

Willie surprises me when he tells me I have to kill Bread. I'm surprised that, with everything he knows about my situation, that one detail, Bread, is the one he seizes on. And he won't let it go. "That clever boy sees your situation. Gonna try to turn the tables on you, Raw. Probly thinks he's gonna pimp you out fo muscle."

With a little square of mirror I can see Willie's huge black hands gripping the bars of his cell and his rheumy old eye. In the dark, he's the color of shadow. My deck wouldn't tolerate a black among themselves, but try telling a castle like me that he's crossing the line. Go ahead.

"How do you know?"

"They's decks like to paint castles as stupid because it gives them a role," said Willie. "They delegate themself your mouthpiece and make trouble for you. Don't like you to be the brains of your own operation. Specially a crook like you."

It would take a ballsy SOB to try something like that. Hasn't been a problem so far, maybe because I've cultivated a reputation for being sly and mean. "Ever happen to you?"

Willie doesn't seem to hear. It's unusual to see him so worked up. "He going to go around talking about how Croft's the number one castle, build you up, but also, between-you-and-me like, say you couldn't find your ass without him."

"So I gotta kill him?"

Willie's uses his old-dog voice. It's the way you'd think a basset hound would sound if one could talk. "They's lots of uses fo a deck. Only one use fo a case like you. In they mind, you like a prossitute that won't fuck. Don't know your place. Don't work f'no one. You think they goan let you be, now?"

Most convicts know very few things for sure, but what they know, they know. Some of them can barely tie their shoes without a manual, but they have the genius of vultures and jackals when it comes to being marked. I always wonder, where is that level of insight when they make every other decision of their lives? The worst part: not all of them are decks.

There are two spots in the chow hall favored by convicts with influence: under the high windows on the far end, and near the door. Castles sit at their own tables near the door. The morning after Bread made his proposition, I notice a few guys from a certain table under the windows looking in my direction. Red eagles tattooed on their upper arms poke out from their sleeves. Full members of the Skins also have the large eagle across their backs, outlined in red and the rest filled in with the same blue-green ink used on prison forms. They're stealing glances in my direction.

From the moment the guards clapped bracelets on the Rook, it's only been a matter of time.

Everyone knows my situation, and they all figure if I'm not dead within the month, somebody's going to own me. No surprise to anyone that the vultures are circling. They figure I'll need cover, but there aren't many who could stop the Rook even if they had a reason to: maybe the Skins, probably Vanderventer, but even they couldn't stop him directly. Not the Rook. They'd work through the system. That's how they'd figure to get me owing them my life.

Sitting across from me are yet another pair of red eagles, this one on a huge pair of castle shoulders. I'm sure the hacks thought about transferring Blake when he joined the gang. The idea of a big case with the eagles must have scared them bad, but the gang's been smart enough not to put him out front. Blake sees me glancing at the table under the windows and smiles. He's always made an effort to be friendly to me, the way someone does who's waiting for the right moment to try and sell you religion. He's never talked to me about the Skins, yet, but I have a feeling that's about to change. He's got something in his teeth, and he's waiting until we're alone.

Soon convicts begin to trickle out one and two at a time, then the hacks close the chow hall and the long line forms to leave. Blake makes sure he's next to me while we wait to shuffle slowly out. He doesn't say anything right away, but I can feel him working up to it. Then he doesn't quite touch my arm. "Hey, Raw."

"Yeah."

"How you been holding up, man?"

He's got that blank intensity of someone who could only be a waif, a criminal, or a tent revivalist. In the body of a bear wrestler.

"You know I'd like to help you out. What are you going to do?"

"I'll work it out."

"I'm just sorry we can't get together on it, man. We've been keeping an eye on the situation, but you know how it is."

"Yeah."

Blake's walking half out of line so he can talk around my shoulder, but a passing hack doesn't bother him about it.

"I've been talking with the Brothers, trying to work something out."

Maybe he's still got his blinders on, thinks the Skins are about something. They'll get a convict various chemical furloughs like inhalers and other pharmaceuticals, everything but narcotics. Vanderventer owns those. A regular racket of theirs is to corner a fish and take everything he's got. Then they'll beat him bloody and say, 'Welcome to The Max.' Then he can buy his things back at a big markup.

The line separates by cell block, and once we're back inside C Block, Blake is free to talk to me face to face. He looks concerned, and it looks strange on him. He's in his forties but still has the overheated born-to-lose metabolism and the strange innocence of a much younger psychopath. I can tell he's not going to leave me alone.

"I have a number you can call," he says. "Best I could do."

"A number?"

He hands me a rumpled piece of lined paper torn from a notebook. On it are ten digits, no dashes. The numbers are large in a fast, square hand, like he probably prints only in capitals.

"Call and talk to this guy, have someone get him the fee. Sorry it can't be a favor."

"Appreciate that. I'm alright."

"Hey, man…"

I want to get out of this conversation. Soon he'll ask me how I feel about the Skins, and I can't afford more enemies, now. If they make a serious approach, I'm not sure I can thread that needle.

I say, "Thanks, anyway," and start to walk away.

"But the Rook."

I know. He can't imagine what my plan could possibly be. Once I'm out of sight in my cell, I crumple the paper in my fist and flush it. Only suicides and drama queens believe things couldn't be any worse.

The Skins aren't an unexpected development for Willie, and I can feel him nodding in response when I tell him about it that night after lockdown. It's amazing the range of expression you learn to sense from the man in the next cell even though you can't see him: frowns, shrugs, nods, like it's right in front of you. Willie's one conceit is his big blue babyshoes. I can see the tips of them if I put my head to the bars.

"Blake stupid?" he says.

"He's no genius."

"He lookin for a daddy? Cause it don't matter how big they are."

"No."

He was quiet a minute. Then: "Sho. First they cain't do nothin for you. But then they come back at you with, Maybe if you was one of them."

"Blake says he's pushing them to help me out."

Willie only laughs.

"I know. But he's always had a thing about me. Thinks he's my kid brother."

"Then he just the one to send. But you think he won't turn on you like that-." Willie snaps his big fingers so I can hear it loud and crisp. "You been eatin cockroach bait. They cain't do nothin for you cause they waitin for you to ask *them*. They just come around to get you thinkin. Then they play the fool."

"What if they ask me?"

"Everybody in this place knows you on the wrong end of things, now. They ask you and you say no, then they been dissed by a bitch. That's how they see it."

"Yeah? How many of them have to die before they get over it?"

"One. You handle what's comin, yourself. Live dangerous. Get a six-inch blade and stick it in the Rook a few times."

"And wind up in here for another twenty?"

"That's goan happen anyway, now. Probly this smart deck goan do it to you."

That's like a slap in the face. It seems like a hell of a leap. I have to recover for a second, then say, "It's not him I'm worried about."

"This deck mouth got plans fo you. 'Sides, you kill the first one, the other ones goan stay away."

"There's no way to let the Skins down easy?"

But all Willie wants to talk about is Bread.

Months from now, I'll reflect on how right he was.

I wake up in the dark, but I know it's almost dawn. Must have been the noise of the kitchen staff getting unlocked, which puts it around 4:30. I lay awake for twenty minutes before giving up and getting out of bed. I press the round button over my sink and bring the cold water to my face and then sit heavily again on my bunk to wait the hour and a half until 6 a.m. count. I don't know what I want time to do: speed up? Freeze like a second-storey man in a spotlight?

At five minutes to six, I stand up and move to the bars, and I look out. I know they think my being in prison is just the usual castle willingness to be incarcerated, the indifference to freedom. In reality, the point is to get out free and clear, if I can, with no legal encumbrances. After that? I'll never get caught   again.

The Skins watch me again at chow, and I know it's coming. Across the table, Blake stares into his food, clearly thinking about what he's not saying. He doesn't hide himself well, and I distantly wonder who he killed to earn his bones. After chow, I go to the weight pile for an hour as usual, and the place feels conspicuously empty - so much that I wonder if I've forgotten something, like a holiday. Guys in my deck keep together more than usual. I keep watching the door, but no one shows up.

I shower and then grab a few minutes to myself in the yard before work. The cons covering the benches and tables like pigeons, playing out the perpetual games of checkers and Mexican train, are already starting to drift toward Industries. I start to think it won't come today. That's when I spot them moving through the yard in my direction, against the tide. It's Blake and a ginger-haired deck called Blister, shirt tied around his waist, with the full-sized red eagle across his back. They do that sometimes, to show off the eagle for a few minutes before a hack tells them to put their state-issue back on. I take a breath and don't watch them come. One jackpot leads to another. They look serious enough to lay out the whole thing, right now: 'This monster is going to kill you without connections, but you don't want to smear shit on yourself by talking to us? I want to hear you say it.'

Something like that.

The Skins do things no one else does. Last year, they killed a deputy state director of corrections at his house in Kansas. Rumor is there's a special area of Mount Washington just for them, where Brothers who've killed guards are supposedly starved and prevented from sleeping with bright lights. Convicts call it Skinmax.

I'm supposed to be working on busting out.

Blister hangs back a little and lets Blake take point. Maybe Blake told him we're friends.

"Hey, Croft."

I turn back in their direction. They're smiling and friendly.

Blake says, "Good news, brother. I was able to plead your case. The Brothers definitely have some sympathy for your situation, man."

I nod. Blister is looking at me more keenly than Blake is but trying not to show it.

Blake says, "You can throw away that phone number." He taps the round of my shoulder. "I know you got no ink, man. How would you like some?"

I say, "I was planning on keeping a clean hide. In case someday I want to be a cop."

Blake turns toward Blister. "That's just his sense of humor. Croft's a righteous con."

"That's good," says Blister. "A lot of these guys take themselves too serious."

That's what his mouth says. From his eyes, you'd think we were strangers trying to pass each other on a highwire. He wants my answer. Other cons still on the yard know exactly what this conversation is.

Blake says, "Are you up for talking to some guys today? If it goes well, I think we can help with your problem. Take care of it ourselves."

I look off into the distance. Maybe they think I'm considering their offer.

Blake says, "What do you say, brother?"

"A few more months and I'm out. Clean."

Blister's smile fades. He says, "You want to get out all at once though. Not a piece at a time."

"Appreciate the interest," I say. "Let me sleep on it."

"This is serious, man."

"That's why I want to sleep on it."

With no expression, he walks away. A lot of tough cons would chase after him at this point, beg for the chance to do what he wants if it will erase the disrespect.

Blake runs his hands up and down the long, coiling snake tattoos on his forearms with a rasping sound. "You know, I never wanted to join a gang. I was one man, and I was a case. That was what mattered. And then I got in a situation. My Brothers gave me a way out. That's why there's loyalty. There's family."

That's when the work call buzzer goes off. Blake claps my shoulder and goes off to work. I stay where I am, watching them both go. They'll be back because they know I have no real plan. And next time, they'll come at me harder. Maybe I should have asked for a pigsticker and said I was going to take care of Rook myself, like Willie said.

I try to feel sure that Willie is wrong about it already being too late, that things have gone around that corner and getting out next year is a pipe dream already growing small behind me, and it's just a question of who I'm going to do the time for - if I stick around.

Blake's large form is still distinct a long way off. Take care of Rook themselves? I probably saved their lives.

I'm shooting hoops in the yard when Bread finally shows up again. He's got a week of stubble and a gray, sagging face. They must have thrown him in a box after he pulled his stunt. My deck is standing in a semicircle on the basketball court, catching my rebounds while I shoot monotonously from the foul line. I think of telling them that's why backboards were invented, but if they want to stand there, fine. With only a week to go before Rook gets out, I'm not capable of much more than bouncing a ball while I try to think. When Bread walks over, the others part for him. I palm the ball. I notice distantly that the sore spot from the tetanus shot is gone.

I say, "I hear someone pissed on the Rook."

"I didn't get much out before they dogpiled me."

I try not to act too interested but give myself away by talking out of the corner of my mouth: "What did he do?"

Bread flips a coin and covers it on the back of his hand. He glances over at a group of blacks loud-talking each other on the other end of the court and says, "Charged the door. Grabbed at anything he could. Too bad it was a hack's sleeve. They put him in a box. See what a couple of weeks in there does for him."

"Weeks?"

"Sprained the hack's arm before the sleeve ripped off." He holds up a pair of fingers. "Did it with just two fingers."

This is disturbing for a couple of reasons. First because it probably adds to whatever Rook is planning on doing to me, and second because it's a box. Black as death. Underground.

It's a good thing for Rook that he didn't get a firm hold on the hack's wrist and shatter it.

Bread gets right down to business like he didn't just spend a week in a box. No yard talk about how fucked up the system is. "I can lay down a few thousand bucks of my own to grease the wheels, but these guys will shake me down without protection. I'll say it's yours. You've got someone on the outside funneling it to you."

I stare at him because now I see it: he'd been transferred here because there wasn't enough coffee in the world for them to deal with him at Chesworth.

"Think about it, Croft. It would take me months to organize an operation and protection to use what I've got set aside. If it's yours, nobody fucks with it and nothing slides. And you've got ready-made soldiers. I have a supplier on the outside just waiting for a call."

He speaks well, not like a convict. Good elocution, but there's also something greasy about it. Usually I can tell if a guy is educated, but I'm not sure about Bread. He's somewhere between a personal injury lawyer and a fry cook, but I have no idea where. I bounce the ball a couple of times and set like I'm going to shoot, then bounce it a couple more times. I look around the yard and realize I'm unconsciously looking for red eagles. Maybe that's why I haven't already told this crackpot deck to peddle his wolf tickets someplace else.

I take the foul shot, and the ball bounces wide off the rusty red rim. Pratt chases it down and stands there holding it to his chest, not sure whether he should toss it back to me yet because I'm in a conversation.

"How much do you bench?" Bread says. He flips the coin again. "Troy does five fifty."

If Bread could afford to flip a few thousand bucks to make a lot more, he might be able to *buy* Rook more time in the hole. Maybe. And it would be his writeup, not mine, if someone didn't take the bribe. If it's him handing out cash instead of me using a pigsticker, he assumes all the risk.

Bread waits for my answer with his eyes.

I experience a fleeting feeling that's like a woman blowing on dice in my palm when I don't exactly want to roll. I turn away and say, "I can top that." And just like that, I'm around a corner and into something new. It was easy.

"I know. Get it up to six hundred. They have to talk about it."

It sounds like an order, but he doesn't backpedal from my warning look. Guy pissed on the Rook – doesn't make him tough, but it does make him a kind of absolute reality, someone you can't ignore.

"I'm already stashing Prax. I'll get tested any time."

"I'll take care of it."

"You?"

"One catch. You work for me."

That cuts the thread of my curiosity and gets me seeing red. I know what a deck sees when he looks at me and what they'd ask me to do. Not calculus. I don't pop necks. I'm a crook, and a good one at that.

"You work for me."

The repetition of his statement, the confidence in his voice, as if he's manipulating a dumb animal. I start circling closer to him on the court and looking around to see where the hacks are. It's that look around that lets most cons know the situation is serious. Everyone but Bread takes a step back.

We're in plain view of the gun bulls in the towers. With the glare of the sun, no way to tell whether they're watching. Still I stop close behind Bread and my eyes run along the fragile bones across the tops of his shoulders. I begin to raise a hand that I'll place on his right shoulder to force him down to his knees. It's a strange age we live in, where the pride is regarded less than the backbone, but I can break one without a felony rap.

Bread talks over his shoulder to me. "Rook gets out in less than two weeks. You remember, the guy who lifts tractors?"

This sounds like a threat. The guys in my deck seem to agree because they go pale.

I lay my palm on his shoulder. It's just warm bones. "Sorry," I growl, "Self employed."

"We could run this place. I've already had a couple of conversations, and there's some interest."

With that, his gaze shifts slowly to his right, and I follow it across the yard until I'm looking at a guard named Phister. He's looking right back at me. I drop my hand from Bread's shoulder, and the heat of it stays in my palm for a moment.

Bread talks low enough so that only I can hear, rotating in slow circles, not looking at me. "Everybody's going to want a piece of your action. You're the strongest with Rook in a box. We won't have any problems. With the deals I'll set up, the loot will be real in no time."

Willie is right. I do want to get rid of this guy. He might try and stop himself, but I can see he's going to argue with me if I say No. Nervy deck.

I say, "Last I heard, somebody already runs this place."

He moves into pharmaceuticals, the Skins will eat his face. Narcotics, and Vanderventer will take him out if he does more than a trifling business.

"And somebody ran it before him. We'll start small."

I'm still aware of Phister. At first I thought he was just watching, but now I realize he has an interest in my response. Already on Bread's roll? Is this a more interesting conversation than I'd thought? Hacks aren't hard to buy, but you have know who to approach. Bread must work fast, in his way. He hasn't been here long. Who is he? A crazy person can come across as energetic and assertive, and he might not say the one thing that gives him away for days or weeks. It happens. Could be a lot of other things, too. Prison is full of irritated pride and delusions that make men exaggerate, lie, and take credit where none is due. Other hand, Bread has the merit of being about money and not some convict creed (and money) with a lifetime commitment.

The boys in the deck don't know what to make of it when I don't tell Bread to get lost. He looks at a watch, says, "Think it over," then walks off and curls a finger at them. They look around at me and at each other, thinking of their own problems, sniffing opportunity, then follow him like the zombies they are. The guy holding the ball can see I don't want it, and he bends and sets it on the ground like it's an egg, in a crack where it won't roll away.

I'm standing near the fence and looking out a few minutes later when Nick Karoulas comes sauntering back. Of all the guys in my deck, Nick has at least a pair of wits to rub together.

He starts talking before I ask. "Well, he's not crazy. Not that I can tell. Friend of a friend in Chesworth says he's actually pretty sharp."

"What was he into?"

"I don't know. When I tried bringing it up, guy suddenly had to be someplace."

He gives me a significant look.

"Does he know how to be careful?"

"He wants to meet tomorrow morning in the old showers, talk about his plan. Wants to spend his own money, what do you care, right?"

A pair of wits. Not much more.

"So, what do you say? See where it goes?"

Sounds like someone wants to give it a try.

It's a longshot this isn't just another prison pipedream, even if Bread is in the Book. You can get in the Book by biting a hack's ear while shitting yourself. But if he turns out to be even half legitimate, at least I might get out of the rain for a little while – until Vanderventer kills him and his brother Eddie turns him into a lampshade. Maybe I can set aside the genius plans I've come up with so far for a few minutes tomorrow morning. I can always curse myself afterward.

In a situation like mine, the Rook would be too stupid to be employed, extorted, or blackmailed. He'd work himself into a rage and get himself and everyone else destroyed, and there'd be nothing left but a smoking crater. I've got the sense Rook doesn't. That's good news and bad. People act crazy for a reason, try to come across ignorant of consequences, like they're wired up all wrong and might take you to pieces before they remember the hole exists. It's the same in the streets. Once someone knows you don't have a hair trigger, they take on a predatory shine.

We meet early the next morning in the dry shower, in the oldest part of the SO. Bread, my deck, and me. The old shower is a lot bigger than the new one upstairs, with high bricked-up windows and benches bolted to the walls. Built in the days when tuberculosis took every sixth man. Bread looks comfortable pitching to an audience. He talks with his hands, but not so much that he appears feminine. He mimes holding up a wall and framing a box. He talks about heroin.

The cons in his audience probably expect an ace, something crafty and unusual. What they get isn't long on originality. Small amounts coming in through visitors, for starters. Then occasional shipments coming in with outside deliveries like dry cleaning and food. Finally, the bulk of the contraband comes in through hack employees, including guards. They keep waiting for the ace. It keeps not coming. "I'm talking about *weight*," he says, "Not a hobby to pass the time. Step up or fade away, boys."

They look around at each other. Seven guys: three robberies, two murders, an ag assault and an arson. That is the way I know them. I can see the big unanswered question working its way to the surface – once they realize they have to ask. Finally Frankson spits it out. From his tone, he thinks it is both a stupid question and the only question. "What about Vanderventer?"

Bread looks a little surprised. It actually takes him a minute to understand what they're worried about, but then he warms to the sell. "You guys are the ideal small operation because you can vouch for each other and you've got a brand nobody will fuck with." The crossed moneybag tats on their arms and necks that make them my deck. "If everyone believes it's Croft's money and you're his soldiers, who would fuck with that?"

Bread's eyes had switched over to me as he finished this reassuring little speech – a look just for the grownups. The others watch me now, too. They know the Rook has monkey-wrenched my rules, but not by how much. I can't imagine what I might say. I'm already sitting in a dank toilet listening to decks talk about what they like to stuff up their noses. If I say anything, some vital organ will fall out of my mouth.

Bread is perfectly confident. Hasn't been here long but isn't a true fish. He's been down before, doesn't seem irrational, and if he thinks he can walk in and do this, that's plain unusual.

3

Willie says the little things are going to start soon, Bread showing me who does the talking and who does the listening. The smart deck and the big stupid castle who'd stand out in the rain if someone didn't tell him to come inside.

It's two days since the powwow in the shower. The guys in my deck bought Bread's schtick - I don't know whether I'm really surprised - and for the first time since I was a fish, I've been working out alone. Forgot what I was missing. Too bad it can't last: I'm doing deadlifts when the Claw, the arsonist in the bunch, creeps up with his withered claw-hand tucked into the hollow of his chest. "Hey, Croft?"

The Claw has never actually spoken to me before. I ignore him, and he follows me while I walk in a circle to stretch my back. The others are probably talking strategy and carving up territories in the imaginary prison in Bread's head, the one where everything magically falls into line. As for Bread, he must not want me too deep inside his scheming because he doesn't seem to mind that I'm not too interested. I'm not expecting any developments – not in the short time before Rook gets out. Just keeping an ear to the ground.

The Claw says, "Croft, Bread wants to know, uh, if you can come to the hog shop for a minute."

Sending for me.

I bend down and grasp the bar harder than I need to. Then I start to pump, and breathe, and close my eyes on the negatives. My balance is no good. The arch goes out of my back, and my form is ugly.

"He says it's important for you to be there."

I drop the bar with a sound like a car wreck that shakes the whole Service Operations building, and decks all over the weight pile jump. The Claw seems to be sucked backward in time, he retreats so fast. Castles crane their necks slowly, like bears.

I breathe deeply and bend to the right when my left ribs don't quite expand. It's the 25th. Rook is getting close to the week mark again. I don't want to find myself going under the fence or having to stick a bedpost in his eye and know that I didn't give other avenues a real try. So I raise my palm like a butler and smile a rictus at the Claw.

He heads out of the weight pile and across the corridor to the stairs. We have to go down and then walk the length of the SO to get to the little guard cafeteria, what they call the hog shop. The SO is the size of a three-story parking garage with one level underground, and the cell blocks each attach to it like the fingers of a hand. A Block is the thumb, where they house crazies, snitches, sick people, and fish waiting to be classified and assigned a cell. The weight pile, central showers, library, the workshop, and the rec room are on the top level; the cafeterias, kitchens, and chapel are on the lower. Guys come back to the joint when they realize they can't assemble these different pieces in the adult world, outside. I follow the Claw down the stairs, where we pass Blaine Mitchell and Lou Stibb, a couple of bank robbers in Willie's deck. They don't break their conversation to acknowledge the Claw when he gets out of their way. I turn a little for them. They turn a little for me. On the first level, we take a right past the cafeteria.

The corridor outside the chow hall is a control area. In a big enough scuffle or a riot, at both ends magnets let go of heavy metal containment doors. There are small ports in the doors so that gas can be launched inside. The other control points are the entrances to the cell blocks and the long corridor leading to admin. The seams in the ceiling give them away. All that's needed to defeat them are pencil marks on the wall along the plumb line and a mop handle. If there are going to be men on both sides of a door, laying down bedsheets will work; they can haul up on both ends.

I watch the Claw's small, slightly bent back in front of me. The way he walks is a movement learned from some old source of pain, and it isn't normal, although it's meant to look that way.

We turn again to reach to the small guard cafeteria with the new stainless steel lunch counter. It's quiet here, this time of day. The Claw stops outside the door.

The hog shop is lit only by a silent tv screen. I slowly make out the slouching figures, inside. Bread is sitting on a table with his legs scissored, one foot on the bench and his other heel on the floor. Standing across from him is a dealer I've seen with Rook's deck, Bingo. He's a small, very light-skinned mulatto. Looks angry and defiant. Standing too close behind him is a guard called Stromm, porky Swedish bastard, puffy face with tiny eyes like a pig. Purely because of his looks, I've never liked him. He's a meatball who probably lives in a smelly apartment, and he has a topheavy figure that pours over his belt and looks like a child's drawing of someone big and tough. All the guys that made up my former deck stand around them.

I'd heard through the wire that someone in Rook's deck is sending up appeals because Rook has been in a box too long; can't imagine what else this is about. How does Bread know it's Bingo? Stromm's presence is another surprise. He's got no real rank but has been around a long time, a lot longer than me, has a lot of pull with the bad hacks. It seems like too short a time for Bread to have a guard like that on his roll.

"Bingo," says Bread, "you know Croft, don't you?"

He says it without looking at me, knows if he has to look away from Bingo, it's spoiled. I don't move at first, just register what's expected and briefly wonder whether I like the role. Then I move into the room and stand at an angle to them, close to Bingo and partly facing him. Bingo's back is to the door, and he doesn't quite turn. Stromm backs away imperceptibly as I get closer.

Bread doesn't miss a beat. We're in the hands of a professional.

"I guess Bingo is a little worried about his friend Rook, and he knows a lawyer who might be able to help out. Seems like you can only keep a person in d-seg for so long."

Bread's already laid the tracks, so I just huff and chug my way along them. It's comfortable, easy, a sensation I don't trust at all. I inflate my lungs and let the air out in a long, considering growl. Bingo leans away from me and watches the floor.

"I guess you know," says Bread, "That Croft, here, is also concerned about our friend Rook. Thinks a nice box is the best thing for him, right now. Isn't that right, Croft?"

Bread's made it smooth. Smooth deck bosses have ruined many a weak-minded case, taking care of the angles, paying them better than they'd get for real work. But most criminal enterprise is like that. It dulls the wits.

The gang watches passively, like it's television. Stromm strokes his blackjack and says, "We have policies around here, Bingo. We don't like it when inmates question our policies."

"I'm just saying," Bingo whines.

"Croft is going to show you the new policy." Bread still doesn't look at me, his eyes suddenly locked on Bingo in a stare of startling hatred.

Someone behind me closes the door and shuts out most of the light.

My comfort dries up. Does this sonofabitch mean neck popping?

The others all take a step back.

I'm already standing very close to Bingo, behind his left shoulder, to intimidate him, so I can feel every nerve in his body is firing. He's standing there like a naked man, hairs prickling, spine wired tight. We're close enough for me to feel his body heat on my skin, but I feel all the hollowness of my pretending. There's no more blood and force in my arms than there would be if I were slicing vegetables.

I do nothing, just stand there breathing and not looking at Bread.

"Croft."

The members of his gang are looking around with their eyes because we're getting off-script.

Bingo doesn't hear Bread anymore. He is cranking his neck in my direction like someone trying to look into the sun.

His brown eyes are liquid like a woman's, trembling and somehow ready. Because he's looking at me, he doesn't see Bread take Stromm's blackjack out of the loop on his belt. "We don't have time for this," he growls, raising it up.

The blow makes this unripe honeydew melon sound when it catches Bingo above the ear. I blink like a balloon popped in my face. Bingo does a half twist and begins collapsing, but Bread had grabbed his shirt to pull him into the blow and now uses it to drag him backwards onto a table, sliding him into position like a medic. Then he starts pulping Bingo's head and neck with the blackjack, arcing high like he's breaking logs. He hands the blackjack back to Stromm and starts using his fists on Bingo's abdomen and groin, making him flop. For a few seconds, everyone is frozen by the ferocity of it. It's in all their pale faces now that they're a deck and not a gang. Then Bingo pops up electrified and starts wheeling off the table, and when the others wake up and catch him it's like he's trying to pull out of a giant wad of taffy. They hold his arms and legs. They give each other orders in tight little responsible voices like surgeons.

I'm still not moving, still have the same idiotic bad-cop expression frozen on my face. Beside me, Stromm is wiping off his spring-loaded blackjack with a handkerchief.

When Bingo's movements become sedated, Bread turns to me and says, "Do it."

I stare at him. Do it? I search his face for irony, find none.

"What are you waiting for?" he says. "Rip his fucking arm off, or something! Come on!"

The others are holding Bingo still but not doing much more. They weren't counting on this and look like a bunch of boys caught shaving a dog.

I keep on staring at Bread and nothing else, wondering where he got his perspective. I honestly can't tell if he's holding himself above the rules or is somehow missing a big piece of common knowledge.

Then Bread actually steps up to me and, lips flattened by anger, says, "Don't just stand there. You need to do this."

I forget the room and what's happening. All I know is some deck is holding his angry face up to mine. For a moment I notice every ugly line of it. I feel something black and red move up my chest. Then he turns away again in disgust and walks to the table where Bingo is held down. He thinks, walks partway around the table, runs the flat of a hand down one stubbled cheek and sniffs through one nostril. "Alright," he says.

He hauls Bingo's prone form down to the bench seat so he can prop his leg on a chair and jumps up and down on the knee till it pops and the joint sags against the pantleg like the rolled-hay leg of a scarecrow. A couple other guys in the room blink like a fistful of flour just burst on their faces. Bingo wakes up for a few seconds with a silent scream. His mouth looks like a hole cut out of a bloody sheet, and then he's lolling. Bread, breathing heavily and sweating now, pulls him to the ground and dances around on one of his hands until looks like a crushed spider. Stromm watches with his chin pulled back into his neck, like someone pulled a bad fart. Then Bread grabs a metal chair and looks around at the others. He shoves the chair into Frankson's hands, and they argue violently for a moment before Frankson suddenly turns and slams the chair down in Bingo's neck, unleashing a solid bolt of blood that sprays across Dodd and Nick, making them gasp. He hands the chair to Nick. Then they're handing the chair around as they get tired, like a gang rape.

I'm leaving now, my broad back turned to the spectacle. I move down the hall listening to it, my shoulders high, knuckles tensed, flexing and breathing. The sounds are slow to fade, behind me.

For a moment it's too dark in the corridor, like there's something wrong with my eyes.

He's doing all that because it has to look like I did it. Bread's creating a monster.

I should have stopped it. It's great for Bread if it looks like I beat a man into white-flecked sausage, but Stromm's presence there isn't a guarantee that the DO won't charge me for it. As I walk, I can feel consequences attaching to me like flies in a butcher's yard, and I feel myself reddening almost as if in shame. I want to get mad, but what I've just experienced is too strange.

I get back to my cell and blow out my breath, my eyes hunting around the sockets for the sense of it. Now I know why Bread's in the Book: same reason as all the others. For having a personality that's like a piece of abstract art. It's only been a few days, and already someone's been murdered in front of nine witnesses. I blow more air through my nostrils. Was it commitment? Lack of any sense of proportion? Depends on who Bread turns out to be.

An hour later, he shows up on my front porch for what is to be the first and next-to-last time. I'm staring at the pages of a battered pulp detective novel, the cover so softened by hands it almost feels like threadbare velvet. When I first see him, I feel an instant of ugly anticipation that's like a cold raindrop hitting me between the eyes, but the next second it's coated over with a steely reserve. He's smiling when I look up at him, like we're old comrades and the sight of me is reassuring to him.

But what he says is, "What was that, today? Did you choke, or what?"

I don't mention my concerns. I can tell threats won't do anything to him, and telling myself I won't go down alone doesn't do anything for me. "Choke? Why would you think that?"

I rotate on my bunk, conscious of sitting on a lump of pills and matchbooks and a few bits of wire with the insulation stripped off the ends. I don't get up for him.

"That piece of shit was right in front of you, and you didn't do anything."

"You seemed to do just fine."

"You let other people handle your beefs?"

I don't care for the way he keeps trying to put me in a conversational box, so I stand up and say, "We're having a communication problem."

"This was for you, today. You heard what it was about. Taking care of your problem, and you stand there and watch."

"I watched you set me up for a murder rap. We're cellmates twenty years from now, tell me then how you did it for me."

He never responds to that. "You know why these other trash never make money, never get anything done?"

I'm dying to know the answer.

"They don't know how to work together. They think just because they're in here, they have to be this wolf character who doesn't need anybody."

Before I can appreciate his message, emphasized with a slight tilting of his head, Bread suddenly switches gears. Very little happens, outwardly, but I see something change. His eyes dance for a second, and he's suddenly on to the next thing, like he has a pot boiling. "Don't worry about it. Just back up the play next time, brother."

He walks away without dropping his eyes, like I disappeared from his vision. I don't move. The more little half-gestures he lays on, the near-wink, the way he almost forms a pistol with his hand or moves his eyebrows up that big forehead, the more he seems cold as dry ice. I turn my head ever so slowly to watch him. It's hard to put together the things he does with the way he looks and talks. I can't explain it, but I get the most persuasive feeling I've just been talking with someone who isn't even human.

This won't be the last time I look at Bread and get the impression I'm looking at something that should be in a specimen jar, in the kind of place where they keep the last living smallpox and polio virus on ice.

The rest of that day I watch the hacks closely, expecting them to take me into custody. If Stepner isn't busy, I'll go straight to his office, where he'll accuse me of killing Bingo. Otherwise I'll wait for his interview in the hole. If that happens, I've decided that Bread will answer to me for his arrogant lack of caution. I go to lunch, four more hours at the furniture factory, dinner, weight pile. All of it tense.

I've heard stories about cons being taken to the hole for the first time, how they'll go along quietly all the way to the cell doorway and then stop and look at the silent little space with the solid door and tiny pebbled glass window, not knowing when they'll ever be allowed out again. There's a moment, right then, when even the most docile inmate can't step over the threshold. He has to be pushed, because insanity is waiting inside. And he knows the bulls, knows they can pace the corridor listening to him beg and cry and scream to be let out, and to them it will no different from the sound of toilet pipes flushing in the walls.

The sun goes down without my noticing. After lights out, I realize I'm getting accustomed to not sleeping well. The extra-bright emergency lights in the yard go on for a single minute sometime around 11:00 as part of a test or mistake, and it looks like a baseball stadium for that one minute, which is how long it takes me to forget about it again because I'm too keyed up. It's late when the realization begins to really sink in that if no one's come for me by now, they probably aren't coming. I sleep like a gator anyway, my eyelids sliding open sometimes for no reason.

When word about Bingo hits the wire the next day, the decks are worried but the castles give me these long, curious looks. They know it's not my style, and they're wondering why I'm letting a deck run my name. I'm not exactly working for Bread, and he's not exactly working for me. Most of them have probably put it together with the Rook situation, but I'm still embarrassed. I'm also still thinking about the DO. I catch myself holding my breath when I'm sitting still and not thinking of anything. The day feels too short and too long at intervals.

Castles are too polite to each other to say anything. Except Willie, of course. Willie's had something stuck in his teeth since the day I talked with Bread in the yard, and now there's Bingo. Right at lights out he's got his hands wrapped around the bars.

"Hey, Raw."

"Yeah."

"You know this deck gonna make you a slave, boy."

I don't answer. Willie knows about Rook, what the hell's he want me to do about it?

"You know what he tells people about you? That you need him. That you wasn't shit without him. He buildin you up for a fall, that's the truth."

Willie's hands are the size and color of old catcher's mitts. He's seven feet tall and used to play basketball before they found out he was a case. I never asked about it, but I heard he let a group of docs cut him for money, back when, and that he was never the same. Out on the darkened tier, a couple of unlocks are going back to their cells from a late meeting.

"Hold the Rook over you forever, Raw. Run you. Then one day you can't remember yourself."

There's a moment of silence as he waits for me.

I say, "Willie."

"Talk to me."

I feel myself growing cold and small. "Nobody can stop the Rook, if he's out."

"Willie ain't scared of no Rook."

"Why not?"

"Cain't affo'd it."

I'm in the lunch line. It's been two full days since Bingo, and I'm still walking around. I can't figure what type of connection Bread might have with DO Stepner, especially for someone who's been here so short a time. Can't be Stromm - he's too rough and has too much of a reputation. They say Stepner's a cat, because he's careful. But Bread's got something. Both of us skating on Bingo's murder - while claiming credit for it, in a way - that's no mean trick. If he can do that, then maybe extending Rook's time in the hole isn't such a stretch. I still don't know if I'm happy we got away with it so clean, because it means something's going to be next. Guy like Bread hits a jackpot, he thinks it's God telling him to keep gambling.

Behind the steam tables, in the kitchen, convict cooks are dropping fruit (apple slices, today), sugar, and yeast down an old laundry chute meant for dirty towels and aprons. In the basement, laundry workers will stick it in a certain washing machine, add water, and let it ferment for a few days. Apple pruno.

The guy ahead of me looks back at me after Bread taps him on the shoulder. Bread wants cuts, but the guy just watches me. He's a seasoned con looking at a big crook who's just doing his time, and *he* knows it's the ballsy twit tapping him on the shoulder who doesn't get the picture. I might not care if someone cut in front of *him*, but *he* is in front of *me*. Then they're both looking at me like a pair of scientists with competing theories. I'm troubled when the old con finally lowers his head and walks off.

Bread takes a couple of little cartons of nonfat milk and two small squares of stale key lime pie from the lunch counter, but no real food. "Why don't you sit with us today, Croft? There's no point being coy."

I don't answer. I want him to feel the weight of my shadow on him, to feel eggshells beneath his feet, but instead he starts grabbing extra milk cartons and loading them up on my tray like I'm his kid. "Come on. I insist." He walks off. I look at all the milk and am dimly aware of a series of nods it sets off between the convict cooks and the hack standing at the end of the long counter, Palecki. Two is normally the limit. Castles going for extra milk is a sign of bulking.

I watch Bread. He works fast. Maybe a guy who'd been here and come back could work that fast, or someone high up in a major gang, but not Bread.

Then he sits down and waves me over to sit with him and the rest of his gang. I'd never sat with them when they were my deck, and I have no inclination to sit with them now. Most castles sit with their own kind, though not all of them. This is still different. I'm known as an unfriendly castle, and the biggest when Rook isn't in the room. And these guys are a drug gang. And I know what Bread's going to do when I get over there, if I go. He's going to talk too loud and laugh too much, and he's going to put his hand on my shoulder and lean in to tell jokes so everyone can get a real good idea how chummy we are. He's going to do that, and then over the next few weeks he's going to burn himself up like a candle, living too fast and hard on the Inside, and I don't want to be close while he does it.

I stand still for a moment, my big hands gripping the toy-sized tray stacked with too much food and milk. I measure this against the trouble he might save me with the Rook. Sometimes, for a while, the devil you don't know is better.

The guys in my former deck stop talking and act cagey when I come to the table. I stand behind two of them who see a shadow and then scoot aside so fast one of them falls off the bench like it was a skateboard, and then they're jumpy as hell. A man finds out a castle has been quietly standing behind him, he becomes a gazelle. I sit. An oil slick forms a greasy layer on top of my stomach, and I can hardly eat.

I look at the light in the high windows across the room, and when my gaze slips down I find myself looking at the Skins' table. Two of them are already smiling at me like I'm wearing mouse ears.

Bread eats his two slices of key lime pie in small bites that linger on his plastic fork. He feeds the conversation and the volume just like I thought, but not with a lot of hand waving and dirty jokes. Instead, he lets things wrap around him, the other guys looking at the sides of his face for what he expects. "Croft," he says, "How many times have you been down?" He asks me all the questions the guys in my deck have always wanted to ask but didn't quite dare, and I answer, feeling like a ventriloquist's dummy.

I still can't believe he got himself sent to solitary and took a piss on a case I have nightmares about. But it isn't courage. The decks aren't scared of Rook for the same reason ants aren't scared of Rottweilers.

Then I don't hear anything for a couple of days, which is about the worst thing that could have happened.

Rook will get out of the box on the 6th.

April 1st is a bad day when the full weight of the situation and my lack of a solid plan hit me. I wake up in the morning with a feeling of bullshit about everything Bread has said, feeling stupid and afraid. Did I really believe Bread could buy himself enough influence before my clock ran out? Or ever, for that matter? Less today than yesterday. And I didn't think so yesterday.

I stand for count, go to chow and the weight pile, then a QA shift in Industries, eat chow again by myself, go back to the weight pile and work like I'm going to make a month of progress in one session. I look at myself in a grimy piece of polished metal riveted to the wall that serves as a mirror, wondering what this guy could possibly be afraid of.

Then the sun goes down and 10pm lockdown comes. I spend part of the night breaking the heads off dozens of matches in the dark of my cell. Grind several dozen sulfur match-heads to powder and they'll make an incendiary that can burn out most locks in a few seconds. The metal will glow red hot and buckle like a viscous fluid. It's a piece of a part of a plan.

I half expect Willie to ask me what's going on – I know he doesn't sleep well – but somehow I don't think he will. He may not hear much better than he sleeps, but it's impossible to tell. He reserves the right that the oldest cons have, to sink into themselves and let the world turn without their help.

I keep going. I wonder what people in other cells make of the little sound of breaking matches in the dark. I almost don't hear the hack walking along the tier until it's too late, don't know where my head just was, and all I can think of is to sit there with the coffee can part full of match heads hidden behind my inside hip. Pretend to be a guy going through one of those long nights, thinking, worrying himself old. It's nothing unusual to see, and the hack goes on by.

I break off more matcheads with my thumb.

Escape won't be incredibly difficult. The ones you hear about are the crowd pleasers: complex schemes that take months or years. Most real escapes are relatively simple and direct, and involve exploiting an obvious weakness. Common criminals get stuck on spaces and things they can touch, which is why they can't pull a halfway decent bank job to save their lives. The real details are times. Shift changes. Lights out. Head count. There's the time before they realize someone's missing, time until a proper search can be mounted. The walls and bars belong to the prison system, but the system doesn't own time any more than the bank does. Time is a free agent. Time and perception.

After midnight when I'm truly tired, the plans fall apart in my head. It gets cold in the small hours, and I can smell ozone and a snow that never comes.

"I told Bread not to sell to that junkie queen Drupal," Frankson tells me. He's changing my plates between sets of decline bench press while I look up at the ducts in the ceiling. "She can't ever pay, and I told him we'd just have to throw her a beatdown. And guess what happened? I guess he knew it would have to be someone. Bread says the message is as good as the money."

Seems like Bread can think up a slogan or two for any kind of situation. His operation is the same raw-knuckle, bottom-of-the-barrel scraping that you always hear about. Visitors muling small amounts, penny-ante deals, teaching lessons to deadbeats. There's no new angle, not even a new gimmick. It's already the fourth. I could confront him about the Rook, but that would be like asking a guy who says he can fly why he hasn't jumped off the roof. I have three days left and will probably have to pull the trigger on my own scrap of a plan. The snake wrapped around my guts coils a little tighter.

I begin my set.

I've been in places much harder to break into than this place is to break out of, but it still takes time. And my idea coming in - with nothing but bad choices - was to trade five years to get clear of the law and then keep a low profile. It wasn't to get seventy percent of the way there and wind up a fugitive, anyway. Maybe that's why my plans aren't further along. Just haven't wanted to swallow that pill.

Frankson and Parker watch me work. The rest of the gang is scrambling to smuggle scag into the prison and sell it to anybody desperate enough to go outside Vanderventer. The members of my former deck wear different faces, now: alert, ready. Anybody could see they're into something new.

I finish my set and rub a cramp out of the muscle beneath my right armpit. Frankson says, "Hey Croft, you ever tell off a hack?"

He's sure talkative.

"Bread wants to throw a scare into this prick Weisner. We find out he's got this nephew he takes care of and could use a little help at the bank, so Bread offers him a taste to do a little favor. Totally generous offer, but the guy acts like we smell bad."

Yeah, sounds like a real prick.

"Thing is, now he doesn't want to let it go. Says he's going to tell everybody from the president down that he got 'approached'. Now nobody's sleeping too good. Guys on both sides of the bars, you know?"

Makes sense to me, Bread being so tone deaf that he approaches a squarejohn hack thinking he's going to turn him on a dime. A low, throbbing anger like a toothache catches up with me, worse because I predicted this. Like I thought, Bread had kept on rolling the dice until they came up snake eyes. I don't dwell on it because I've moved past it. I'm getting out. But how would I have felt about this if I wasn't? Bread taking a lot of bad risks with my name, and I find out about it from Frankson?

"So if he was to just get a little scared, just once, maybe he'd think a little differently."

I finish squeezing the tightness out of the back of my neck and stand up. Frankson holds out one of the ratty towels that hotels sell to the prison when they're too threadbare for the guests. I let him stand there holding it for a moment, then pinch it between my thumb and forefinger and snatch it out of his hand. Then I turn from him real slow and walk away.

Sometimes I think better in the shower, so I stay in a while to see if it will work. My head is like a radio between stations. If I stay, Rook will get out or Bread will run us right over a cliff and turn my nickel into four more just like it. If I go, writing off four years just to go on the run will feel like carving out a rib. I'll keep getting ready.

I've just gotten back to my cell and closed the door when Chris E brings me the list.

Under ordinary circumstances, he would never come to my cell, never bring me anything. And I'm *edgy*. He hands the piece of paper through the bars of my cell door like he's handing a cupful of bloody meat into a lion's cage.

"What's that."

"It's a list," says Chris. "Bread wanted me to give it to you."

I feel hunted. I turn fast and make him jump. He jumps back so far I can't reach the piece of paper in his hand. Then Chris doesn't want to get any closer and looks like he is thinking about tossing it.

"Don't you throw that at me," I say.

He steps forward and puts it in my hand.

On the little receipt-sized piece of paper are four names in a loopy script.

"What is this?"

"It's the ones he thought you should handle."

There are any number of conversations I'm not about to have with this deck on my front porch. But an actual list of necks I'm supposed to crank, and not an hour since Frankson said I could really help out by threatening a guard. For a minute I nearly forget all about Rook, looking at that scrap of paper. I don't move. I almost get very angry, but then I say, "Thanks, I'm low on toilet paper." And I start wadding it up.

Chris E's face shows surprise. "You mean...you're not going to do it?"

"Do what?"

"Take care of them."

"What do you think?"

"I don't know, man."

"You don't know if I should?"

"Come on, Croft, you're confusing me. He just said to give you that piece of paper."

I'd looked at the names, and they are people I know to see or by reputation. All bad risks for a sticking or a fight. I can see why Bread would want someone else to 'take care of' them.

"But you're going to do it, right?" he says. "Otherwise-"

"Otherwise someone will have to be more careful? This is four guys. That's the number that ought to get stomped in three months. This seem low profile to you?"

"I guess not."

"You tell him that."

He's too nervous and not really listening.

I'm just now starting to get really angry. I know Chris can see it because he takes another step away from my cell door. Bread is sending messengers now with lists of things for me to do, and not a word about the Rook situation. Taking me from hot water to deeper hot water. Knowing things are bad for me and calculating on it. I realize it, now: I don't think Bread's delusional. Not at all.

Someone else is angrier than me. Willie's long arm comes stabbing out of his cell with a pointed finger for a speartip. "*Get* the hell outta here!"

Chris scrambles away.

I turn in place again by myself like I'm rounding on someone. I have to focus, now. I have to plan exactly how

I'm getting out of here. It might be a little easier for a castle like me than for a deck, but a stupid plan works out about the same for both. There better not be any more distractions tonight. I'm having such a hard time putting the pieces together in my head, it's almost comical. There are guys who go through life like that – and even when they buy it, it's like a lame pratfall.

It disturbs castles when guards punish one of us harshly, and it disturbs the guards when castles work underneath decks as soldiers because there usually isn't the same hate between hacks and castles. Some castles remember the way the streets were for them and then look around and think one place is as good as another. As for the guards, they know the decks are their real enemies. Both sides usually give each other a little elbow room, but Rook has been in an iron box for a month. That's not lost on anyone.

But now he'll be out again in a day or less. I haven't eaten or slept much. A couple of times I've almost blacked out in the weight pile. I either bust out tonight or face him tomorrow; either way, years of patience and planning are ruined. Even if everything goes perfectly, I'll be a fugitive. Instead of being laid up in a nice hotel planning a score, I'll be in some dump waiting for them to kick the door in.

I've given up trying to think in my cell and gone outside. It's a foggy morning before work call, but not enough for them to clear the yard. The gun bulls in the towers still have a clear shot. I walk but don't feel like I'm moving. With the fog and the overcast, there's no sense of space.

Bread has been far from my thoughts the last twelve hours, and if someone asked me, I couldn't have said who isn't talking to who. Doesn't matter, anymore. Now that I'm looking back on it, my dealings with Bread are this strange and discordant episode, something I can't exactly understand. It's as if there's a high-pitched ringing in my ears when I try thinking about why I ever let it get started. Just something that happened in prison. Something a guy with my face but a different name will barely be able to remember, this time next month. I'm glad. I have a kind of premonition that things could have gotten really bad in a way I don't quite grasp. A kind of rottenness, not frightening but gross and unfortunate, a feeling of ill-luck and disease.

I walk, and the fog dampens the sound of my footsteps.

Distantly I wonder whether he's come close to being able to do what he said he would do, or whether he'd ever planned on doing it. He is probably still trying to get someone in the kitchen or the mailroom, someplace where things come into the prison, or another hack willing to risk a turn in the joint, himself. I feel a twinge of disgust. Maybe he got away with killing Bingo, a problem I hadn't even known I had, but he's a one-hit wonder. He's Danny Frye, the white jazzman of Southside Chicago, who recorded Licorice and disappeared. Bread didn't do the world the favor of disappearing.

I look around at the fences and crumbling buildings and think, Or did he?

My escape plan is like a used car: it runs, but it's dragging a muffler. Usually there's a soup of facts: layouts, routines, details in the landscape, and if I just sort of let them in and look at them and don't handle them too much, they'll start to knit into something, and it will be better than what I would have got if I'd drawn diagrams. This time I'd left the soup alone and it had frozen. I'll probably make it. I probably won't get shot. I watch the games of dominoes and the disordered chunks of ground mist like hanks of torn whitebread hanging above the dirt, and I wonder how I've slipped. It's something I never would have let happen a year ago, I'm sure of that. Why do things seem unreal? I'm standing at an angle to nothing, and my eyes squint up like I'm this dull child.

I still have to make a phone call.

Blister sees me and starts coming toward me. I get ready to tell him I don't have time for him, whatever his opinion on that is. He looks oddly relaxed, though. He smiles and says, "Where's the celebration?"

"What am I celebrating?"

"I'd like to know how you did it, but I won't ask."

When I don't respond, he looks at me like I'm putting him on.

"Not in the mood," I say.

"Some advice, friend, learn to take the good with the bad." He looks out over the yard. "Another month in solitary."

I stare at him. "Who."

He laughs.

"The Rook?"

"You've got to be relieved." Then, thinking I might take it wrong, he softens it up by saying, "I would be."

I watch him very closely, until he looks put off by it. He lets it go, says, "Take it where we can get it, right?" and walks away.

I watch him go, knowing he wouldn't pull my chain about something like that. I don't move for a minute; just my eyes. The mist on the air tastes of burnt pennies, and everything is too bright. Then my neck and my eyes both move independently while I look at nothing in particular, the way they would if I'd heard a twig snap behind me in the woods. I don't allow my mind to race; I can sure feel it wanting to. I'll wait a little while, make like I'm not too concerned, then ask Bread if something has happened. I'm just thinking that when he shows up.

His honey blonde hair is combed over to the right. It's darker at the roots where his hairline makes the breadloaf shape high on his forehead, making it into a heart. He's expressionless but looks almost angry, the way people do when they feel they've done a lot of work that others don't appreciate.

He stands in front of me and doesn't say anything right away, just gives me a kind of level stare. He knows I must have heard the news. For the moment, I have no idea what to say.

Then, cold as anything, Bread says, "I held up my end."

I just look at him. I want to blink my eyes and take a deep breath in relief, but I do neither.

"So I know I can count on you, now."

For lack of anything better to say, I take a poke at getting him to confirm it, say, "It's not a long-term solution."

"I know I can count on you to help protect your own money."

Something changes direction in my head. Three times in the last minute he's spoken to me in that dead voice, like he's somebody else's lawyer.

"That's a shuck," I say. "Remember? It isn't real."

"We had a deal. I held up my end."

The minute a guy like Bread knows you want something, no matter how insignificant, he puts you on a treadmill. Or tries. I'd been feeling relieved and grateful and never thought he'd come at me like this, now. The unpleasantness of it sharpens me right up. "You've had my name from the first day. If I threw my shadow a few times, that was a bonus."

Some of the deadness leaves his voice. "What are you, a lawyer? This is a golden opportunity."

"First it's my money, then it's an opportunity."

"Can't trust a guy who knows how to say it?"

"I can't figure out what you're saying. And Rook will be out again in a few more weeks." I can't believe this conversation. Relief and anger are pounding through me at the same time. In five minutes I'll have a headache.

"This isn't the beach, and I'm not going to go around putting my head in a cardboard cutout of you anymore."

"So don't. My name stays bought as long as Rook's out of the picture. That's the deal. Don't break it." I give him a look that, for most cons, is like a cinder block flying through the air at them. Message: Rook gets out, you better hope he gets to me before I get to you. I feel it sort of become true as the words leave my mouth.

And then he walks away, without warning. It's not an admission of defeat or helplessness. Instead, it's like someone hanging up a phone. I stand there in the misty morning, my legs made of concrete. After a minute I look for Bread among the decks standing in groups around the cold yard, but I can't see him.

4

Merc Creighton's crew runs the kitchen. They're waiting in the storage cage between tall metal racks filled with five-pound cans that dispense like artillery rounds. Bread doesn't look around before he goes in and then doesn't touch anything like he's thinking of germs. His gang piles in with him, and I go in last. When I come in, I see the eyes widen on Merc's guys and then shrink back down, like they'd been goosed.

"Have you met Croft?" Bread says. Must like saying that with me standing behind him. Have you met Croft? Says it about once a week.

I don't want to be here any more than they want me here, but I stuff myself in the small space and look at them. A squint comes over me almost like my eyes are trying to shut them from view.

The two crews nod to each other; Merc and Bread shake hands. "Rolling in kind of heavy, aren't you?" says Merc. He's obviously impressed, and his voice has the slightest breathy quality. Bread plays it off.

"Not at all. You've got your guys, here. We've got ours."

Some part of Merc and his guys, a part they try to ignore, wants out of the little room now, but I'm blocking the door. This casual placing is rehearsed. I'm sure that Bread had made it sound like the standard thing, the crews meet on an equal footing to discuss the deal.

I look around as they start talking. There are no brand names on the food cans. One just says "Tomato Paste" on a white wrapper. There's "Cherry Filling" and "Yams". I've never been back here, before, but I've seen some similar places. I've gone out the back way from a restaurant, a hotel or two, when something blue came in the door. Never actually ran. To a quickly scanning eye, even a castle like me can be invisible if it's walking calmly. Even surrounded by white-crowned chefs and blue leaps of flame from skillets doused with bourbon, someone who knows how to dress and knows how to walk can usually breeze on through.

Unlike those other kitchens, the prison kitchen stinks of bleach, and all the meat's been killed twice: it's ground or shredded, mechanically or chemically separated. Cheap places don't stop at butchering. They like to do more work. I look back at the giant can of Tomato Paste and it hits me again, the tough part of prison – it's not a hard place but a simplification of real life, like it was laid out in Crayola. The conversation between the two convict captains filters back into my consciousness.

Bread's holding up an empty food tray with its little compartments. He turns it upside down, and the tip of his index finger is holding a tiny baggie against the bottom of the tray. "Like that," he says. He mimes handing it over the lunch counter.

Merc's skeptical. "It's been done before."

"And I bet it had a good run."

"Worth it, huh? Yeah, we could run it for a while. Till someone gets caught."

"Until then, just deal straight. Nobody gets his feelings hurt."

He half-turns his head in my direction.

Merc says, "Speaking of that. Seventy-five percent is a little steep. How about more like thirty-five percent?"

His guys are nodding their heads.

Bread turns to look full at me. I shake my head.

Also rehearsed. Tiresome, because Bread had seemed to think I wouldn't be able to remember my lines. 'Croft, what do you do when I look at you?' Twice, he asked me this. Six years ago I stole a pair of Robinson helicopters out of a news station hangar, value of two-hundred K apiece. What had the next biggest thief in this little room stolen? Sixty bucks from a gas station?

Merc pales a little. "Fifty."

Bread doesn't bother with the look, just says, "Seventy five, or I walk out of here and you don't do business at all."

"Or maybe I just do business with someone else, instead of risking my neck going around the Champ. Thought I'd get a better rate, with the added risk."

Then Bread does one of the more interesting things I've known him to do – there aren't many. Without really moving or saying anything else, he frames the room. He makes everyone inside feel the confines of the space with his silence. I feel myself grow larger and my presence more immediate.

"Seventy five," says Bread, "Or I walk out of here and you don't do business at all."

Merc pales more. "This is bullshit. I thought you were on the level. And anyway, who am I speaking to, you or him?"

At this point, a dirty hack named Peterjohn pokes his head around into the cage. He's on Merc's roll, glances around the doorframe and then his gaze climbs up my arm until he's looking at my face, and then he's gone again.

As long as I don't actually get convicted, any rumors about me – rumors, affiliations, suspicions – don't matter and won't affect when I get out. I'm going out max time, so there's no parole board to worry about. My file is just a piece of paper unless it becomes part of a new legal case against me. So far, I haven't come to that line, and I don't plan to. The script for today – obvious and lacking character as it is – is something I didn't argue with.

Bread just stares at Merc. So do I.

Merc shuffles like his clothes are too tight. "What if I was to just tell the Champ about our little conversation, today?"

Bread: "I can think of at least three problems with that."

"What problems?"

"Getting out of this room alive. Staying alive if you get out. And him killing you himself for being a part of it. I've heard about his brother, Eddie." Bread never says Vanderventer's name.

Nick Karoulas chimes in, here. "Probably make a belt out of you."

There's an ugly energy in the room, and a sudden humidity. If these decks clash, maybe I'll just stand here like a sphinx. Peterjohn can testify I never raised a hand.

"Seventy five?"

"You keep twenty-five for passing out trays, which you do anyway. And hey, if it works out, maybe we can renegotiate."

This lightens things a bit. Merc looks over Bread's shoulder at me, with a light mockery. "Pleasure doing business with you." Then, as an afterthought, "No disrespect, but I always heard you guys stayed out of the biz."

"Don't believe everything you hear."

That sudden tiredness is still with me. I'd like to open up my head, scoop out the jelly that contains the last five minutes, and flick it off my fingers. I only have so many of these slimy prison deals in me. Day before yesterday, I watched Bread, Dodd, Frankson, and Nick stomp a guy half to death over fifteen dollars. Later I'll get irked because I'll start thinking Bread wouldn't go at everyone so hard if it was his own reputation out front. It's a double bind because I'm not supposed to care, but who likes getting driven like a rental car?

There have been a lot of deals over the last couple of weeks, and there's still no special strategy outside of having me along to pull a face. No trace of any genius or heavy connections on Bread's part. No sign that he's going to slow down or be more careful. I'll worry about that soon enough. For now, my interest is simple: if he could get Rook's hole time extended once, he can probably do it again.

The funny thing is how no one seems to grasp the natural ending to this little enterprise: the moment when Vanderventer takes notice and it becomes like a hair that tickles that dark, jealous, half-crazy nerve sack that gangsters and short men carry around in their heads. I've watched the gang go around dealing and beating without any discussion of it in between, like they're a real enterprise and their big worry is how to drive up their stock another quarter point. Now I watch them try to build a roll of hacks. Occasionally I'm there myself, as a prop. Have you met Croft?

Those smudges of dark blue walking the tiers and counting convicts take on a new significance for the gang. Starched shirts, padded shoulders, hard-soled shoes and tight jaws. Bread and Nick, Frankson and Dodd make intense conversation out of them, who they can get for what, the kind of talk that would make the honest guards violently sick.

A few hacks are just waiting for action on the side to make extra money, but they don't want to be taken in by some hothead con who's going to cost them their job, or worse. I know how to bribe a cop on the outside, so I figure the way to approach a hack about getting on a roll is by watching and listening - not choosing some perfect moment to spring. You see who they're chummy with, find out about their situation. Maybe they're a Weisner and need money. Maybe they're disgruntled. Maybe then you leave a twenty someplace by accident, something you can deny. Then maybe you leave it there again. That, or you figure a way to place them in your debt – warn them about something that's coming. Then you ask them for the smallest of favors in return, and the seed is planted. Weisner is what happens when things go wrong. From the approaches I see Bread make, I believe I could do better. If I were inclined.

His successes aren't adding up to anything good, either. There are guards like Osegovic and Phister; Robey, who is close to Stromm; Ratel on the night shift; and Palecki. Easily manipulated because of greed, vices, debts. That isn't necessarily all of them – I think Bread is playing some inside baseball, when it comes to what I know – but these guys are discipline cases and repeat transfers, not unlike hot potato convicts. Stromm is the only solid catch, and he must be costing Bread a pretty penny. So Bread's got the kitchen and a few other small sales outlets, and he's got a supplier and a roll of dirty hacks with gambling problems and love affairs with the bottle. It's a timebomb. And it's not enough for him. He runs it like it's fast food and he knows it's fast food. One day soon they're going to find him in tiny pieces all over the prison.

For now, I generally follow the schedule Bread sets, like a bus driver. I hang over petty deals like a gargoyle, and I don't complain. Just a hump with a flask and a bottle of the pink stuff in his desk drawer. Being a crook was supposed to be my way to avoid this kind of life, but I can handle it for a while. I've put on my grey hat. It's not the first time – sometimes the world demands it, and I'm a man of the world. But the grey hat is something a guy gets paid to wear so he'll keep his head down and not ask too many questions, and do a job. You put it on. You take it off. It's not a dog collar.

It's not a dog collar, and I'm not here to get sent down for life. I haven't said it outright so far because I figure it's common knowledge, but I don't pop necks for deck convicts. I'm lying in my bunk waiting for sleep when something ticks into my cell from the dark tier, outside. It's a small sound, but a convict is alive to little things. I'm awake at half past because, in a state of grey, falling asleep involves slowly swirling around a shallow drain. I've adjusted to the darkness, and I can see well. I roll out of bed to retrieve the paper kite - I can be quiet, for a big castle - looking around for the guard that left it, but he's just an anonymous set of footsteps walking away. I open the kite and glance at the writing, and sleep gets pushed back at least another hour. I look out into the darkness. There are widely spaced night lights on the tiers so the hacks can see where they're going and so somebody who shouldn't be out of his cell won't have the benefit of total darkness for sneaking off. I look back at the paper. Folded twice, just like before. Same loopy script, like before. I can't read it exactly, in the darkness of the cell, but I can see the musical pattern of the letters' stems and tails, and I know it's a list of the same four names.

I crumple the paper and hold onto it in my fist.

I don't know if it's more gall or more forgetfulness, or the two entwined. I don't know if this is simple insistence, the collection of a favor, or a message. Maybe Bread has trouble separating these things in his mind. Sometimes I think he has a strange hole in his head where these things normally get cleared up – or else I've got one in mine. One thing I feel is true: I've already spent more time trying to figure it than he ever did.

No big deal, just send me a kite. It's all just fast food, and I'm wearing the uniform. What's another ten years with good behavior?

I shift my gaze back to the darkness, and it seems to be alive. When I look long enough, strange motes are eating the darkness and excreting it again. There are guys who don't make it out of prison. Smart, capable guys, some of them, for reasons that are never fully understood.

By breakfast time, I've remembered to put on my grey hat. I go to chow late so there will be no empty seats at my usual table. I take the list with me and sit at the end of a half-empty deck table by myself, far enough away not to spook them. I wait a few minutes, then take the rumpled piece of paper out of my pocket and let the nervous men at the table see me staring at it over my breakfast of powdered eggs and cold toast. Then, as I get up with my empty tray, I set the piece of paper down and drop my spoon on the floor. I turn, then bend, pick up the spoon, and walk away. It looks like I've forgotten the paper. I don't turn back again until I'm at the cafeteria door. One of the men at the table has scooted over and is sitting within arm's reach of the paper.

The names will be on the wire within the hour. Each of the four bruisers will hear that I was carrying around a list with his name on it.

If Bread's as smart as he thinks, he'll realize that he's not having problems with them anymore, even though they're still walking around. That will have to be good enough.

The next night I'm just outside the weight pile at nine p.m., an hour before lockdown, wanting to get some sets in when Bread sees me. As he turns in my direction, he looks strangely unfocused for somebody with a bee up his ass. He looks almost like his turning and stomping in my direction is a coincidence, like I'm not even here. So I'm surprised when he stops in front of me with a half dozen guys and asks me point blank when I'm going to start pulling my weight. He says it as if he says things like that to me all the time and that is our relationship. He has a short memory.

"What's that?" I say.

He seems to have a lot on his mind. He'd been passing by and just happened to see me, although from the vague way he looks at me, I'm just a blurry shape in the landscape. He's on a roll and looks like he clubbed someone before me and there is going to be someone else after. "We don't do these collections and settle these bad deals for you to stand there and watch, for your entertainment."

In the upper half of my body there's a sudden surge of blood. "I don't turn you inside out when you use my name to make your money. I figure that's my job."

"No more free lunches," is his response. "What do you spend so much time in the pile for if you don't want to use it?"

The gang members with him, mostly guys from what used to be my deck, study the smooth floor of the SO. He's all alone in this, but it doesn't seem to bother him a bit.

I stand over Bread, and he is entirely inside my shadow. "I think you're confused, right now. You don't need my name anymore, you let me know." Then I realize with electrifying clarity that little has changed for me since this deck has come into my life. I'm still putting up with garbage and worrying about what's going to come down. I say, "I'll tell you something else. You're not being careful."

"I'm not the one who was in trouble. Get your head out of your ass."

I twitch and almost make a grab for him. He doesn't see it – his guys do. Bread's eyes are locked on my face, so he can't see my shoulders. There's a slight screech in his voice like there's rust in his throat, and his face is blank and almost rubbery except for the skin crowding around his eyes. It's hard to believe, but I'm tempted to think he's really mad at someone else and is finding it more convenient to take it out on me. I'm not too proud to believe it can happen, but it's never happened before, and it's almost too strange for anger. Most guys, they hammer their thumb standing next to me, they run out of the room and close the door before they shout.

Then he turns his back on me and walks off. His angry, accusing face still hangs before me like the afterimage of a light bulb, stirring anger in my gut.

Despite my irritation, if other circumstances were different I could almost laugh. A lot of the time, the people we think have been given something extra are actually missing something, instead. I'd find that easier to believe, in Bread's case. I watch him go. He's still too small-time to be turned out to the wilds of Seamax on his own, and we both know it.

Even if he lived, he'd be set back a year. Still can't realize a musclebound case like me can see the situation. In his mind, I can't realize something like this. But like the lyric from the old blues song, his mind is all in his head.

His real name is Phillip Conroy, and he jailed in Chesworth State Pen for five years before he came to Seamax. He got out of the van and went straight into the Book, which means he brought along a reputation for violence. That much I've been able to find out about Bread from people I know. And he's dyslexic. It still doesn't make any straightforward sense to me, what Bread's been able to do since he got here, and nothing about any heavy connections in his file.

What he expects make as little sense. On the outside, when I'd study an architect's vellum or the engineering on a main, I had a little pair of reading glasses I would wear. Simple things with black frames that would sit halfway down my nose. They stayed in a leather case in my luggage, and when I put them on, somebody was going to be calling his insurance company soon. There is an indirect, primeval understanding of that dignity among castles on the Inside. We are not our size. It would be the most obvious thing in the world for the deck bosses to yoke every one of us into being their soldiers, the kind that are in and out of the hole all the time on somebody's say-so, doing all the neck popping and fighting each other. And maybe it was that way, years back. Not anymore. Now there's a code. One thing you never do as castles is fight one another for deck money. Another rule that's more of a guideline, the way there's no hard and fast rule against being a punk: you don't work for a deck boss as an enforcer. I'd feel that way anyway, and for once the prison agrees with me.

I can't tell how much Bread knows about the rules, although anyone would be able to see the outlines by now. There were a few days when I was almost convinced the castle code was one of his strange blind spots. Now I think he finds it quaint. There are people who are like burn victims with their skin peeling off every second the world doesn't behave right. And here I am, stuck in the past, won't pop a neck and he can't wrangle me into doing it.

I've got these antique notions, and it finally seems to Bread that I'm not going to let them go. So he decides to set me up.

We're in the yard behind home plate during a bad baseball game when the players and the audience are pissed off at each other. Just me and Bread. It's May, and there is some blue in the high cold sky. Men sit at square cement tables playing dominoes, friends and petty gamblers peering over their shoulders to see who's drawn good bones. It would be poker or blackjack if playing cards were allowed, but they make do. I say, "Who are we supposed to be meeting?"

"Just give it a minute," says Bread.

We don't talk much because I have nothing to say. Bread had struck me as the kind who always had to be talking about something, but that turned out not to be the case. He's full of the kinds of little surprises that make you overestimate him after you've underestimated him.

On the baseball diamond, there are men on first and second. The batter spits a wad of snuff while the pitcher stares him down. An outfielder swats at an insect and touches the back of his neck. When I look away from the game, I see something that snatches my gaze. A pair of dark eyes are staring at me across the yard. Billie Tripps is staring at me.

You don't stare at someone in prison. You don't point, you don't wink, you don't stare. He's just a skinny convict leaning against the back of the low bleachers along the first base line, and at first I think I'm seeing things. Stress getting to me. I worked a couple of times with a bank man who'd get floaters in his eyes under stress; said they looked like fruit flies. I stare back at Tripps and realize his eyes are a little bit off, like he's wearing bifocals. Then I see it's actually Bread, next to me, he's staring at. Bread is eyeing him with a small, fixed smile.

Then Tripps is more than looking. He's straightening up and I see him getting ready to do something. He is striding across the yard. A friend comes with him, and they're a couple of spindly yard rats on the move.

My blood starts pumping a little, not on account of two decks but because I know the hacks will be watching whatever's about to happen.

They get closer, and Bread keeps grinning.

"What the fuck are you smiling at, shit for brains?" says Tripps.

I want to roll my eyes, but I step forward with my right shoulder in front of Bread.

Tripps and his buddy stop out of my reach. They don't look at me, just at Bread.

I already know the real situation isn't here, with these two. It's an announcement to everyone else who's watching. He couldn't make me do this for something I knew mattered to him, so he decided to set me up for something meaningless. Players on the field are sneaking looks, and part of the audience isn't paying any attention to the game.

"I'm smiling at you, sunshine. You and your fuck buddy."

Now the buddy steps up but also stays out of my reach. "What's your problem?"

I can feel a guard's eyes on the side of my face. It feels like a fading slap. But he's not the only one with a special interest. On the far end of the bleachers, halfway up, are Brick Cassio and Eddie Vanderventer, the Champ's brother. Guess he's not busy cutting the tendons in someone's neck with wire cutters or stuffing a live rat down someone's throat.

Bread says to Tripps, "Nothing. Croft just asked me a question. He said, 'Who's the biggest snitch in this yard, right now?'"

Tripps tries to get in Bread's face. I stop him with a hand. He still doesn't look at me. I find him stupid and ugly and want to wash the hand. The tension is making his flesh as hard and electrified as if he's having a seizure, and I wonder again how this is going to finish. If him or his buddy turn out to be crazy or coked up, and it escalates. I measure Tripps for a hard shove. One arm, from the elbow, not the shoulder or he could go back onto his head and die on me. Or it escalates more, and if I don't let them have Bread, I go to the hole and maybe wind up in Rook's box if one of his crew can front the twenty bucks a minute. I can almost feel the cons on the yard tallying up the meaning of each movement. Prison is a place where a cough can signal an invasion. What we're doing now is like screaming at the top of our lungs.

Still without looking at my face, Tripps winds up – I feel him coil down the instant before – and launches himself into the air towards Bread. He reaches the highest point of a low forward arc when I tense my arm, my hand catching him softly in the chest like he's a basketball or a small child and putting him back down on his feet, and his electricity and rage crumble in surprise and sudden hopelessness when he's back standing exactly where he was after blasting every fiber of strength in his body. He sags on his feet looking lost. For an instant his eyes are nearly round with slackness. I feel the hack's gaze hot on the side of my face, but some of the intensity is going out of it. I know that he's still got his stick halfway out of the leather sleeve, reaching across his body with his left hand, holding onto it with his thumb pointing toward the ground. Just a reflex – it wouldn't do him much good if this was a real rodeo.

This is Bread's moment. We have everyone's attention, now. Brick and Eddie have turned fully toward us and dropped any pretense that they're not taking it all in, point for point. I wonder if this little demonstration isn't just for them. I also get the strangest feeling that they have no interest in Bread, find him predictable – I feel it's me they're looking at with curiosity, and something like humor.

"You got something you want to say to me?" Bread says to Tripps. "Let me explain something." Now he uses a raised stage voice: "Anybody who wants to talk to me can talk to Croft. Anybody who tries to fuck with me is going to have to fuck with Croft. But I'm sure he'll let this slide since you didn't know and you're a dummy who doesn't understand anything but queer dicks. How's that sound? Do you want to just forget it, or are we doing this?"

The baseball game is stopped. Hacks and cons start moving closer and then stopping, not sure whether to run. Bread starts rolling up his sleeves and stepping up. As he does this, I twist my hand into Tripps' shirt to get a grip. Tripps twists away violently, like my hand is a giant spider, keeping his eyes down so it's not like he was tangling with me. His shirt tears. He spins away and throws up his open palms. "Wait. It's cool."

His friend can't take his eyes off me, watching across his face, and asks, "We can just forget about this?" The cons watching us don't blink, their eyes suddenly big and hungry.

Bread says, "Like I said. I'll let it slide this time."

They look like they saw a ghost and actually thank him.

The tension snaps. Bread walks away. No one else moves for a few more seconds. About ten feet away Bread turns and looks at me bug-eyed, says in an impatient, raised voice, "Are you coming?"

For a moment I stay rooted and mute. My perspective shifts in a subtle but profound way and I suddenly look back on the situation as one where no one looked at me or acknowledged my presence except to stay out of my arm's reach, and when Bread had spoken of me it was in the third person. I could have been a braindead stooge with elephantitis, and it would have gone the same way.

I'm tempted to throw him to the wolves. All I'd have to do is look at Tripps and his friend, say, "He's all yours, boys," and walk off in the opposite direction. Right now Bread's like the captain of a submarine, deeper than he can swim on his own. And his stock just rose a few more points at my expense. How did I get in this position?

That night in the weight pile, I'm doing preacher curls when Willie spots me. He looks like he's been looking for me. Willie doesn't go looking for *anyone*. Apparently it can't wait until lockdown. He's heard.

I feel like a hunted animal, these days. There's no one I would less rather see, right now. I'm embarrassed enough as it is, and in his way, no one is more serious about standing separate as a castle than Willie. He wouldn't put it like that, but that's what it is.

I pull the bar up one last time and rack it. My arms are so swollen it's almost painful. Willie sits on a bench beside me and watches.

"I don't want to talk about it," I say.

He takes his time. Willie's getting old, and he claims his privileges. "What you think I'm gonna tell you?"

"I really don't want to talk about it."

I run my fingers up my face and into my hair. In prison, the difference between a person and a sack of groceries isn't money or race, it's an ounce of forbearance, a moment of weakness.

Again Willie doesn't answer right away. The seconds stretch. Then he says, "How much longer you in here?"

"Fifteen months."

"Fifteen months."

He doesn't seem to calculate so much as taste the words. What is fifteen months? What sort of animal might it be if you starved it?

"You gonna spend it sittin on that bench?"

I figure he was upset, maybe even angry, until he was actually sitting beside me. I wonder whether he's aware that I never know what he's going to say. It's been a couple of years since I gave up thinking I could guess.

"You don't need those twist curls." He holds the outside of my arm just above the elbow and twitches his thumb back and forth in the muscle. "Already got a head on that bicep, but it ain't long. Do hammers."

Looks like he's not going to tell me what I already know about my situation. Nothing to add.

I start on the curls with Willie watching like a coach.

If he's been thinking about what happened, then he's not the only one. No one has said anything to me directly – at least not yet – but I've felt a little like I'm going around without my outer layer of skin. Some tough castles years ago had staked out a position of dignity and superiority with a few simple rules, and here I am giving away the farm. Yeah, that's me.

Bread starts gaining momentum, and something I suspected begins to get a little more obvious: he's done all of this before, and more. The impatience, the way everything moves too fast. There are spry young athletes who play by rules, and then they take second to a no-talent thug who puts them into the boards at the last instant. After that, they break the record for fouls.

Bread's attitude toward me must come from his previous experience. He assumed I'd be stomping on necks for him regular, and the idea is still in his head like an infected tick. If he has humiliated me, I've rented out a room in his head, too. He comes back to his cell while I'm guarding the door during a count, he can barely look at me without pulling a face. Another time he turns away slightly to shut me out of his vision, and I see his profile harden as he blanks past me close enough to smell his body powder. Even the success of his yard stunt seems to have honed his awareness of how wrong I treat him. Maybe he'd like to kill me. How did he ever survive so long on the Inside with a nervous system like his, getting all bent out of shape and cross-eyed when his expectations aren't met? Maybe he had a tiny stroke in the center of his head six months ago, and he's been living on borrowed time.

Whatever it is, we don't hold it together, we both become prey. Bread wants me to think he has mental lapses and forgets that, he's so temperamental. I don't buy it.

When a deal is set for 1:30 Tuesday in the old shower, I have to hustle because that's when I come back from getting my Praxlatan and Defenerin in A Block. I come quietly into the dim room with walls full of cheesy cracks. The deal isn't interrupted on my account, and I watch a large beetle lumber across an old twisted shirt. It's not exactly the conference room at the Ritz. Bread completes the deal and watches the backs of the Lobos gang members as they leave, then looks into the floor. His own gang waits a full minute while he says nothing. Then, to the floor he says, "Buy a watch."

His guys all look at each other.

"I'm talking to you, Croft. You forget how to tell time?"

Six weeks ago that statement would have been like a pale arm rolling a pineapple hand grenade into the middle of the room. Today my former deck acts like he's talking to his own kid. They play with their feet. A lot of times, out in the world, this happens to a case because of his size, not in spite of it.

I watch the side of Bread's face, and I still don't buy it - that he's forgotten what he is without me. There's also the old double bind: that I'm not supposed to care what a bunch of decks think about me. I look at him like he's being adorable.

Dodd misunderstands and smiles like it's a good time.

Bread says into the floor: "Be back here at five o'clock on Friday."

"We'll see."

"Five o'clock. Friday."

A rib I moved doing pull-ups last year goes tight. It's right next to my heart and floods my chest with a watery feeling.

Three times that same week someone in the gang comes to talk to me urgently about something going down while I'm still eating. Couple of times I actually catch myself shaking a leg for a minute or swallowing half-chewed chunks of food and make myself stop. The last time it happens, I have this suddenly sick feeling that I've somehow been stuck with Bread my whole life. It throbs in my veins like poison.

Even then, there's another angle that plugs up the violence I feel: with each rebuke, with each irritation, I'm a little more sure Bread's going to get the Rook another turn in solitary. I'm not quite sure how I know, but I do. Maybe he's just trying to get his money's worth. Who knows? I decide to conserve my energy. If the timing's not comfortable on some deal, I don't show up at all. From what I hear, Bread doesn't take it well. Also reassuring. As long as he stays bent out of shape, I figure he's still resenting the fact that he's going to do me a favor. For his own reasons, but still a favor.

Frankson is shuttling my weights around the pile one day and tells me something he's said to Bread about me. "You got to finesse him a little bit, I said. That's all. But he says it doesn't work like that. We got to be smooth, fast." He snaps his fingers a couple of times, sharply, then shakes his head as if he has no idea why.

With a sudden, wry amazement, I realize we may really be headed for it, after all...over nothing. In my line of work, every few years someone needs to go away, but usually it's a nutjob or an addict of some kind, someone who *can't* stop their behavior. It's never been like this.

I have to remember to blink.

At lunch that day, Bread is at the table he's claimed, his gang around him. He sits there looking almost sulky behind two slices of pie and no other food, eyes flat and shining, deafmute, and his gang ignores him as if they're used to his fugues. They reach across him and are careful not to touch him. When he does speak, half the guys at the table jump up to fix him a coffee. Mister Man. He has round-the-clock eyes on his cell and money to burn, and the convicts stay out of his way. Even if they don't think he is The Man, it's The Man who'll have to handle him. I pass across his eyes, and he waves me over with two fingers like I'm a waiter. And like a waiter, I pretend not to see.

I'm starting to think Bread's never left anything or anybody alone in his life. Other gang leaders are playing a role when they're being scary and possessive, but Bread's not that good an actor.

I sit facing away from the table where he eats with his gang, so he can wave to the back of my head. After a few minutes, for no apparent reason, my smugness seems to reflect itself and become frustration. I eat with restless legs and flushed cheeks, and my heart starts trotting. This illness is new to me. The symptoms cling for a few hours and then leave me drained, and I'm surprised to find I've got a headache. I don't get headaches. This one lasts the rest of the day. It's these stupid games. Some people like books and movies about prison on the outside, but I was never interested, not even on the day I got my uniform and bible. Trying to sleep at night, I swirl around the edge of the drain. Sometimes I'm going down, only to be spit back out. In the morning, faint, colored bags cup my eyes.

This is what gets to me: on the outside, anyone who spent a little time around me, I became someone they couldn't explain away. I don't fit a lot of preconceived notions. But if normal society asks a person to be legible, prison demands it - others need to be able to see instantly who you are. If you're bad, you have to look bad, act bad, remake yourself for the lowest common denominator or get fucked with all the time. You live under the constant judgment of people who can't hold onto a job or a marriage.

I need to burn off some unpleasantness, and it's a decent night in the weight pile, regulars working hard, not a lot of yard rats trying to figure out how the machines work. If I squint my eyes, the place could almost be a boxing gym or a fire station. I let it soak in: sweat, hand chalk on the air, clinking of forty-five pound plates like teacups on a tense barbell.

I do reverse-grip curls and then clean a heavy barbell up to my shoulders, making the muscles pop. I live in the throb of my heartbeat. A few feet away, a bad case called Bubblegum Grunnel bench presses and talks at the top of his reps, singsonging yeahbitch, yeahbitch. After a set he springs off the bench like it got hot, picking up the song as if he'd never stopped singing. His eyes focus between men out of contempt - he never looks at anyone he isn't going to fuck or kill, and I can feel the meanness coming off him like the stink waves off a cartoon skunk. Across the room Troy, bigger than Bubblegum and possibly even my own size, is tricep-lifting a stack of forty-five pound plates over his head by a rope down his back. It's all expected. It all belongs and doesn't move me.

Weisner, the guard who threatened to report Bread for attempting to bribe him, wanders in at some point, strolling like a beat cop. Squarejohn, but an experienced guard with friends. He doesn't pay me any special attention. Sometimes I have to hear about him, how he's afraid of castles because he saw a guy pulped real bad one time. His combed-over hair makes his head appear slanted; there's a dark length of curls draped across the top of his forehead that looks like the edge of a lasagna noodle. Irishman's slightly dreamy blue eyes beneath that, and hard grey lips. A lot of urgent messages go flying around if someone sees him coming out of the warden's office or getting a phone call in the middle of the day. I ignore him. I feel alright.

Then I turn and see the Champ. Must have come in during the last couple of minutes. The one who is eventually going to put Bread, and by extension me, out of our misery. Vanderventer is there, curling with one arm at a time. His usual entourage is with him, like a deck, except that they clown around with impunity. While I watch, in the same five seconds he loses his temper with one of his guys and then starts laughing. I don't watch too hard but glance over as I walk in a circle and shake out my shoulders. Then Vanderventer is walking it out, too. He carries his right shoulder higher than his left, so you can't tell if it really is larger than the other side as the posture seems to suggest. I could never say whether there is a deformity about the shoulder or collarbone on that side, or if it's just how he carries it, like a psychological tick. He bounces the shoulder like he's back in the ring. He puts the dumbbells down and starts jumping rope with the small wrist movements and smart feet of a boxer.

I sit back down on a weight bench and prop dumbells on my knees before hoisting them to my shoulders and starting to pump. I keep watching the other side of the room. Even the big iron freaks in his area are very aware of Vanderventer. They throw glances, smile whenever he laughs, make sure they aren't in his way. Brick Cassio and Clem Johnson might have been a pair of nephews, how casual they are with him, as if everywhere he goes becomes their living room. Clem's cherry red baby shoes draw the eye like a pair of bloody socks.

It's about time for me to be getting out of this place. That's knitting itself up neatly in my mind, about now. I'm not at all sure what Bread's going to do about Rook once the time comes, especially since I'm not giving him anything: not doing what he wants, and not taking my punishment for it. And even if things were sweet between me and Bread, there'd still be the fact that the whole plane is going to crash into the mountain.

Vanderventer wears fine gold chains over his sleeveless black shirt and has hairy arms. He has a good smile and loves to joke, which he can afford to do because his record of savagery reads like a satanic bible. Everyone who works for him or knows him at all calls him the Champ. He'd won the boxing tournament three seasons in a row before they tore out the old ring. Before my time. Brick and Clem turn away respectfully when Eddie comes in to whisper something into his brother's ear. The Champ nods seriously, then Eddie leaves again and the jokes start back up.

It occurs to me to wonder whether I could've got Vanderventer interested in keeping the Rook out of my life, before Bread came around. But I wasn't thinking this way, then.

5

It's dark in the furniture factory except along the row of machines at the front, near the door. A little deeper inside are piled cordwood and heaps of defective materials. Near the back there are equipment cages, the pipe room, and the powerhouse. I take my clipboard with me. June sixth is getting close now, and I'm not going to get caught with my pants around my ankles again. That guy wasn't me. There's been this kind of eye-opening irony to the last few weeks of my stay in Seamax, and if it's grated on me in one way, it's sharpened me in another. There's less hesitation, this time. More control.

I move through the darkness, my footsteps quiet because of the fine dust on the concrete floor.

I'm tired of it. There won't be another lap around this racetrack, for me. With the irony has come this narrowing suspicion that Bread could have gotten Rook more than another month in solitary the first time, if he'd wanted. I don't know that it's true, but I suspect it. The quality of suspicion, except in the stupidest sense, is missing in a lot of castles on the outside. They're so big, they get relaxed. I'm the opposite. For the sake of argument, you imagine the other guy is one step ahead of you. Then you suppose he may be two steps ahead. That's where it becomes intuitive – you go until it feels right. So now I wonder, has Bread been taking me for a test drive? If he does anything at all, will he get the Rook another month? One thing that all frauds and manipulators have in common is that they don't build tables and chairs, and they don't build monuments. They build treadmills.

I fold over the top page in the stack of papers on the clipboard, revealing a half-finished sketch of the power switches and the connecting wires at the main fuse box. I set the edge of the pencil tip against the paper while I study the switches for the breakers, and eventually the pencil begins to move. The problem is that the labels on all of the breaker switches have long since worn off. When I'm done, I'll take the drawings to Botch Mazel, who does electrical work when the hacks don't want to pay a contractor weekend rates. Botch used to be an electrician before he took an axe to his old lady. He'll tell me which fuses to pull to black out the yard and towers on one side so I can make it dark when I want to.

I can burn through my lock and lay down a section of the fence with just a day or two to prepare, but if I try running to freedom through woods and fields in the dark, I'll only end up in some trigger-happy sheriff's spotlight. So I'll need a ride. I don't know if Michaela will still be around or have the same phone number after three and a half years, but

I'm still going to call. My guess, she'll agree to come. Probably still can't leave that German husband who mail ordered her from Russia, whose face she scarred after one of his beatings. Broke off two of her own fingernails holding on to a doorjamb while he dragged her by the ankle. It's been a while since I thought of Michaela. Tough little nut, and a steady hand at the wheel. If she's around, she'll take my call. She always takes the call. 'It's you', she says. 'Tell me what is it, boss?' I think I'm her vacation. People who live in hell visit purgatory for their fresh air and sunshine. She'll come.

I sketch quickly with a practiced hand, and I don't have to look back and forth much between the paper and the fuse box. It's not unlike sketching the inside of a bank from memory while I sit in a car, outside. I pause for a quick glance around, and the thought strikes me that very soon this may all be a part of my past, and I experience a slight strain behind my ribs at the thought because I want it bad.

I move back toward the front area of the factory floor where men work with lathes, saws, and staple guns, and I pass an old factory motor that weighs a few hundred pounds, bolted to the floor next to a compressor. I've pre-loosened the bolts attaching it to the concrete with a ten-pound wrench but left them in place. This way it will only take me a few seconds to pry it up. I figure I can get a running start with that heavy motor and achieve enough momentum to bow the big fence over, then just walk right up it when it's half laid down. After that, the second fence only goes three feet underground. With a couple of pairs of leather gardening gloves, I can probably just pull it up and slip under. Then: Canada. For a while.

It's close to chow time on Monday evening. June has brought some heat to Seamax, just not the kind of sleepless doldrums that comes in August. It's a quiet time when cons live in their own tiny worlds, and the cell block feels almost like a New York tenement on a summer day. My own little storm cloud follows me. There's no peace. Only plans.

I go to the chow hall. I get my tray with a little pyramid built of milk cartons and move toward my table. When I'm about halfway there, someone steps into my path. Barely gives me time to stop without running into him. A hack. He's got a wavy length of hair across the top of his forehead like the edge of a lasagna. He's got an average build and lined eyes. He's Weisner.

The general noise in the chow hall is enough so that whatever he says to me, if he speaks in a normal voice, will be lost to everyone but me.

"I want you to know, it's over."

Because I don't know what he's talking about, I resort to the cool stare that convicts reserve for guards.

"You understand?" he says.

I stare.

"You don't have anything else to worry about from me, as long as you remember one thing. You are the lowest form of life on earth, no different from these other shitpiles in here. They just stacked the shit higher, in your case. I go home to my family every night. My house, my yard. There's a reason you're in here. You're not competent for real life." He makes a little circle with his finger around his ear. "There's something missing in your brain. You deserve to be dropped down an incinerator chute by an imbecile who peels potatoes for a living. But it's over, you son of a bitch. I'm not a problem anymore." Then he moves closer, like he's going to whisper a secret, and I feel him spit on the edge of my jaw, a cool wet line. "Don't worry about me. I'm done."

He looks up into my face for another moment and gets more of my cool stare in return. I can feel that my look is unbroken, and in the way of all convicts, I'm denying him the satisfaction of whatever contrition or injury he wants to see. That's instinct. The reality is, he's frozen me. I'm shocked, and I don't move.

Then the shock changes. It turns hollow and rotten like a week-old jack-o-lantern. Some regulator that's been straining inside me quits altogether, and my metabolism cycles up in an uncontrolled rush at the same instant that everything becomes somehow pointless. Then I seem to watch helplessly while things fall down inside me. They're like gears dropping out of a clockworks or pipes spilling from an engine. When Weisner turns his back and walks away, I still don't move. I can't tell whether it's because I'm paralyzed in some way or because the way I'm feeling is so unexpected that it's interesting, and the moment I start moving again it will be lost. On the surface I know that I should feel confused and startled, but that's not what is happening deep in the three-dimensional center of my head. While this hack's spit dries on the side of my face, the same spot where a taekwondo master once gave me a special chop that didn't stop me, I paradoxically remember a hotel restaurant in Philadelphia where a guy held a gun on me under the table. I remember the Asian hostess who had excellent cheekbones and seemed to want to be near me. I remember biting into a five-star burger made with bison meat, pink in the middle, a disc of havarti cheese on top, while the gun was pointed somewhere below my belly button. It wasn't a bad feeling. The whole scene comes back to me now with intense clarity, like I can almost reach my arm into that space. I remember the place was fifteen minutes from closing and the chef still came out to ask how our food was, and how the guy across the table from me eventually felt foolish and put the gun away, and we left with a deal. It's paradoxical to be thinking of this because what's clawing its way to the surface amid the collapsing machinery in my head is a rage so total and blinding that I'm shocked it exists. It's like watching my skin open up without pain as a live insect crawls out of it. I have no idea what's happening to me. The paradoxical memory is like a ringing in my ear, like the one after a deafening sound at a frequency you'll never hear again, ringing itself away for the last time. Then I have no capacity to imagine anything. I see Weisner's back moving away from me. The sight of him doesn't tug at the anger. It's bigger than him. I stand there waiting for it to pass. Finally it collapses, like a surf, spreading out in toxic yellow froth, depositing its load of trash. My head feels hot and swollen, my heart is two horses galloping through slick mud, my hands and feet tingle. I feel like I drank poison and I don't even know when.

I look around, and there's nothing in my environment that could have caused this, even with Weisner's help. Then I look back at Bread, who's talking in one direction but smiling at me with his eyes in another.

I set my tray down on the edge of a table, where a pair of convicts scoot away from it, and I begin to move toward Bread where he sits with his gang. He sees me coming but doesn't stop talking. My feet carry me toward him without my bidding, and I seem to float. Then I stand behind the backs of half his gang and talk at him – over him, whatever he's saying – across the table.

"Seventy-two hours," I say.

He keeps telling some story to Dodd for a few more seconds, then stops and looks up at me. The men sitting with their backs to me are leaning slightly away and turtling their necks.

"Seventy-two hours until the Rook gets out. What are you doing about that?"

"How about a little respect? I'm in the middle of dinner."

"I'm asking you about something that needs to be handled now. That should have been handled a week ago."

Then he answers me the way I've been answering him. "Don't worry about a thing," he says, knowing the exaggeration will make his statements seem less reliable. The deck cons around the table smile into their plates. Prison uniforms haven't had stripes for a long time, but these guys are zebras just the same, their numbers hard to tell when the eyes want to focus somewhere and the nerves are up.

When I don't leave, Bread seems to get away from himself, his face reddening. He says, "You want to have a conversation about the deal?"

I lean down so that my hands are on the edge of the table, and decks beneath me scoot away without getting up. The table bends under my weight. My upper body gives a sudden pump, and the table with the attached benches and the weight of twenty men moves three feet with an abrupt groan. Plastic cutlery and cups of water and grape juice go to the floor, and men at the surrounding tables stop talking. "You've sent enough trouble my way to keep me locked up the rest of my natural life. I asked you what you're doing. I won't ask again."

Our eyes lock. Bread stands up, slowly, crimson blooms in his cheeks. "Walk away," he says.

Only a few tables are aware of what's happening over the general wash of hundreds of convicts talking and eating, but other men are beginning to turn and watch. I see it in his eyes.

I lean further over the table. "I asked you a question. One way or another, I'm going to get an answer."

This goes far enough, the whole prison will know we're quits. He becomes nothing but a hot-headed petty dealer with a deck instead of a real gang, but with a real gang's enemies. I press my palms into the table, bending it until there's a faint crackling sound.

Bread looks very aware of stage we're on. He lets all the looks hit him and meets my stare. "No."

Then he keeps staring back at me and doesn't budge.

My brow takes on a life of its own and drops into my eyes. Anger and confusion - confusion at his control and lack of fear - settle in. More men are watching, now. Bread doesn't even look hateful, just like a man controlling a bad situation. This kind of control in a man given to moods and vapors and fugues, it makes no sense.

"Walk away. We still have a deal. *Walk away.*"

For a moment, I can't make myself move. I feel the pulse of caged violence in my arms. Why did I come stomping over here like an animal? When I have to back off, it's going to be like swallowing a box of thumbtacks. I don't wait. I do it all at once. I push off from the table, bending it like a trampoline, and walk off feeling like someone just clashed cymbals next to my ear.

I'm debating whether to stay in the chow hall and try to force some food down my throat – because I have to think clearly, tonight – and that's when I spot Vanderventer eating in his favorite spot, the left end at the back of the room, far from the hacks and the feebs, close to the windows and the light. He eats with his right elbow on the table like a trucker, that one outsized shoulder next to his chin like he's narrowing his profile. He has an off-center widow's peak with a contour that appears to give his head a bean shape, and a charming crooked smile.

I decide I'm not hungry and turn again to leave. I glance back from the doorway because of a feeling and am bolted in place by something dark and penetrating. Vanderventer is looking straight at me. Even at this distance, it's unmistakable. His eyes are dark as a Jewish woman's, like twin bore holes. I look back, trying to glean something from the set of his face, but he breaks his gaze and goes back to laughing and eating, so fast I'm left almost wondering whether it ever happened.

I walk away thinking, Bread, you dumb bastard.

I dread the coming of night because – if the last few are any indication – my thoughts will keep churning, I'll feel like I ate too much sugar, and I'll wish for the daylight to make me stop feeling like I'm aboard a boat. There's little in my cell to distract me. The only thing I've got better than mainline is a plush towel. Most cons who've been in a cell longer than a few weeks have personal items like photographs, address books, medications, keepsakes, candy. My cell is more like a dentist's waiting room: toothbrushes, apple juice, baby powder.

I pace and try to come up with specific instructions for the phone call I'll probably make in the morning, but I'm distracted. Amid everything I'm simmering about, Weisner's statements float momentarily to the surface, and I wonder what had made him madder than he'd probably ever been in his life. And me. That massive spasm of sick rage was like a dead hand that reached out and touched me, and I can still feel it. I assume Bread's failed or never really tried to keep the Rook locked up, so I try not think about it. I try not to consider that he still has a few hours to do it. Most of all, I tell myself there's nothing I can do to affect it, either way. It's up to me to get out of here, now.

Shortly before lockdown, I find myself on the way to his cell.

I should stay away from him, I know that. But then I'm moving through the tunnel into the SO.

Bread knows the situation and knows what I need, and it occurs to me again that he's no genius. He's like a ratchet. If a competitor has his mind on the situation fifteen hours a day, Bread has his mind on it eighteen hours a day. I actually feel alright, now that I know I'll be fine in any event. I've got enough powder from sulfur matcheads to pack the lock on my cell. I've got a factory motor and a poorly planned fence. I've got a five-foot-tall Russian woman who'll be waiting for a second phone call with a hot car and a .38 special. I make the call in the morning. Private knowledge gives me a cool feeling. There's also a loose tingle around my nerve endings from this afternoon in the chow hall, like small air bubbles under the skin. I'm two people, tonight.

I go into D Block. As I cross the space, I go through a little draft of cool outside air that gives me a new thought. Even if Bread comes through now, I should make the call anyway. The way I felt with Weisner, the way I feel in the early mornings, that won't be the worst of it. Something's slipping. It's all over for me, here; my plan has failed, and I should concede that and get out before something irreversible happens. The *worst* thing that can happen is that Bread tells me he's got my problem covered, and we keep scraping along. It's time to go. I could make the call now and maybe even go tonight.

Instead, I stop on Bread's front porch, and he's inside with the door closed. Something about him says he's seen me even though he's turned partly away watching his little color television set.

The show is Changing Seasons, a soap he'd picked up during a stretch in isolation in Chesworth. Every con who's spent any length of time in solitary has a soap or two that he can't go without. Changing Seasons seems even worse than most, a cast of second rate models who can't act amid flimsy sets, but you'd never know it to look at Bread. It's strange to watch him engrossed in scenes at funeral parlors, a kind of place he'd never go unless he was the one in the casket.

Maybe I expect him to talk first, but he makes me ask. The obvious way he keeps me waiting and gives me vague answers is prosaic and expected and makes me hate the situation more than I hate him. Bread doesn't act bothered by the fact that I'm dogging him about this twice in the same day. It crosses my mind that it may be flattering to his ego. "I told you I'd take care of it, didn't I?" he says.

"You expect me to sit back and trust that?"

"I expect you to do whatever you want, just like you always do."

"He gets out, it'll be no better for you."

I'd revealed my little crystal of knowledge, but Bread doesn't seem to hear the words.

"I told you I'd take care of it."

"I see you tomorrow, you don't know me. You got that?"

Saying the words makes some echo of the rage wake up like a hungry thing and tingle again in my nerve endings.

Bread ignores me. His face is a sullen mask, as if there's no sensation in it and it's beyond his power to change its expression. I want to smash through the bars and teach him that whatever inner thundercloud has him in its grip, I can be worse. I started to sweat in my pits a few hours ago. I can smell myself.

"You hear me? You see me coming, don't be in the way."

Suddenly I don't know what I'm doing here, capering, taunting a crazy person. It sickens me.

Then Bread looks up again from the television. Even though his face looks like rubber, I can somehow tell he has a feeling of rightness about this – he has something I need, and things are the way they should be. "Get some sleep."

I don't move, just stand outside the bars of this deck's cell while he turns away from me again to watch television with a numb expression. I can't tell whether it's the most invisible I've ever been or the most transparent. Suddenly I don't know whether to laugh or stamp my feet. I watch Bread, and he looks smaller than usual, on top of his blanket, his front porch like the entrance to a woman's boudoir and not a place to be standing. Good thing I'm not staying. Good thing I don't have to deal with this strange, blind, crippled, vicious deck anymore.

I go back to my cell to stand for last count, then pace. As I look ahead to tomorrow and getting out, it becomes more obvious how I've mishandled everything the last couple of months and how escape can't come soon enough, now. I'll be hard on myself, once I'm out, for this sloppiness, for having to run. Finally I lay down and endure a night when my brain wakes me up with little shocks every hour, like a boss catching me asleep on the job.

I'm awake while the kitchen crew gets unlocked at 4:30.

When I stand for 6am count, there's a clock in my head. I don't know what time Rook gets out of the hole the day after tomorrow. I eat and then walk around like a plane waiting for its turn at the runway. My stomach isn't exactly churning, but it seems to have turned hard. I know the plan and what I'll say to Michaela, and figure I'll call soon. That gives me a cool sort of feeling, the kind you get when you know something the other guy doesn't, and it feels good after weeks of keeping a grey hat pulled down tight to my eyes.

But then I wait. Instead of picking up a phone, I float through half a QA shift I won't be able to remember minutes after it's over, the sun slipping higher in big photographic leaps. Then I'm walking toward the chow hall. I tell myself I'll call after I eat, that I don't still hold out an irrational hope of being able to stay and cash in on the last four years of sacrifice. I eat, twirling my spoon in tasteless tapioca pudding...then I go back to work. As I go, I feel like a guy driving on through a bad storm with water up to his axles.

I'm on my way to the weight pile before dinner, still planning to call, when Frankson catches me and tells me Bread wants to see me at his cell. On autopilot, I almost tell him to get lost, but my body and voice are slow to react and almost languid. I follow him without a word, through the SO, south toward D Block. Up the four rusty metal steps out of the sunken corridor from the SO to the floor level of the block. The hacks on the tiers are watching me because this isn't my cell block. We reach the top of the stairs, and I'm strangely out of breath.

After that it starts out exactly the same, a repeat of yesterday.

I stand outside his cell, looking at a setup where everything is a cut above mainline. Radio with cassette deck, miniature tv set, silk sheet, shelf bulging with pudding cups, name brand soup cans, plastic-wrapped pastries. Down pillow, some kind of plastic mirror big enough for him to see his whole face at the same time. Better than mainline, but not well thought out, like the uptown apartment of a guy who lives to work.

Bread reclines on an elbow like a Roman, looking through a Spanish porno mag, not looking at me while I stand outside his cell with the bars shut on me. It passes quickly, but for a second I feel an echo of rage so severe I can't believe Bread's unaware of it, unafraid of it, since it's so bad *I* am almost afraid of it. It occurs to me what really burns me up about what Weisner said to me: they were my own words - words I might have said to people around me here - coming out of someone else's mouth. My own words that I'd never said because I'd gotten so sensible. Without meaning to I hang one hand on a crossbar like Bread is outside and I'm on the inside. I know him a little by now and know that if he's making me stand here and wait this long, it's because he's done something or has something I want. I've never felt rays of hope shining on me before while being ignored by a deck convict who knows I'm waiting on him. Man pushes everything to the hilt, and sometimes I'm outright fascinated by what a strange thing he is and why I don't leave the best parts of him on floor for the porters to clean up with rubber gloves. I'm about to walk away again when he says,

"It's done, Croft. It doesn't matter what happens, now. Rook stays in the hole long term."

I stop. I'm not relieved. I don't feel anything, not even my own body. I say, "Are you sure?" stupidly.

"What did I just say?"

I want to tell him never to say that to me again, but I just stand there.

"So we have an understanding, now?" he says.

I start to walk aimlessly around the cellhouse, feeling like a foot that fell asleep. Objects around me — bars, rails, windows – start to pop like birds breaking from bushes, suddenly becoming vivid in my sight. You never know the pall that's been over you until it's lifted. The shallow breaths you've been taking, like someone stuffed the bottom half of your lungs with cotton - then you pull the air all the way down. At the same time, something troubles the edge of my mind as I walk. Something I saw and only half remember. In Bread's cell. What was it? At the foot of the bed next to that ledger of his with the black cover, his little book of vengeance. Something that didn't belong.

I've spent years training myself to retain details so I can revisit them later, while I work. What I do is remember one object from each frame. If I focus on that, I can begin to see everything else that was around it. The trick is not to try too hard. I focus on the ledger, and initially there's nothing but blur around it. That's normal. I wait. A few seconds later, I see a nub pencil. A cigarette and a dollar bill rolled into a tube. And then it's there, what's bothering me: a photograph. A photograph of women and children in a school playground. I can even see the kids' faces - a boy and a girl, both with brown hair. Seems like an awfully wholesome item for Bread to have. It can't be his own family. There's not much I'm certain of about Bread, but family is one thing – he has none and hasn't had any for a long time, if ever. I let my mind drift a bit, and suddenly I have the answer. Of course.

Bread has a little reach, after all. Maybe he's proving that in spades, today. He claims to have gotten Rook a permanent detention in the hole, and on his bedsheet is a photograph someone on the outside has taken for him of Weisner's family. I frown. It makes such a neat little turn of events for Bread that I almost loathe my own relief. But then I think: confirm now, loathe later.

I go to the first tier of B Block to see one of Seamax's life-withouts. I walk across the polished cellblock floor to B11 and see Fronthouse inside with another man whose name I don't know. The life-withouts make up one whole side of the lower-B tier. The cell has only one bed in it, and the two men sit on a custom comforter playing chess. At the back of the cell is a shelf heavy with law books.

I darken the doorway. When Fronthouse looks up, I ask to come inside.

The Front has wizened, knobby facial features and hands on a small and almost youthful body. He'd been an attorney on the outside. Now he's a jailhouse lawyer. You might think he spends all his time on trial issues and appeals, but the Front is mostly kept busy with bankruptcy and divorce. He is also privy to information from representing cons in their formal interviews with the Disciplinary Hearings Officer.

I ask what has happened to the Rook.

The Front moves his bishop but doesn't take his hand off the piece. He says, "I understand your interest, so I'll tell you. DO Stepner is normally by the book. I know what you hear, but I haven't seen any sign of it. Then out of nowhere he revives an old conspiracy investigation, a year old, with no new evidence. On top of that, he recommends solitary confinement until the investigation is concluded. That means indefinitely."

The DO doesn't work under the warden but as an investigator for the regional office. Stepner can send prisoners to the hole for longer than 60 days, even recommend transfers.

Fronthouse takes his hand off the bishop, studies his move with dissatisfaction, then looks at me. "They dragged the big boy out in chains so they could sit him down and tell him he was going back in for God knows how long. I'll be honest with you, Croft, I tried to stop it."

I nod.

"For a minute, I thought he was going to go berserk. But then they led him out the same way they led him in."

Something about that idea hooks me in the stomach and pulls, but only for a second.

"The idea that it's not cruel and unusual really makes me wonder about people. Half the men who stay in the hole longer than six months come out in straight jackets. It would be better if they just horsewhipped a guy like they did in the old days. That's something I would never have said on the outside."

The Front's chess companion chimes in now: "Or they'd hang them for a minute, until they blacked out. I read that somewhere. I don't know which one I'd choose. Not the hole, I guess."

I say, "Are you going to appeal it?"

"No, because I don't think it would work." The Front looks at me over his glasses. "Even if it did, then I might have a whole other mess on my conscience."

I don't know what to say to that, so I just thank the Front for telling me. As I walk away from his cell, I feel strain falling off of me like the layers of an onion. Like coils of heavy rope sliding off the back of my neck. I stare up at the stingy amount of sunlight striking into B Block through the high small windows. The new situation slowly becomes real as I keep walking, like an instant photograph developing. Two months of dragging the weight around with me are slipping off. Then I start feeling irritated with myself for letting it get to me that way.

I have restless legs for a while, don't want to stop anywhere. I buy some things I don't need from the commissary, pace the yard.

I eventually hear it on the tiers that a terrified young convict who'd needed a deal was put into Protective Custody hours before Rook was sentenced by Stepner. Now it's all over the wire that the boy's cellmate had been charged and transferred out last week, and the boy picked up a snitch jacket off of that. Maybe the DO set it up that way and jammed him so he'd give up something on the Rook in exchange for PC. Stepner would know the cons have a way of putting two and two together. If it happens to equal five…close enough.

I think about it as I lay waiting for sleep that night, the chain of events that Bread was able to set off. There are maybe a few cons this part of the country who could have set something like that up.

In my mind, I've already started abandoning my plans for escape. I wait for the future I want to start putting itself back together in my mind's eye. I remember an upscale mountain lodge with a fieldstone fireplace and timbers recovered from an old whaling ship. I've always had it in mind to steal a great piece of art, like a Van Gogh. A heist thought to be impossible. My work of art. For some reason, that future refuses to come. I feel disconnected from it, like it's an idea I had for a movie. They say you're institutional when even your dreams are about prison.

I roll onto my side but don't sleep right away.

The last thing I'd said to Bread when he broke the news to me was to ask something I hadn't thought to ask Fronthouse: "He's in the hole, but they didn't put him back in a box." Not exactly a question.

Bread had already lost interest in the conversation, or wanted me to think he had. "Who cares?"

6

Summer comes, and Bread's operation grows. There are new faces in the gang. All the muling by friends and relatives has stopped – he's got guards and other hacks doing the job, now. It's faster and less risky, and supply isn't a factor anymore.

Other small operations are desperately trying to survive during the second half of June, and there are two attempts to stick Bread before the July 4th holiday. Both fail, one because of luck and the other because he had a few seconds of warning and fought so hard the two big hunters couldn't get a blade in him before the hacks showed up. It only helped his reputation. Some people are eager to say it was Vanderventer, but if that were the case, there would have been another attack within the hour. Most people in Bread's gang are making steady money now, so it will take more than a rumor or a failed sticking to scare them off.

I'd heard a hack ask this question as Bread passed him on the tier, and the question remains: what's the Champ waiting for? Bread's risen so fast, I think maybe Vanderventer is waiting for him to flame out. Or maybe it's some deeper plan. (If it was my call, I'd wait for Bread to consolidate all the small-time action and *then* take him out, putting one of my own lieutenants in his place.)

Maybe part of it is me. I'm supposed to be the power behind the organization, but I don't think there's much talk of going after me directly, for a couple of reasons. To understand it a deck only needs to imagine trying to insert three inches of sharpened spoon between the ribs of a chest sixty four inches around. I don't know, though. For a disciplined organization there's always an answer to one convict with strength, especially if they don't have to deal with him in real time, can sit back and connive.

During June and July, the violence escalates. Bread concentrates on heroin and morphine, the big sellers, stepping on the scag with sugar and powdered milk. There are always guys willing to do the knifework that comes with that: the Skins might run the drugs in Redlow or Spinnerville, but in Seamax their real money comes from gambling and extortion - and contracts. There's been almost a murder a week, this lovely summer. I don't know how the stuff comes in or who Bread's hack mules are – that's Bread's inside baseball – but with a bottomless drug supply, Bread's living on the edge of a knife. He's on the verge of going from a big small operation to small big operation. That will make all the difference.

He's no genius. Sometimes his own guys have to deal with his little vanities and the subtle things he doesn't pick up on. But he never stops. From the moment his eyes open in the morning, he's trying to control everyone and everything. Even his blind spots help him by feeding his energy – he doesn't worry about things he doesn't see. I'm sure it's nothing new under the sun, and I can see why guys like him wind up on top of shitheaps like this. It's what they do. That, and nothing else. Who knows what's inside them?

I don't think Bread enjoys pushing the envelope the way some hotheads do. In his reality, there's just something wrong with a world where he's not on top, and he isn't one to stand for that. Except for that one clerical error, he seems to have no feeling about the work.

It's hot in mid-July, and the sun is swollen with humidity. Ants have claimed the southern part of the SO's first level, moving in lines over the dock and the floor of the corridor inside, watering themselves from the leaky pipes. The heat keeps the yard empty during the middle of the day. Hacks disappear for long stretches, playing cards where it's cool and drinking Cokes with a belt of cheap rum or vodka, from bottles that roll around old wooden desk drawers while they're looking for pencils for a write-up. The Skins go around with their shirts off, arms hanging limp and dangerous like pythons at their sides. The gang's business keeps me busy, and I don't have much of my own time – a funny thing, in prison. When I hit the weight pile, the sweat drips off my nose and runs down my chest in tickling rivers as the heat presses in. I wrench the weights around not to build strength, but to get rid of it, drive it out.

Here's a fact. It isn't easy to get someone alone in prison. It's often done, but it always takes some maneuvering. There are about six hundred inmates in Seamax, about a hundred and fifty per block. Barely medium-sized, and it's not as overcrowded as some. But it's crowded, and few of its nooks and crannies are private for long. I'm on my way to the weight pile after morning count, not yet knowing someone has designed to get me alone this morning.

I've just finished climbing the B staircase that comes out near the weight pile, and I see a familiar figure leaning against the wall of the corridor up ahead, past the pile and the showers. It looks at me and nods, takes the bottom of one foot off the wall and turns to face me. Brick Cassio is one of Vanderventer's lieutenants. He is aptly named. He's tall and solid and tucks his uniform pants into heavy work shoes. He has brick colored hair, brick colored freckles on the upper half of his face, and a solid jaw. He also has smooth skin and an upturned nose that makes him look like a bratty kid. His arm curls at me to come on and talk.

I'd slowed down when I first saw him. Now I stop completely. Come on, take a walk with me down this empty corridor, where we can discuss how successful you've helped to make a competitor.

He waves me on with his whole arm, friendly like, his body language imploring and faintly humorous.

I don't want to show hesitation. I begin to walk again. I take my time and let my center of gravity flow down into my legs until my feet feel thick. That way, not much short of a cement truck is going to topple me.

"Got a minute?" Brick says once I'm close enough.

"A minute," I say. Just because he's one of Vanderventer's lieutenants doesn't mean I'm going to fall all over myself. I slow to a very deliberate pace.

We fall in together, walking south toward D Block. I keep my center mass low and try to extend my sense of hearing down the smaller connecting corridors. We walk together side by side, and Brick doesn't say anything. Neither do I. The unspoken history between us – between the organizations we represent – begins to fill the space around us. There are several things that might be about to happen, none of them good. I suddenly wonder, Have I caught Bread's strange disease, letting myself think that somehow the shoe wouldn't drop? For my part, all I'd have to do is throw a fist out to the side, without even turning, and Brick would be in a world of hurt. He knows this, but he's totally relaxed. As we approach the D stairwell at the south end of the SO, he says, "The Champ wanted me to talk to you about something."

"What's that?"

"In here."

He opens the door to a small utility room that's always locked except when Botch Mazel is inside, cursing and banging on pipes. Brick goes in first and flicks on the light. I follow, but already I can feel my patience wearing thin. If it wasn't for the cloud of doubts that's kept me thinking about Vanderventer, I would never have come this far, much less close myself in a piperoom with this deck in the morning while I want to be hitting the pile.

The room is about six feet deep. I come inside, stand near the door, close it.

"Alright," I say.

"How you doing today?" says Brick.

I don't quite let a smirk show on my face.

"Okay, I'll get to the point. The Champ is thinking you must be pretty frustrated with the your situation, these days. Jammed up with the Rook, stuck with this upstart, Bread. I can't imagine he sees the lines too good, this guy. Something like that will make the road bumpy, make you feel the time more than you want to."

It's one of the most reasonable things I've heard in a while. I don't say that, though. I want him to think I believe he is trying to brace me, keep him off balance that way. For the moment neither of us is throwing his weight – mine physical, his organizational.

"The Champ respects the old lines. You know that. Maybe it's not a perfect system, but it works. Smooth time. And this other guy, he may have helped you out, but at what cost? How long till he gets you a new conviction, guy like that? Unless he already has?"

I twirl a finger for him to get on with it.

"Champ's got a proposition for you."

I turn my head away slightly and act bored. I'm still a castle, whatever my situation is, and this is still deck intrigue, whatever his organization is. Inwardly, I find it strange that no one has walked by in the hallway, yet. I haven't heard a single pair of shoes, and this isn't the quietest time of day in the SO.

"Distance yourself from Bread. Cut him loose. Then the Champ makes sure Rook stays locked up."

"Keeping him locked up is a favor. A payment. For that I 'distance myself'? That's awful cheap."

"Bread's paying you to do something. The Champ wants to pay you to do nothing. You don't like deck bosses, right? How is this not better? I know we both respect the old rules. We respect each other. And you don't respect Bread."

I'm not sure whether this is Brick talking or Vanderventer, but it is either a lot more perceptive or a lot more honest than I usually get from convicts.

"That's it?" I say. "The deal never changes?"

"If it did, would you go along?"

"No."

"And we know it."

"What if I tell you never to bother me again."

Brick shrugs with his palms in the air and a smile spreading on his face, as if the idea of violence and finality for him is like sliding into a warm bath. "It's nothing, either way."

Nice. A casual, inside-out threat that Vanderventer can probably carry out. I still haven't heard any passing shoes, out in the corridor.

I say, "Alright."

"Alright what?"

"Alright."

"Really?"

Now I laugh a little, through my nose. He thought I'd be a tougher sell. Apparently he doesn't know how I feel, after all. These days I'm always walking into places I don't want to be. If it might be dangerous, I go in first. Otherwise, I walk behind.

"You don't like him too much, do you."

I look directly at him. "I don't like anybody too much."

At this point, Brick is excited, shifting his weight, smiling. He says, "Excuse me," then reaches past me and knocks twice on the door we're behind.

The door opens at my back. I'm not worried about a surprise attack because I've just agreed to their deal. The door comes open slowly, just drifting, as if from a draft in a horror movie. The hinges squeal. Then Vanderventer is standing there, grinning with half his mouth. The open neck of his shirt shows springs of black chest hair, and he has the smell and presence and slow way of moving of a physical man who can deceive with his intelligence. I realize we're both wearing almost identical grins. Went down for a string of relatively minor crimes: B & E, distribution of stolen goods, parole violation, resisting – there was absolutely nothing to foretell what he would become. Sometimes, I think I almost like him for that.

He says, "I was just standing out here, thinking." His gaze traces the doorframe. "In this place, inside these walls, there's almost no privacy. But I've got someone like Brick here with me all the time, on top of that. All the time. I'm never alone like I was the last couple of minutes."

I say, "How was it?"

He sticks out his right hand, the one attached to the outthrust shoulder. I shake it, and we keep shaking. He's got a good grip for a deck, but he's not trying to impress me with his grip. "What's your man's line on Stepner?"

"I don't know."

"Will you try to find out?"

"Favor to do nothing, huh?"

"A favor for a favor. When it's over, Rook stays locked up and we never met before. I don't know your name."

"I'll try to find out."

We keep shaking for another few seconds, unnaturally long, and when we release our grip, it's like letting go of a chess piece. Too late to change your mind. That's immediately clear.

Then he's gone. Wham-Bam. Even the hacks don't get much of Vanderventer's time.

It's Tuesday, drug day. 6am count is called, and then castles move out tier by tier. We report to A Block with the crazies. There's a secure door to get into the block that stays locked, and the smell inside is slightly different, a hint of piss and iodine instead of the standard cologne they could call Restless Nights. When it's my turn, I take the little paper pill cup where the nurse slides it under the Duraglass, rattle the pills around, then fling them onto my tongue.

I don't know how much Bread pays the hacks who work the little pharmacy, and I've been sort of curious to see how far I can play this. Usually I jam the pills under my tongue and slide them way back almost to the gag point, but I can tell the guard with the latex gloves, pen light, and tongue depressor doesn't really check. Not me. Today when I open my mouth wide, the pills are sitting right on top of my tongue.

The guard shines the light in my mouth, looks down his nose and lays the wooden tongue depressor on my teeth. Then he snaps the light back off and says, "Next."

I turn away feeling troubled. I'd like to have a better idea of Bread's game and who he's got. There's surprisingly little I could've told Vanderventer yesterday, and I wonder if that's an accident.

There's a metal garbage can just outside the pharm door, and I spit the pills into it like bullets as I go out. A ponderous ripple moves through the line of waiting castles.

Vanderventer's deal keeps the Rook put away a lot more cheaply. It's a good one. Getting rid of the feeling that my grey hat is slowly giving me brain cancer, that's even better. I'd thought going to him would probably be seen as desperate or taken as an insult, but him approaching me changes the logic. There's no reason to doubt Vanderventer: he'll do what he says, and probably won't be too taxed by it, either. I've thought about who in Bread's gang I might ask about Bread's line on Stepner, narrowed it down to a few. I'll just have to corner one of them and shake it out of him; then tell him very specifically what's going to happen to his anatomy if he tells Bread.

I'm still a little too keyed up to decide on the details, but I can figure those out tonight. Right now, knowing that Bread and my career as a bodyguard are living history has given me an itch: I go to the weight pile feeling stronger than I have in months.

The barbell frowns with three hundred pounds of plates on each end. Up and down it goes, slow, steady, with the delicate plink of the plates tipping against one another. The world gets simple again. Looking down myself, I can see the twin domes of my pectoral muscles cresting. When my arms are straight, the triceps bulge over my elbows. I was big on the outside, but never like this.

Across the floor is a deck who used to play pro football. He's forty-five years old, and still he's pounding out reps with four hundred pounds on the bar. It's taken him years of sweat and drugs, stretching, controlled breathing, to stay in this kind of shape; in short, science. That's the difference between him and a castle like me.

He's learning his limits.

I'm learning the opposite. Bread, Rook, Vanderventer, and a lot about the last few months begins to blend together and fade away as I pump. Now that there's a good chance I won't be hard-assing the time, the particulars don't seem to matter much.

Part of me is glad for a case like Rook, mega-huge and unruly. He's a reminder to the decks—you don't know us. You don't know what we can become. Bread pissing on him only means that some decks think they've got it all figured out: like dogs, they don't understand potential. All they understand is what you can threaten them with right now. A deck is a deck not because he's small but because he's stupid and trifling.

I decide I'll just learn the one small piece of information Vanderventer wants, and wash my hands.

I leave the pile after my workout, and my little stormcloud finds me again as I walk. I wanted to do my time and not get caught up in the big sideshow. All so tough, I think. All so hard and smug. They get used to the small world. A dirty hack ringleader like Stromm starts to think he's Boss Tweed. A successful convict gangster thinks he earns as much as a bank president. They can have their perspective. I'll have mine.

It's been six weeks since Bread made solitary Rook's long-term home, and we haven't had one of his heart-to-hearts in half that time. When he does come to talk to me, I have a suddenly sick feeling. I've just about reached my limit with him. That he also looks close to his limit is of no consequence. He comes into the nearly empty television room where I'm reading and just stands there with his ass against an ancient pinball machine that guys have shivved each other over, looking at me, watching me read. We don't often deal with each other directly, anymore. I see him here and there and live with the consequences of his actions. We're really the next thing to strangers.

The tv is playing low on the other end of the room. There's the thin smell of old sweat and floor cleaner that I will always associate with empty common rooms in prison. Bread stands there while I make him wait. To him that is insane. It fits nowhere with his conception of the world, and I wonder how he ever had the patience to work his way up to anything. At the same time, I live with the doubt that I'm really on top of any situation as long as Rook could get out and Bread is friendly with the DO. Sometimes everything I do feels like farce, an unfamiliar feeling that I don't want getting familiar.

I say, "You're in my light."

He waits a few beats, for theater, then says, "How much do you really know about what's been going on here, Croft?"

It's rhetorical. He's telling me I don't know shit. But less is more, sometimes. Do I care what the decks are sticking in their veins or shoving up their noses?

He says, "We've reached a certain point, and I think it's time for you to make a decision."

"Like chocolate or vanilla?"

"How about smart or stupid?"

I go back to concentrating on my reading. I expect him to get pissed off, but Bread's unusually calm, today. He may not even have meant to insult me just now, but it's insult enough that he thinks he can come in here alone and try to talk hard to me like we're somehow eye to eye. Then I realize with an unpleasant little shock that I'm supposed to be honored he's here in person.

"We're going places, Croft. Things are going to change around here. They'd just go that much more smoothly with you on board."

Funny he still believes that, after the last few months of complaining about me.

And he doesn't get that even if Vanderventer wasn't around, he couldn't handle the top spot. If it landed in his lap an hour from now, he'd wind up picked apart by the hacks and other gangs that Vanderventer managed to push into the dark corners or rope into his own interests.

Instead of telling him that, I bait him, try to find out what Vanderventer wants to know. Now's as good a time as any. "Then maybe you should tell me how I can be sure the Rook is staying put. I hear someone else talks to Stepner, lately."

He waits just a beat too long to speak. Doubts cross the gulfs of his mind, and then I can see it when he's reassured by something. Then says, "No, they don't."

"And you know this how?"

"I just told you we're going places. What do you say? You want to take the trip?"

I can't tell if he dodged the question or just didn't hear it above the constant wheedle that must go on in his head. There are times he really doesn't seem to hear me speak, as if what comes out of my mouth isn't English but some kind of deep-throated babble nobody has time to sort through. I say, "Nope."

He's quiet another minute, but raging inside, now. He jerks upright, his rump moving the pinball machine a couple of noisy inches. "You can't do that. We had a deal. A deal I honored."

Not giving a damn about honor but guessing that I do.

I say, "I should have got that deal in writing."

"You've got no gratitude."

I feel my neck muscles bunch and my teeth begin to grind. "That's right. How do you know Stepner won't get away from you and get me killed?"

Maybe later he'll get around to wondering why I kept bringing up Stepner, but now he's looking at me curiously with his face glowing like a red light bulb. "What are you if your word is no good, Croft?"

The man has the kind of short, selective memory that drives people crazy. He won't understand anything I say to him. Other people being careful of me has no application to him.

It's not until I walk out of the room a few minutes later that I wonder what exactly Bread might have been talking about. What was he up to? As I walk along, the empty corridor of the SO feels like a bazaar of conspiracies. I remember thinking I was going to ring information from some scrawny neck in the gang. If something else is about to hatch, now is probably a good time to do that.

Chris Elbert is an ideal subject to question: scared, weak, but egotistical enough to hot dog a bit if he knows something. I get a smooth kind of feeling. I'll play this cool. I'll do as little as possible to get what I want. I go toward B Block and then along the tier to Chris' cell.

He probably won't be in the cell, I think, but as I move onto his front porch, Chris E is there, folding his clean clothes. He has an ordinary appearance, a little on the tall side and just the slightest bit knock-kneed and limpwristed, as if he'd survived a muscular disease as a kid. He has dark messy hair that's almost black and a thin attempt at a mustache, and there's a big blemish on his chin. I move into his doorway and stand there. Then I ask to come in and move inside before he can answer.

The real benefit of my bulk is the look. In another age, the strength itself might be worth more, but today it's the threat. Chris' body coils up on itself a little, as if I stepped on his foot. "Croft. What is it?"

I move into the middle of his cell and look around, take my time. I make it clear that I'm staying as long as it pleases me.

He says, "What's up, man?"

I stand with the backs of my knees to his bunk and slowly sit down, breathing out. "I'll ask the questions, and you'll answer them."

I feel him leaning away from me and looking around me at the open door out of his cell like it's a paradisiacal mirage. "I can't talk now," he says.

"Why not?"

"I have to be someplace."

"Where?"

"I don't…remember."

"You don't remember?"

"No." His voice is getting small, dwindling to a single point of sound.

"First question."

"It wasn't my idea. I can't tell you about it."

This stops me for a second. Can't tell something to me, in particular? On instinct, I decide I'll ask him anything except what it is he can't tell me.

"Why not?"

"I can't."

"I said why not."

"Why are you asking *me*? I'm not even involved!"

He's retreating up the other corner of the cell now, up the wall, like a spider.

"I'll give you to the count of five."

"I can't! I can't!"

"I used to know someone who could clamp down on a guy's head-" I mimed it by facing my palms toward each other in front of my chest, elbows out. "And say which eye was going to pop out first."

"I can't!" he screeches. He's winding himself up so badly that all I have to do is keep sitting here and he'll have to tell me whatever he's hiding or his own nervous system will shred itself. That's when a hack stops by.

He's a newjack, barely more than a kid. I'd be surprised if he's twenty-two.

"What's going on in here?"

Chris stares at him and says nothing.

The young guard looks back and forth between us. "Whose cell is this?"

Without a word, I get up and walk out. I shoulder past the kid, and he lets me go. I go back toward the SO. A minute later, he moves on and continues his walk around the tier. A few convicts watch him, this young, apple-cheeked Newjack. Some with contempt, others just to stare at something – anything – that doesn't belong here.

I get almost to the corridor out of the cell block before I turn on my heel. I stomp right back toward Chris E's door.

The newjack had walked some distance away, but he sees me just before I reach the cell and starts jogging over. "Hey!"

I don't pause. I walk directly into the cell. Chris had been standing at his sink and goes pinwheeling away from it, back toward his bunk. I wheel after him. He gets up on the bed and stands in the corner, raises one knee between me and his body. I reach up and take hold of his arm. Just take hold of it, that's all.

"We're gonna kill him!"

"WHO!"

"Please!"

The kid is back outside the cell now, not coming in, sap in his hand, shouting.

No time for games. "Who! You tell me who or I promise you–"

Then the kid, thumb hovering over the button of his radio: "This is the last time I'm going to say it!"

I half whisper, half growl at Chris: "I'll be back in twenty."

I turn and walk out of the cell and down the tier exactly as I did the first time. Thoughts are popping a mile a minute in my head, about Bread trying to kill a snitch, a hack – that would be something he would know I'd disapprove of, something he'd order them not to tell me about. I don't want that heat while my name is on the roster, and it would be a stupid thing to do, anyway. Was that Bread's big plan? Which one, then? Weisner had already thrown in the towel. They must have just discussed it, or Chris wouldn't have known exactly what I was asking about like that.

I ruminate on it as I head back toward my cell. Kill or maim a hack, the system has its ways of handling you. You see it sometimes with guys who've hurt them, and sometimes with a guy they've just taken a certain shine to. I've heard of unnecessary dental procedures without anesthetic, desperately sought furloughs suddenly offered and then cancelled at the last minute. There are the cell doors that mysteriously don't lock, giving access to thieves and predators. The lost personal mail that finds its way to a blood enemy. A guard might claim to have visited or had sex with a loved one, or to have detained and abused them after a visit. It might be all of the above, with a grand finale of 'shot trying to escape'. The hacks take a real kitchen-sink approach to tearing a guy down. Right to his soles. Some convicts get a reminder about who's got the most dangerous gang of all. No way I'd let Bread kill a hack while my name is mixed up with his.

Because of what I said, Chris figures he has about twenty minutes before I come back. That means he'll wait a couple of minutes, then try to sneak off to Bread's cell, where he'll have the protection of the gang. I step out of the SO's central corridor just as he's passing it on his way between cell blocks. He turns on his heel and tries to scoot away, but I snatch the back collar of his shirt and lift him onto his toes. Then he's doing a ballet across the floor, and just as quiet except for a small noise coming out of his throat because the top button of his state-issue is caught under his Adam's apple. I walk him a short way down the corridor and push him up against the wall below a burned-out fluorescent light.

"Wait!" he says. "Just wait! I'll pay you whatever you want."

"Don't change the subject."

"I can't tell you anything. You try to stop them, they'll kill me. Why are you doing this, anyway?"

He stops to swallow something sharp. His breath is bad.

I slip my fingers around his throat. Jowls that are normally hidden make a soft bulge along his jaw.

He gargles: "You can't tell anyone. The Champ. Everything. Would be. Fucked. You. Too."

"Why can't I tell the Champ? Who's Bread going to kill?"

Vanderventer's supplier. His source. Or his main hack. Who is that? McMeany? French?

"You too. Champ. He'll kill. You too."

"He won't kill me. I work for him. I'm working for him right now."

Chris eyes bulge so extremely that when he twitches them back and forth, they move his eyebrows. I let him go, and he doubles over at the waist. A pair of convicts pass at the end of the hall, see something, and choose not to see more. Chris watches me carefully while he coughs.

Once the coughing slows down, I say, "Tell me what's going on right now, we'll go see him together. I'll tell him you helped watch his back."

Chris just squints, shakes his head as if confused. "We can't."

"Why not?"

"Bread's right. You don't get it, man." He tweaks his neck and spits on the floor, then looks up at me from the tops of his eyes, his mouth smiling. "He's the one we're going to kill."

That's when the newjack comes around the corner with two of his friends. The kid is red in the face. "That's him. The big one."

One of the other two is Wimpy, a hack I know to see and by reputation. He has twenty years on the kid and has been at Seamax longer than I have. My head is full of what Chris just told me, and I blink at them as if they're transparent. The kid starts to complain to Wimpy, and the older guard tells him to keep quiet. They approach me together, ignoring Chris except to give him a brief dirty look. Wimpy puts a hand out when the kid goes to speak again. He studies my face and says, "You got something in your teeth?"

I blink at him again and shake my head slightly. I have to control my breathing and ignore a sourceless flashing light behind my eyes.

"Think you better get back to your cell for the rest of the evening," says Wimpy. "Think you better not be seen out again tonight. Tomorrow's a new day."

"That's it?" says the kid. "Are you kidding me?"

Wimpy gives my shoulder a slight shove as I begin to walk away, turning his own body but not mine. I go along. Making light of everything, he loud-talks the kid: "Make sure he gets home. Tell his block sergeant he's grounded till work call tomorrow."

It has to be a joke. A deception of some kind, to throw me off. But off of what? I pace around my dark cell at a few minutes after ten o'clock. If Bread really tried it, he would fail, and then Vanderventer would wonder why yours truly hadn't warned him something was coming. Warn him? He'd think it was a joke. He'd double over laughing. So I have to wonder: how come I'm not laughing?

Because I know something he doesn't. I know a little bit about Bread. Not much, but I know he thinks limits don't apply to him and consequences are just bad luck. I'm not sure anyone really appreciates that. And on the very remote chance Bread succeeded in his scheme, he'd be stepping into a vortex of violence nobody could handle, with only me to protect him. For me it couldn't be smoke and mirrors like it has been: I'd have to commit a felony assault every day. I can see why Bread had ordered his guys not to tell me. And now – standing at the bars of my locked cell door – I won't be able to find out anything else until tomorrow. Some tube of muscle in my chest turns over in frustration, making my heart do one soft and one hard drumbeat before returning to normal: buh-BAM.

I sense movement or hear a soft sound from the next cell. Then Willie says, "Raw, what you thinkin about so loud?"

I don't want to say. Instead my mind twitches like it had blinked without my eyes, and I remember something else that's been troubling me all day. "Willie, we ok?"

"What you mean?"

I try to make my voice neutral and smooth, try to remember I'm keyed up about other things. "Today in yard. I stopped to talk to you. You just walked right past me." A sudden anger boils up, and I smash it back down. All of a sudden I have to know. "We ok?"

There is a long silence, then: "Whatchoo talkin bout?"

"You just walked right by."

"Hell I did."

"You didn't?"

Another silence. "Hell I did."

He sounds defensive, the second time, and Willie doesn't lie. I feel myself deflate. He's lost a lot of his peripheral vision. I say, "Maybe I'm wrong."

"You think I done you like that?"

"No. Forget it. I don't know what I'm talking about."

For a minute we are both embarrassed. I wonder distantly: how does a place smell different because the lights are out?

Willie says, "I got things on my mind, these days. Gettin old."

"It's my fault."

"You on your game?"

"I'm on it."

"This thing you stewin on tonight. You handle it tomorrow?"

"I'll handle it."

I sleep toward morning, then wake up like a crackerjack when count is called. My cell doesn't unlock. I experience a single instant of outrage so white hot it's almost like cold panic, and then a low feeling of forced patience washes through me. I remember I'm locked down until work call. I wait at the bars and press down on all the thoughts that suddenly try to crowd with ugly force into my skull. I watch the chow line form and move out tier by tier. A few minutes later, an inmate wheels a cart into the cellhouse with breakfast for the lockdowns. I eat mine without tasting it (shame) and do my best to keep my mind blank so my thoughts won't climb all over me.

A few minutes before eight, I get unlocked and make time to the yard. I look at the brightness of the sky feeling dislocated and even a little stimulated by the break in routine. It occurred to me sometime early this morning that Bread might have told me what he planned to do when he came to see me last night – if I'd said I was on board. Then I'd been interrupted trying to get it out of Chris. Now I need the details from someone else. If Chris has already told Bread about our little talk, that will be harder but not impossible. Who, then? In the chow hall, on the yard, they'll be sticking together now. The next person I see ought to be Frankson, in the furniture factory.

No one else in the gang works in the factory. We'll be alone together. I pace while I wait near the metal detector and hope he's at work, today. Other guys waiting on line can tell I'm agitated and stay away from me. When I spot Frankson behind me in the line, it takes a conscious effort not to grab him immediately.

Frankson operates a lathe on the work floor. I wait almost half an hour to show that I'm in no rush, then get his attention. I gesture for him to start walking toward the back of the production floor and lead him to an equipment cage off the main factory area. I take a second to study him. He gives a little nod of the chin to say, What's Up? His brow furrows a little, deepening the vertical hate lines beside his nose, but he doesn't seem wary of me. He doesn't even seem surprised by the fact that I want to talk to him, even though I have never set out to have a conversation with him, before. I suspect Frankson has always thought we are comrades, of a kind. He has a triangular scar below one cheekbone and a sharp black widow's peak with a little curl on the end. Before Bread, he'd always been so broke that he'd been given the ironic nickname of Frankie Diamonds, after the gangster in the Wright play.

"What's up, Croft?"

I just stare at him until he gets uncomfortable and says "What's up?" again.

"Look," I say. I'm instinctively disingenuous, thinking that almost any shuck will get me closer than honesty. "I already know. I know all about it. I just want to know why I wasn't told."

For a moment he looks surprised, then almost shamefaced. "Don't you think, you know, that's a conversation you ought to have with the boss?"

"I'm asking you."

"It's nothing personal, man. He just thinks you're, I don't know, cautious. It's a good thing in a lot of situations."

"He told you not to tell me. And you didn't."

"Yeah, ok, I didn't. I still don't see what the big deal is."

"You're still not telling me."

"Ok, so what are you gonna do, kick my ass?"

I drop the shuck. "How's he going to do it?"

"Forget about it. It's a good plan. Be nice when we don't have to worry about that jumped-up prick anymore."

"When?"

He squints at me. "Hey, don't worry. It's gonna be good. Look, what are you asking me about this for?"

It's funny, Bread told his guys not to tell but didn't try to keep them from me, didn't even give them too strong a warning.

I look over both shoulders and take a step closer to Frankson.

He takes a step back. "Alright, alright. He goes to see a visitor, nobody shows. On the way back, Bread and Nick take him in the hall."

Just like that. I think a moment and then shake my head. "He's never alone."

"He'll be alone if he thinks his old lady come to see him after two years. In the Neck he will be, anyway."

The Neck is what they call the long corridor between admin and the rest of the prison.

I say, "They'll never pull it off. Everybody knows they can't get to Vanderventer and walk away clean."

"That's *why* they'll put it off, man."

I'm shaking my head. "Not this guy. Not Bread."

He gives me a look like I've spent the last three years on a desert island. "Yes, he can. I'm not the smartest, but I've been in this place fifteen years. I been through Sullivan, and I been through Vanderventer, and I'm tellin you, Bread's the worst son of a bitch that ever walked through these doors." He shrugs. "It's why we love em."

His statement is like a stone falling down a well and making no splash. I listen to it go and go.

"When?" I say.

Frankson smirks. "Eight thirty."

I look at my watch. It's eight thirty-two.

In the production area, I get Popeye's attention by waving an arm and then jerk my thumb at the door. He shrugs at me across the noise of the room. I jerk my thumb at the door harder and walk out.

Popeye has to jog to get to the doorway by the time I reach metal detector set in the fence. The checkpoint hack looks up and sees Popeye waving me out, and I go through without breaking stride.

The clouded daylight is an assault on my eyes as I cross the yard, the fresh air like ice cold milk in my lungs. The man had pissed on the Rook. Pissed in his face. He'd shown no fear of me. He would really try it. I tell myself it doesn't matter, that Vanderventer has been around too long. He'll smell a setup a mile off. And there are all the hacks on his roll.

So why am I in such a hurry?

Last night, I'd thought Wimpy was taking it easy on me. I thought it was just the understanding that castles aren't at war with the hacks; that, and the fact that he might need a favor sometime from another hack who is on Bread's roll. Now I think he's probably in on it. Locked me down just long enough so I couldn't get in the way of this.

I blow through the door on the south side of the SO. Two men have to grab the wall to avoid getting knocked down. The hack escorting them, a few feet behind, yells at my back as I continue moving. "Hey!" he yells, but he isn't really telling me to stop, just honking his horn.

Maybe I can stop Bread even trying, if it isn't too late. I'd be a lot more afraid of Vanderventer's revenge than Bread's, even though I wonder whether Frankson could be right about him. Maybe I've been in prison both too long and not long enough, so I'm no longer keen but still don't understand the joint.

I turn left into the main corridor behind the chow hall, toward admin and the visiting area. I jog a few steps and fall back into a walk, barely.

I turn right and walk along the east edge of the SO until I come to the Neck. About a third of the way up the fifty-yard stretch, it's closed off by an extendible gate of finger-thick metal slats. The gate is open about a foot and locked off that way, and a bad hack named Ratel stands in the opening with his arms folded on his chest. He doesn't register any alarm when he sees me, which means he hasn't been told to watch out for me, specifically.

I approach, and he fixes his body in the small opening, widens his stance, and uses his best command voice. "Closed off for now. Back the way you came."

When I don't respond, he says, "*Now.*"

I know I'm not going to just turn away. The stakes are higher than that, now. Larger than a writeup or even a month in solitary. I feel almost as if I'm floating outside myself.

"Something's about to happen."

"You're about to get charged with fucking insubordination, that's what's about to happen. Do what I say."

I stand there, rooted.

"Did you hear me?"

"Get out of my way."

"*What?*"

I take one big step forward, and Ratel jerks back. He can only watch as I wrap the fingers of both hands around the mesh of the gate. It's a heftier version of the kind used to cordon off parts of shopping malls and ball stadiums, good for stopping one, two, a small group of convicts, not serious riot containment. With a wrench of my shoulders I rip it out of the lock position and send it accordioning back along its wheels with a crash. Ratel crouches and throws his arms up over his head, but quickly gets up and starts shouting at my back as I jog up the neck. I hear the chime when he keys his handset. He's shouting into the radio, now.

I come to a second gate, this one locked off completely. Holy hell, I think: are they locking Vanderventer in with Bread? I curse, throw a foot into the gate. It shakes along its length, holds. Then I stand practically touching it, facing it, and reach my hands up to take hold near the top. I rip it out of the track with a few tugs, and it falls forward. I keep going.

Now it sounds like there are two or three hacks behind me, following but not too close, talking into their radios. Hello, hole.

I start moving again, and one of them must have smacked the back of my knee with his sap. I feel a sudden weak numbness in my right leg, stagger but don't fall. I keep on going, right off the radar grid of normal behavior that will get me out of prison on my scheduled date, and up the Neck. Bread isn't going to win this one. He isn't going to put me in the position he wants me in. I'll spend a little time in the hole, or Vanderventer might even be able to make the whole thing go away. Still, shouting in the back of my mind is an incredulous, sane voice: *What are you doing? What the hell are you doing? Four years! Four years!*

I'm only about twenty yards from admin and the visiting area, beyond the rotunda, when three hacks jump on me from behind. At first it's just a shock. I don't even start feeling the weight until I go another ten yards. They can't put their heels into the concrete floor. They yank. I refuse to go down. Two of them each take an arm, and the third hits me in the middle, wrapping his arms around my upper legs and pushing with his shoulder like a football tackle – and for a deck, he feels like he probably played some ball. I don't fight or go down. One of them is trying to talk sense into my right ear, while another is growling threats into my left. "Goddam you," the one on my left arm says. He's trying to work the arm behind me and failing.

I could trudge half a mile this way, but the stupidity, the indignity of it is starting to make me angry. I stop and manage to say, "Alright–" before a long, low, loud bloop comes over the hacks' handsets. A code call. I know the code hasn't come from one of the hacks hanging onto me because one of them yelps at the sudden noise and drops his handset. "Fuck!" he says. They stop struggling and let go of me. In a few seconds, the dispatch guard in the control room will tell all the hacks what is happening in a relaxed, robotic voice.

We wait.

'Code blue, code blue, visiting area, inside entrance. We have a code blue at the inside entrance of the visiting area.'

Code blue. A violent attack requiring a forceful response, medical attention, and forensics. The hacks run in the direction of the visiting area, leaving me alone.

I stand in the corridor, my clothes twisted around my body, the back of my knee throbbing, my eyes blank. I don't bother standing up straight for a minute but stay hunched over.

When I begin walking back toward the main part of the prison, it's past a lot of running guards who ignore me. They don't know they'll be dealing with me next, as soon as Ratel and his two pals have a minute to tell them. That is, unless all hell breaks loose and they keep having other priorities.

Most everyone else is still at work. I go outside to the yard. May well be my last fresh air outside of a cage in the snitch yard, where hole residents get their half hour a day. It might only take them a few minutes to come for me. Hours, if I'm lucky. I'm not much of a smoker, but there are times you want something to do with your hands, and this is one of them. Five minutes pass. I try not to think about who'd killed who. Instead, I feel the air and try to listen to the sound of the prison. When fifteen minutes have passed and I still have the yard to myself, I start to feel conspicuous and like I'm tempting fate. I slink off to work.

In the furniture factory, I can see that nobody has had heard anything. To everyone here, it's as if nothing has happened. Frankson watches me out of the corner of his eye but otherwise plays it cool and runs his lathe. I can see that he feels it must have gone down right unless I managed to foul it up. I make the rounds with my clipboard and keep expecting the hacks to show up. The first thing I see will be their silhouettes in the main bay door. Because I'd resisted, they might not even offer me the chance to come quietly, this time. Or maybe they'll call a lockdown for better control and come at me with the rhino.

They don't come before lunch. We shuffle out through the metal detector, then to the cell blocks. When they call chow, I watch the lines shuffling through the SO. Each slow step I take makes me anxious to see: who will be missing lunch today, Bread or Vanderventer? I don't see either of them, but the lines stretch out of sight. Once I spot one or the other, I'll know whether to call Michaela and tell her to pack a .38 and some bandages and drive the last mile with the lights off. Or will it be so clear cut?

I step partly out of line to look ahead. Bread and Vanderventer are both usually inside the cafeteria before me. I get to where I can see a sliver of the large space, and the line is stopping and starting like we're in line to buy movie tickets.

It will be bad, either way. Bread will get me locked up in the hole for a thousand years for trying to interfere...or Vanderventer will think I knew about the attempt on his life and didn't say anything.

The chow line shuffles up to the steam tables, all normal. Once I'm inside and see the sweep of the cafeteria, I'll know who's missing immediately. But I once I get in, I don't look right away. Instead, I get my meal and four cartons of milk and move to my table, focusing on the five feet in front of me. Once I'm settled, I allow myself to look up at Vanderventer's spot.

He's gone.

I look to my right at Bread's table.

He's gone, too.

They're both absent, and I don't know what to think, and the hacks still haven't gotten around to me. My skin prickles like a tomcat's. I look down at my food, and it might as well be made of cellophane. Eventually I drink two of my cartons of milk. I wait for one of the two gang leaders to come in, but neither does. Forty-five minutes pass, and then, crazy: I go back to work once again as if not a thing has gone down, and the same lack of awareness waits for me there. Prison can be like this: a drama that would go all night on the outside – people fleeing, chasing, bent on revenge or love – is forced to happen in bits on the Inside. The convicts work and take smoke breaks with their weak sister supervisors. I go into Popeye's office, and he raps on the doorframe a few minutes later to ask about reports and tell me to go ahead and brew coffee, if I want. French roast.

Dinner comes and goes, and still the two men are missing, along with a couple of other guys from each table. Bread's guys are a little too quiet and eat too much. Vanderventer's crew is closed up like a Venus fly trap. Then dinner wraps up, and the line shuffles out to the cell blocks, and men go about their various activities. I go back to the yard. Again I spend time observing things I may not see again for a while: the bruising sky, walls and fences - I just try to enjoy being able to look at distant objects. I stay there until about 7:30, when the hacks say to roll it up.

I head for my cell, tired of the nervousness of waiting for the hacks to come and wondering if they'll just come the moment my cell door locks tonight. On the way, I notice something: except for a few other stragglers coming in from the yard, the SO is quiet. That's strange. As long as chow isn't on, there should still be guys in the rec and the weight pile, but the silence doesn't lie. When I go through the tunnel into

C Block, it's thick with convicts. There's an intensity on tiers. A lot of whispering and looking around, a few guys going from group to group like worried spiders in a web trembling with flies.

I stop one of the first guys to cross my path, a bald white convict with soft, young, eager eyes that don't go with his badass tattoos. I put a hand on his shoulder, and he skids to a stop. I ask what's going on.

The intensity I listen with gives him the jitters. He tells me that someone is dead, tells me the name and who he heard it from, then makes some commentary on how fucked up it is. He keeps talking because I keep staring at him. I can't seem to do anything else. My feet have grown roots, and there doesn't seem to be a drop of moisture in my body all of a sudden. I look across the tiers and see the tension and excitement, and somehow it looks like a big stage set.

Then it hits me. It starts as a sniff through my nose and winds up dropping down my throat and deep into my belly. I start to laugh.

I'm not paying any more attention to the guy I stopped, but he starts nervously laughing along with me and looking like he wants to be anyplace else. I turn away from him and keep laughing. The laugh feels like gas escaping from rotten matter, and it's truly comical - because this is a big joke. Men moving along the tier give me a wide berth.

The laughter scares me a little because I feel disconnected from it. I don't feel like I'm laughing, and there's no mirth in it. (And most prisoners never laugh, just like they never smile; when you do hear the sound, it's because of something hideous or crazy.) It splutters like an old car as I walk along the tier, dies suddenly as if it never happened, then rises back up my throat again like vomit. Instead of going into my cell, I keep walking around the tiers and feeling the tension. The laughter in my guts becomes a solid tightness in my belly, and I begin feeling anger and anticipation that starts in my skin and works its way inward. Blister catches my eye from the catwalk connecting one side of the tier to the other and pumps his eyebrows. He isn't quite grinning and looks like a kid on Halloween night. Nobody else is casual; they all stand with their own decks or gangs, and they keep trickling in from the SO like it's raining in there. I don't see any less-familiar faces: everyone is staying in his own neighborhood. The hacks look ready for something. I see a couple of guys come up to them with the usual issues and complaints and get swatted away. There's a lot of radio chatter. It's July and the sun is nearly down beyond the rim of the earth, and the sharp heatless color coming in the high windows seems to add to the confusion.

Everything is about to fall to shit in an amazing way.

There's a loud noise like someone slamming down a book from the small C Block television room as I pass by, and a bunch of cons come flooding out of it, heading in all directions. When I look inside, there is nothing strange about the room itself. No blood, no fire. Then I look at the tv, the sound volume turned down too low to make anything out, and see a news shot of the outside of Seamax. A pair of long black vans has pulled up in the circular drive beneath the dome of the administration building. A spotlight from above wanders over some clipped shrubs and an American flag, then hovers on the vans. The Seamax S.W.O.R.D. team is climbing out with their body armor strapped on, clutching their nine millimeters behind their clear shields.

I watch them on the screen, jogging in neat files toward the main entrance. Everything about me stops. It's really true. The television drones on. For a minute I feel like a big hollow imitation of myself, and then I just feel cold and shocked. I can't believe it. I wander out again, my face tight and eyes empty.

Then I hear whistles and stomping and shouting everywhere, echoing throughout the blocks and the SO. It seems like I can hear the whole prison at once, even the other buildings. Everyone is stimulated by the break in routine, and it's going to be an ugly lockdown. I start heading back toward my cell.

Tough as he was, who could've predicted Vanderventer would be taken out by an upstart, and the prison wouldn't even know about it until he'd already been dead eleven hours?

Worried as they are, the cons sense that the shadow which has fallen over the prison scares the hacks at least as much as it scares themselves, so they become surly and slow. The hacks try to move crisply in navy blue lines along the catwalks but seem to get stuck in grey mud and catcalls, men moving in the wrong direction, confused, ignoring, asking pointless questions. Cons, even cons who hate each other, develop extra sensory perception about opportunities to cause trouble and practice defiance together. The noise level jumps again. I can feel the thrumming vibration of the grated tier beneath my feet. Some cons just like the hysteria because it's something different; others I think are trying to tip things toward a riot. I walk at a deliberate pace, faster than the cons, slower than the hacks, and for most of them I'm not here, just a boulder in the current. I see other castles walking along to their cells the same way, a head taller than the rest.

The hacks blow whistles. Someone in Command Operations tweaks the siren for a second, causing a burst of loud, climbing noise that dies suddenly. Its effect is opposite the one they wanted, and the noise level jumps again. Hacks fight their way through crowded tiers. A piece of burning trash drifts down from someplace on Tier 3. A con sticks his fingers in his mouth and makes a surprisingly loud, piercing whistle, and I feel it in my sinuses. Someone backs into me. I shove him aside. A serious fight breaks out across the cell block.

The spectators to the fight form an unbreakable ring like the front row crowd at a cockfight, screaming and waving their fists while a wiry, athletic hack pulls them apart by their shoulders only to have them collapse back together again, like he is trying to separate grey water.

The place is howling, the energy raw and aimless, like we're bringing in a new year.

The killers had struck at the same minute, in different parts of the prison, killing Vanderventer and two of his toughest guys. He'd died only about twenty yards from where the three hacks jumped on me and unsuccessfully tried to wrestle me down.

I see a convict who'd been either threatened or crowded climb over the Tier two railing and then hang-drop to the ground level. Hacks tackle him hard.

I go inside my cell. I can't seem to think, can only let the noise wash over me. Willie is in his own cell but doesn't try to talk; it's too loud.

The S.W.O.R.D. doesn't come into the cell blocks. At least, not into C Block. The surge of rowdiness lasts another five minutes or so before the hacks get everyone put away and lock the place down, but there is no break in the noise.

That night the prison feels like a crazy place. At around 9pm, a single savage shout rings out through the block saying something I can't understand, and it sets off another round of gleeful craziness. Right up until lights out everybody has his hands wrapped around bars of his cell, talking, shouting. The hacks are feeling rough. They don't like the fact of a coordinated attack or who got hit because of all the disruption it will cause – tonight will be the least of it. Supercops go around banging on cell doors with their saps and making threats. They're trying to head off a riot. It is possible to riot even in lockdown: convicts can still throw things, light fires, destroy plumbing and cause floods, refuse to comply with commands. The watch lieutenant isn't doing cell extractions yet and probably won't until things calm down. It's a low boil. S.W.O.R.D. is on standby. If they come in, the first thing we'll hear will be the dogs. At lights out it feels like nobody is sleeping, just waiting in the dark. Debtors, junkies, people who beef with someone in Vanderventer's gang or belong to it or do business with it, and others who just want to know how to avoid trouble, everyone is wondering. There's a guy called Bread. He'd seemed small-time but had too much money and protection. He'd survived an attempted sticking by a couple of hardcore killers who don't miss and had pissed in the Rook's face.

There are rumors that he was involved in the murders. But for now the big news is that Vanderventer is dead.

I look out through the bars of cell C216. A lot of people are dead, now. They just don't know it yet.

I look out. I feel my eyes staring and their roundness bulging with little conscious thought behind them. The noise is terrible. The block smells of smoke. I turn inside the cell and pace just once across it, stopping in front of the wall, breathing too fast. Then I rip the mattress off my bunk and throw it at the bars with a roar that hurts my throat and rings in my ears, and handfuls of Defenerin and Praxlatan rain onto the catwalk and the floor below. I stalk across the cell again, breathing even harder, my heart slamming, and punch the back wall of my cell twice, hard enough to leave blood on it and buckle the surface of the old concrete. A chip the size of a baby's foot falls out of the wall a few minutes later, and I have to get up and stick it back in place with chewing gum.

7

Toward sunup, the cell block finally quiets and I sit in the dark, my mind churning, random muscles tensing up and down my body. For a while, the outside of my arm had twitched every few seconds like a hiccough; then my thigh.

Brass tacks: Bread doesn't have the organization in place for what he's done. No way he can handle the blowback, and my name is attached to all of it. We can't steer it or control anything. I don't even know who will turn out to be worse, the guys who'd been loyal to Vanderventer, like his brother Eddie, or the ones who'd been itching for their own power. What does Bread expect me to do now, go stomping around like an elephant all day to try and keep Vanderventer's guys from wiping him out? Am I supposed to stomp ass until I get juiced up with Thorazine and trucked off to Mount

Washington to live in solitary twenty-three hours a day, year after year?

I try to relax. A cell can shrink to the size of a shoebox in the night, and the scary thought is that it's only your own self control that keeps the walls from closing in. No one else can or will help you. The hacks come because you won't stop shouting, you're off to a deeper, darker, smaller cell. I look around at my sketches and the bed where I've stacked so many nights. It'll all have to go, now. It's like drilling most of the way through a safe, long night of sweat and metal shavings in the eyes, only to walk off at the last minute, leaving a senseless hole. All these nights, this cell, they'll never serve their purpose. Maybe because of the chaos and the hour, I start thinking loose: maybe when I check out, I'll kill Bread as a bonus, since I'll be on the lam anyway. I think about it until I remember he's not worth five minutes of my time on the outside, which is where I'll be that much sooner if I don't stop first to tend to him.

I look out my tiny window and see the first inklings of dawn, the shapes of the clouds giving it depth. Sometimes at night it's possible to see the glow of a refinery or a factory that sits a few miles away. The idea of being out excites me, briefly. I let my mind wander, not letting too much of the leash out, just letting particulars come: rooms, halls, faces. I remember pan seared fish and scallops in white wine sauce, Dominican cigars, silk sheets. I drift back over the time I was in Buffalo on one of the few bank jobs I'd done. Safe enough place to think about even on the Inside, dreary and depressed. The bank is a bank and the hotel is a hotel, but the extra time, the way no one seemed to remember me, the way it was always gloomy and people watched their shoes, the smoothness driving away with the money in the back of the Towncar. There was never a job like it. I could confess to it and they wouldn't believe me. The kind of job I'll never be able to pull again as a wanted man.

In my cell, I watch the light in the window as the sun comes up. The cell and my body are a chiaroscuro, a moving eclipse of black and white. Dawn breaks over the prison like a cold white linen. I sit up in my bunk as I have for hours. The sun burns away the night thoughts like dew, and I can smell the sweat and mop water on the tier again. I feel a sourceless anger that's like a mild sizzling sensation in my brain.

The lockdown lasts through the morning. They let the kitchen workers out at 4:30 as usual, but each man is escorted. The swing guards have pulled doubles and leave with the graveyard hacks when the day shift comes on. I don't want to talk to anyone and stay in my bunk pretending to be asleep. Six o'clock comes, and the hacks come around to count the convicts in their cells instead of having us step to the rail, and then we eat breakfast from Styrofoam clamshells that the guards bring around since the porters are still locked down. There is no work call at eight.

I stew in my cell, feeling ugly, wanting out to think with my legs. I wonder whether I will see Bread in the chow hall later or if he'll be in custody. Depends on how deep the conspiracy went. I work up a few different versions of telling him what an idiot he is but settle on just telling him I'm out. The shorter the better. Don't let him think there's a discussion to be had about it.

That's if I'm free, myself. There are three hacks to remind each other of what I'd done in the Neck. It won't be a priority with everything else that's happened, but that doesn't mean they won't get around to it. Because I'm a castle, they'll come for me while we're still in lockdown and they can control the environment. That's what they'll do. I frown.

Never thought I'd end up rhinoed. I sit on my bunk and try not to think about it but find myself listening to all the hard-soled footsteps, the chunk of their heels on the tiers.

Shortly after noon, I hear the keys clanking at the east end of the block where the SO is locked off, and the three heavy doors opening, one for each tier. A handful of seconds later, there is the cascading thud of the cell doors opening not quite simultaneously. A shift sergeant calls another count. He's too loud and sounds nervous. Men come out of their cells and seem to feel the air with their small hairs. They look around too much, checking in with each other. There's a suspended moment before the block sergeant calls them into line. Then the call comes, and all the men on my side of the cell house turn to their left at once, military style.

Another suspended moment settles in, as if the sergeant is waiting for one wrong move, like he's still getting the aftertaste of something like a big practical joke on the air. None of the hacks looks at me twice.

The shift sergeant yells, "Move out!"

The lines of convicts begin marching off to lunch. Everything is difficult. One line stopping to let another pass into the SO is difficult, as if it's the first time we've done it. A few guys start to turn left instead of right when we get to the junction with the D-B corridor and go toward the stairs. The rowdy convicts love it. There's the feeling all hell could break loose any second even though few really want it. It would just arise, and even the men doing it would be watching their own fists and listening to their own shouting voices like they'd become actors playing themselves in a movie. Every once in a while in prison there's this group telepathy, but only when it's completely crazy.

I see Dodd and Chris E in the corridor coming out of B Block into the SO. They look at me like they're walking a high wire and I'm holding onto one end of it. We pass close to each other where the C Block line marches past the head of the B Block line, and Dodd says, "Where you gonna be, just in case?"

A hack calls out, "No talking in the chow line!"

We shuffle along. By the time we're halfway there, we all know it isn't going to jump off. Not this time.

B Block is somewhere behind me in the two lines snaking through the SO. I have my food and milk cartons and am sitting at my table before I see them lining up at the steam tables. Then I see a hairline that looks like a heart, or the shape of a woman's bottom, hair that looks vaguely peroxided. I follow it with my eyes, looking for a difference in his walk, an injury, anything. There is nothing. No difference. He takes a carton of milk and two pieces of pie, and sits at his table. Incredible.

Next I look over at Vanderventer's table. Vanderventer, Lin Jimson, and Kyle Devaney are missing. Curious thing – so is Eddie Vanderventer, the Champ's brother. I'd heard nothing about him. No one else looks around much. As far as the gangs go, they don't want to show too much interest. Nobody knows the landscape yet, and nobody wants to be the first to learn.

Bread leaves the chow hall after only a few minutes. All the better. I lap up my food and drink my milk in a few cold swallows, then head to his cell in D Block. My anger is like a black bowling ball threaded with red and orange. As I approach the cell, I can hear the bad dialogue from Changing Seasons.

I stop outside his open cell door. He's turned partly away watching the little television set. I don't say anything, at first. Maybe I haven't come to talk. I block the doorway with my body and feel blood pooling in my chest and arms. Eventually I say, "It's over." I'd been up half the night waiting to say it. "It's done. I'm out."

Weisner said it first, but he'd said it to the wrong guy.

Bread doesn't turn. On the television, a beautiful couple stands over a hospital bed with an unconscious form in it, the woman crying. A moment later Bread says, "What did I tell you when we first talked?"

I don't answer.

"I said we would run this place. And we will."

"This is a disaster. There's nothing I can do for you, now."

Bread turns partway toward me. "Relax, Croft."

"You're not hearing me."

"You aren't the kind who'd stick him with a tiny blade. No one even suspects you. In fact, everybody's sure you had nothing to do with it. Your small-time reputation is safe."

"You think that's what I'm worried about?"

When he still doesn't tear his eyes from the set, I step inside his cell uninvited, which for a con is the same as poking a finger in his face.

He jumps off the bunk and rushes up on me, his anger steaming. I can actually feel the heat coming off him from his unnatural metabolism, and he looks streaked with red warpaint from the flush in his naked upper body. "What are you going to do, anyway? *Think*. We took out our last serious competition yesterday. No real investigation. It's open highway. I can't believe you don't see that."

"I'd rather deal with the Rook than have to commit five felonies a day trying to stay ahead of this. They're all going to come after us now. I'm out. You do what you have to."

"Don't think I won't."

I'd started to turn and walk away, but at this I stop. I get right back in front of him, just a few inches away. I'm still standing in his cell, uninvited. "That's a good point. You would. We both know it. But when he's out, will I find you before he finds me?"

I watch his eyes, looking for fear or uncertainty. All I see is the intense stare looking back at me, *up* at me since I'm eight inches taller, the brown eyes kaleidescoped with yellow and green. If I didn't know better, I'd say he looks like he *wants* to fight me. I say, "They'll say Vanderventer's guys did it. No one will doubt it."

Bread shakes his head, the eyes never moving off of mine. "Right after I pissed in his face, I told the Rook that Croft thought he might be thirsty and that this was from him. And anything happens to me, you go down for it. And you go down for Bingo, too. It's arranged."

If it's possible, our eyes lock even harder. I believe him about what he claims to have said to the Rook. Of course he'd said it. Bread wouldn't miss an opportunity to ratchet things down a little tighter.

Not backing off, he says, "I can protect your release date. Whatever we have to do, you get out next August."

"You can't promise that."

"Yes, I can. I can keep the Rook locked down, and I can make sure you get out. You think I want you in here?"

He sees my eyes come unfocused for a second.

"That's right," he says. "Soon enough, I won't need you. You're not much better than the Rook. Even you must see that. But I can't have anybody walking away from me right now."

I feel myself getting confused, his perspective is so crazy. "You don't understand anything," I say.

"Take a look in the mirror." Then he nods around me. "Turn around."

I do. Stromm is behind me. We look at each other, then he says, with his faint Scandinavian accent, "Back in your own neighborhood now, kiddo."

Willie had told me to kill Bread before it was too late. The idea of going down for another felony wasn't within my comprehension, then. Now the longest-lasting and most violent gang in Seamax as far back as anybody can remember will tear the place apart while it runs around like a chicken without its head. Half the top guys will want revenge while the other half go into overdrive trying to be the new boss.

And I'll have to be the biggest, baddest enforcer in a madhouse to preserve the life of a guy I can't stand.

Bread is right about one thing that day, though. The investigation is a joke. Nobody looks into him, and no one remembers me.

I had my worries about the perfect storm, but this is what actually happened. It turned out that the top guys from Vanderventer's gang were geared to fight each other far more than any outsider. Bread and his gang never had to take the whole brunt. It was messy; a hot, bad couple of weeks as we rolled into August, when the Vanderventer "sons" each took a slice of the gang and fought with anybody who didn't treat them the way they felt they ought to be treated. It was one of those situations where nobody does anything, they're all just retaliating for something else, and the desperation and hurt feelings got deeper by the hour. The prison even smelled different: there was a sleepless, meaty smell of too much testosterone and fear.

They should have ganged up on Bread while they had the chance. Rumor was they didn't take him seriously, assumed it would be one of them who took over. That was why I didn't get run as ragged as I'd thought I would having to save Bread and his guys in every corner of Seamax. I don't know if he'd predicted this or just gotten lucky. Someone like that, it's not like you could ask him and expect an honest answer. He'd have planned it all just like he'd planned the sun coming up.

What Bread did do was play one side against the other and then betray them. Near the end, he supported Brick when it looked like Brick would be last man standing. Then I heard Bread personally stuck him in the eye.

Some of Vanderventer's guys who are left hanging around, reeling, actually want sympathy. On an August morning already warped with heat, a middle-aged convict with a salt-and-pepper beard approaches me in the yard. I don't know his name, just that he'd been with Vanderventer's gang. He's alone and looks intense but distracted, like someone set off a firecracker near his head and his ear is still ringing. At first the guy just stands beside me near the wall like he can't find his words. I can see something working its way up to his lips, like he has caramel stuck behind his teeth.

Then he says, "Is he crazy? I mean, insane?"

The guy looks like he thinks I might kill him, but the curiosity already is. They can't figure Bread out. He seems to do all the same things that gangsters have always done – terrify and kill, tell nothing but lies. So why is he able to accomplish more?

I have no answer. I'm also not real interested.

"It's not fair," salt-and-pepper says.

I laugh at the time, even though I understand better than I let on. What isn't fair? It's not fair that Bread isn't normal?

There's no mental disease more crippling than believing the brick-and-mortar world has a sense of fairness, or that it should.

Late at night, I stand at the bars of my cell or at my window, listening to two devils. One knows I have to get out. If they haven't yet, things will get out of control, mistakes will be made, and I'll be in the middle and end up next to Rook in the hole, or maybe even eating a dirt sandwich. Then I tilt up my other ear, and hear this: so much time served, so little left. Everything will be fine. No worries about what some parole board might say because I'll go out max time. Get out clean and not have to worry about my picture in the Post Office, not have to stay in dives all the time.

Maybe there's a third, too, who asks the really hard question. It says I keep ending up with these same two devils, but if Bread's come this far already, why can't I think about trusting him?

I'll tell you why. Because I can't explain it. So how can I trust it?

Cut bait.

Hang on.

Long nights.

Part II
The Cold War

1

In late September, they turn off the big cage fans in the cell blocks, and the cons on the top tier where it's hottest start sleeping through the night again. It's Friday. There's a pot for the winner of a weekly castle fight in the old laundry room, and nobody makes book on any of it without Bread's okay and his cut of the action.

Me, I just stand there and let my bulk speak for itself—for Bread. I'm standing behind his shoulder in the laundry-room where decks are frantically hand-signing bets at Bread's wheelman and two newfish castles are using each other to redecorate the place. One of them suplexes the other into a washing machine that tips over and bursts in a tide of grey water over the crowd's shoes, and the shouting rises louder. The audience is pressed in so tight that they're locked together at angles like a Greek army, pushing and jeering. A groan goes up when the wheel snaps Bread's ledger shut.

There used to be separate prisons for castles, until the system got overcrowded and ran out of money. When they threw everyone together, they got less trouble than anyone expected: with a few exceptions, castles aren't predators the way other cons are. We also don't fight each other for the decks. I watch the action and flex my hands one finger at a time. You can't expect any kind of sense from decks, but I'd like to knock those two around a bit, let them know they shouldn't have had a part in it. We're enough of a spectacle as it is.

Bread won't care because he knows the money will keep some of us coming back no matter what I do. I know. I'm holding the pot.

One of the fighters rubs his elbow into his opponent's eye during a clinch, making him blink, and now the caged light bulbs are probably leaving long trails in his vision.

Across the arena made of industrial clothes dryers and heavy duty washing machines (decks perched on them like pigeons) is Bread's real neck popper, the short, darkly hairy, extremely wide-framed Fiero. Castle. Armed robbery, murder, killer rep. He's new, and he does what I still won't. There's a rumor that Bread special-ordered him from Baxter, said the castles here are all too lazy to earn a living.

I watch Fiero's hairy-knuckled white hand clamp on the lower part of a face, erasing someone's mouth. He yanks the guy backward so hard one of his shoes lands inside the ring.

Maybe the guy didn't pay his marker. With Fiero here, the deck enforcers can put down their pipes and let a real bone-smasher pretend to be me.

Bread doesn't really need me anymore, and I want out.

One of the fighters in the makeshift ring isn't much more than a sandy-haired kid. He's fast and flurrying his opponent with quick punches. Came in and never learned the rules. As I pass by in the crowd, someone asks Bread what would happen if I was in the ring tonight. Angling his head back a little so I can hear, he says, "Too boring. Croft'd just put him in the washer and turn it on. Isn't that right?"

At least I'm pretty sure he said 'Isn't that right?' because I'd walked away. I did it specifically to disrespect him in public, though later I'll find it pathetic that I'd done anything for the decks' benefit. I go around the outside of the ring of cheering men ten deep until I find Fiero, who is standing ringside with someone else's blood stippled across his neck and upper arms. I tap him on the shoulder and he looks up at me with a start. I sling the money belt with the pot in it over his shoulder and walk away.

Bread's sniper eyes track me every inch of the way.

That night I dream about loading shotguns for an assault on some vehicle, an armored car or maybe a bus. The most lucid part of the dream is the anger and determination to destroy anything that stands in my way. I've never worked that way in real life. I dream-load the guns with hundreds of shells. I load and load. I wake up in the last of the dark and the weight of the dream is still on me, the slow thick motions of my hands and the feeling of blind intent.

I fall back asleep and wake up again after dawn, thumb the little round button over my sink and wash my face. Blue-veined grey light the color of a jellyfish glows in my window and casts the faintest of shadows on the floor.

After count I skip the chow line and go to keep an eye on an early deal with Frankson. He's still in bed when I get to his cell, has his legs swung over the edge of the bed and his upper body still twisted in the sheet. "I'm up."

Sections of magazines and Hostess wrappers litter the cell. This is what I work with, now. I say nothing. What can I say? On the outside, guy like this showed up for a job, I'd ask him whose nephew he is. Without ceremony or even a splash of water on his face, Frankson steps out and falls in alongside me.

The corridors are quiet. Nearly everyone's at chow. I'm not worried about the deal, in particular. It's routine. The outlaw biker types just like to get cute sometimes, and you have to remind them that you're there.

Frankson is cranking his fists into his eyes as we walk through the tunnel to B Block. "Jesus," he says. "You think he could set this up a little earlier in the morning?"

Frankie Diamonds. He whines to me like we're a couple of humps griping about the boss. It's a dangerous occupation, talking with other cons. Instead of relieving my boredom, it intensifies it. How they all come with a sob story now. Or there's a girl on the outside. Hearing about how someone loves his girl is like hearing about some weird dream that doesn't make any sense. There's no story.

Frankson warms up when we get to cell D313, where he smiles and opens his arms to the three bad bikers inside. "Paisanos!" he says. I wait outside wondering if it looks like rain.

It's been five weeks since Bread took control. Instead of a rampaging felon, I've become a regular neck popper, at least to the outside eye. No one has any reason to doubt it. They like me better, now. They feel they know what I'm about, and I'm getting comfortable and familiar for them.

Frankson tells a few jokes to the bikers as the deal goes down – they *are* big boys, for decks – and then goes back to bed. He lives in C Block, and we pass his cell as I head back to mine. "Wake me up for my parole," he says. Then I watch him flump back onto a messy sheet, face down, the wan light hitting his legs that look like a pair of pants with nothing in them. Part of his bedsheet is piled on the floor. I find the scene incomprehensible and depressing.

Before I can walk away, a muffled voice comes from Frankson's bunk. "Don't forget the family photo on Monday."

I feel a surge of annoyance. "Can't do it. Working."

"Be a merc, man. Who pays more, Bread or the stinkin furniture factory?"

They think Bread pays me.

Monday morning I stand for count and go to chow, go with Chris E to get his shoes back from a mean transfer with no income, then go to the weight pile, then work. Then it will be chow and the weight pile again. A perfect neck-popper's routine. Outside, it's a winter day that snuck into the season early, probably by its lonesome, and the early air bites like a rattlesnake. I walk across the yard with a lot of other cons shrugged up in their denim jackets, walking right through the metal detector where the line will be long on the way back out. The other cons seem to give me a little less berth than they used to.

Inside the furniture factory, there's the noise and the smell of sawdust and hot oil. Just like in the rest of the prison, my job here is to keep the bad machines working, don't let anything stop production. My face feels like a dead piece of rubber as I poke around with my pencil. I've always thought moods show a weakness of character – dandy actors and rich men's wives have moods – but here I am in a pretty bad one.

I'm checking lengths of wood outside tolerance to see which saw they came from when Dodd steps near me, leans in and says, "Nicky needs to see you."

These days I talk to Nick, Bread being so stratospheric. I thought it would be Frankson who'd try to round me up, but he's not here. Must already be at the family photo, thought I'd be there too. The meet with the Mexicans, all the toughest members of each gang will show up so the other guy can get a look at what he's facing if he breaks the deal. Family photo.

"I'm working," I say.

Dodd doesn't even work here, and I don't like him messing with my shift. When he doesn't move off, I just stare at him. He walks over to Popeye McNeely, the civilian shift supervisor, gets his attention and whispers something to him about me without my permission.

Popeye looks over at me, and I see him nodding. Dodd puts a hand on his back, a little friendly and a little possessive, a gesture that another convict wouldn't tolerate. Then – and this annoys me more than I would have thought – I see Dodd sticking around to tell a joke and Popeye laughing. They talk for a few minutes. It's like my brow is being packed with wet sand until it's heavy on my face. Dodd gives Popeye a cigarette and lights it.

Popeye thinks he's doing me a favor.

Dodd finally leaves, and Popeye waits a minute before he comes over to tell me I'm not feeling well and should get out early, get some rest.

"Croft?"

I'm staring at the door that Dodd left through.

"Croft?"

"Just a cramp," I say. "Feeling fine now."

"You sure?"

"Yes."

He waits a few more beats, then, smelling opportunity: "Cause I got those reports to do, if you're sticking around."

I stare at the door.

"Croft?"

I fix the productivity reports to the Bureau and try to cool my head in Popeye's crummy office while I miss the family photo. The time slips by without consequence. I'm tired of being bothered with Bread's business, but what really hangs me up now is that I'd already told them no. I turn in place and look around at the office. It looks almost like the office of the unsuccessful private investigator in a Humphrey Bogart film. Everything's covered in fine factory soot that's dry when it settles but turns to grease if you rub it between your fingers. Yeah, Popeye the romantic failing P.I., minus a few IQ points and the soft spot. I told them no, so they just show up anyway.

For some reason I'm really feeling the grossness and shabbiness of the joint, lately; to me it's been looking like more of a leper colony than a prison. I remember a con showing me where somebody'd bitten him in a county jail, and how there were only marks from a few teeth as if he'd been bitten by a giant infant. And what do I do? I skip a shift, miss a meal, change my shower time, crawl out of bed. Every big deal, every tough collection. Rook's in the hole, but I'm supposed to be so scared and so grateful to Bread that I don't warrant a taste? The money is chump change, I don't care about it, but I don't like standing in a hole, either.

My bad mood is feeding itself now, like an infection. My shirt collar starts feeling too tight. It's the shabbiness. None of the best people are crooks, anymore. Or they're not getting caught.

I think of Bread and my eyes narrow. Maybe it's a matter of pride *not* to pay me when he's got something else over me. To pay me too would be slack in his knots, in his world where everything is tight enough to cut off the circulation. It's another detail of a bad play I have no interest in, and it feels this big. What's that say?

I sit with a pencil tip hovering over the same spot on a report form for several minutes, my thoughts moldering. A fly buzzes against the dirty little window. I make a mark and drop the pencil, walk out of the office. Popeye is standing near the entrance to the factory, taking a smoke break with a convict.

"Wave me out," I say.

"You're leaving now?"

I walk out and and wait in a short queue to go through the metal detector. Popeye gives the hack a wave when it's my turn, and I head inside the SO. The first floor corridors are cool during the day now. It's quiet with most of the convicts still at work. Weak sunlight glows in small high windows of pebbled glass. The prison is so old that when it empties out a little, it becomes an instant museum. If we all suddenly walked away from it, no one would be able to tell whether it had been abandoned for an hour or a hundred years.

I shower for twenty minutes, but it seems like no amount of scalding water can cook off the tension in my neck and trapezius muscles. I dry off and then stand in the doorway for a minute. What I should do is go back to work or go to my cell and cool my head. But when I start walking, I know I'm headed to D Block.

Nick Karoulas' cell is on the first tier, south side far corner. He's inside, his blonde hair wet and a towel wrapped around his neck. There's a water mark around his collar and a dab of shaving cream in one ear. He daubs it out as I approach the bars of his cell door, which is locked. Never can be too careful.

"Croft. Where were you, today?"

"I want to see him."

Nick looks for more spots of shaving cream in his four-inch mirror, moving it in an orbit around his neck. "Well, he's not gonna want to see you. Come on, what happened to you?"

I get a feeling like I was just hit in the head, and suddenly I don't know what I'm doing here, waiting outside this deck's cell and talking through a closed door. I turn and walk away. It takes him a few seconds to realize I'm gone. These days, I guess enough guys would stand there while he fusses with himself. Once he does realize I'm not behind him, Nick shouts: "Hey! You talk to me!"

I stop and turn toward him.

He has nothing to say until I turn away again.

"He's not there!"

We'll see.

I take the stairs up to the second tier, and then I'm standing outside the one cell in the block that never gets tossed, in my usual spot when there's a count going on Friday nights, when I play guard-ape. A whole operation with my name as a gold standard, turning thousands of dollars a week, and what's my job?

I put my hand on the bars and push. Convicts can lock their own cells from the inside, for safety from other convicts, but the door is open. I move inside.

It's simple, an ordinary con's cell with the grey blanket that seems to be made from lint and old women's lusterless hair, bed nicely made up. But there are two differences. The first is the personal possessions lying in plain sight: the Prime watch on the nightstand, the portable tv, a cloudy mason jar of rings and gold fillings on the windowsill – those, and the fact that the cell door is open when he's not home. The second is the count room.

I peer into a rough doorway punched through to the next cell. It's relatively dark, inside. The bars of the cell are covered by a spare mattress painted grey to look like old concrete. Inside, Chris D is standing over a bed that's been converted into a long table, covered in stacks of small bills and some extra lights.

I move inside the count room. Chris D is busy divvying and counting. To prevent extortion, Seamax policy keeps soft money in short supply, with no one allowed over thirty bucks a month. That limit is meaningless around Bread's operation. Stacks of bills the decks call bibles move through the prison in laundry, in books, in mattresses. They're small denominations, mostly one and five dollar bills, but still many times the total amount of money that ought to be in the prison at one time. Figure thirty bucks apiece times around six hundred convicts, that's eighteen thousand cash at most that ought to be inside the walls. I'd guess the real number might be closer to a hundred grand.

Chris D jerks around when the edge of my shadow falls across him. He looks surprised and then confused when he sees it's me. Then he gets a little scared again when he sees my expression. My face still feels dead.

"He's not here," Chris says. "What are you doing in here?"

Chris's 20-year-old girlfriend had been bigger than him, I'd heard, a Nordic blonde, tall and strong, but he'd killed her just the same in a pointless argument; I know nothing else about him. I care to know nothing else.

I move into the middle of the room, and he shrinks like plastic in a fire. I never look at him. I look all around him at all the bibles, stacked four and five high, at Bread's ledger bound in faux black leather, the drug scales, the envelopes. The dry toilet is filled with bricks of brown powder. Heroin is fading out in the streets, giving way to coke, but stimulants that make you paranoid and aggressive are no way to do time.

My gaze settles on the paraphernalia of scum, in front of me. I can't imagine anything more asinine than a drug. Loved by gross, disorganized personalities that hunger for delusion. To think of living with a drug addict would mean having patience with filth, incompetence, and victimhood that I could never stomach.

"What is it?" Chris says.

I don't answer.

For lack of anything else to say, trying to guess what I'm doing here, Chris says, "It's all here."

"Good," I say. I reach over him and pick up a pile of tiny bags filled with brown powder and cinched with dental rubber bands, feel them in my palm. This is what all the fuss is about. I drop them to the floor.

"Croft? What's up, man?"

I pick up a stack of three bibles and run my fingers along the edge, fanning it. The hand holding the money falls to my waist as I move back into Bread's cell, with his personal stuff.

I let my presence fill the space. I don't get the sense Bread has any attachment to this stuff. Not really. I think he's got what he thinks he's supposed to have, what he thinks other people want to have. If it was a house on the outside he'd furnished, it would be patched together from rich men's houses he'd seen, but for him it would be something he could almost wander off and forget – it could just slip his mind, unless someone else wanted it or tried to take it away.

I feel something behind me and turn to see Chris staring at me with wide, unblinking eyes. He's not really looking at me, but at the money in my hand. I'd forgotten it and almost toss it back to him, and then something hot and ugly rises in me. I raise the money to my chest and regard it. Chump change. But I realize I'm going to take it just the same.

Chris' mouth is open, his head shaking.

Then I go, leaving behind a stunned silence.

In the back of my prison file is an evaluation which says this: "Moderately antisocial, but no indication of any institutional patterned behavior after three years of incarceration…. After talking with him, it is my considered opinion that Mr. Croft may have deliberately underperformed on the Standard Intelligence Test Battery. If he had performed to his ability, he may well have scored above average in every category. Caution is advised: Mr. Croft is more than capable of telling officials and even professional evaluators exactly what they want to hear."

The shrink had been an intern of some kind, resented and feared by his older peers in the prison system because he'd had a couple of brain cells to rub together. He'd seen more than the others but was on his way down the road to being another poor, unappreciated soul in the system. Remembering what he'd written only cast my theft in a more pitiful light.

Petty. Maybe Childish. Sure to have consequences. And yet I don't feel half bad as I walk away down the tier, down the stairs. There may have been a time, once, when I would've thought of a man like Chris as my victim. For a little while when I was younger, I tried showing respect to people weaker and stupider than me. I almost wound up picked apart like a dinner platter. The truth is, we live in a fantasy society where everybody is top dog, and just by being there, somebody with real strength is messing with their illusions and must be punished.

I brush past a convict moving in the opposite direction, making him turn aside.

You don't need to do anything to offend or give a person reason to believe you're going to walk all over them – if it's in their mind, you've already done it. If someone is afraid you're going to take something away from them, whatever it might be, their place or their bullshit pride, it's simpler just to do it. That way you can at least eat your cake while they're working on your knees with a two-handed saw.

A pair of decks talking to each other across the tier fall silent as I move between them, then start talking again.

None of those gradeschool images of bad boys and their victims make real-world sense, anyway. Once the kiddies grow up, the bully isn't an overweight baby whose daddy punched him around at home. We do love that image, don't we? It's usually a shortstack with a chip on his shoulder. Go ahead and hate the castle and the lantern-jawed bullyboy who filled out young. They'll hit you head-on. But when you need to know who carries enough spite every single day to really hurt your life, look for a little guy.

I stash the money – about three hundred dollars in creased and rumpled bills – in my cell. Chump change, I don't care about it. I go to the weight pile, where the scent of iron on the air is like a fine amount of blood in my teeth. To burn through a giddy feeling, I get down to work with a pair of dumbbells and an upright bench.

Prejudice is ugly, I think, watching my veins and my muscles swell. Bread can't see past the neck-popper physique. What I know is that he can't accuse me of stealing from him when there's nothing he can do about it short of unleashing the ultimate ballbusting freak case in the middle of his operation. And if I'm sent to the hole while it's generally believed that I'm with the gang, it will look like he's losing control. He'll have to play it off, act like it was an arrangement. If Chris tells him what I did, he'll have to stick to our little story. Or Chris may find a way to hide the loss and save his own skin.

I share my theory with Willie before lights out. I feel almost amused by it in a low way, but he feels differently.

"You probably right," he says. "You can think fo yourself. You a sly dog." Then he seems to get depressed. "That's the hell of it. These decks. That's the hell of it."

When I don't go the hole, I steal more. Fifty there, a hundred here. Shakedowns, mostly. I tell myself that I need it for something practical – like some gate money for the day I get released – but maybe it's more of a gamble. Why else do I pick certain couriers, guys I know wouldn't be trusted with too much? If I was to take too much, say maybe the whole count one of these Friday nights, Bread would forget all about saving face. It would be war. But just enough so I can't be trusted?

Normally Bread would want me for something at least every few days, but things get quiet. I don't hear from anyone until the second Thursday of the month, significant because it's the day before the second Friday, when the big count happens. The timing must have something to do with a laundry, a mail drop, something going out of the prison on a regular basis. Dodd stops beside me in the weight pile while I'm blasting out decline presses on a bench propped up with a cinder block on one end. A prison gym doesn't have all the equipment, but convicts will improvise.

"Hey, Croft."

Dodd's face appears above me. He's an outlaw biker, tall with a very high forehead and a fu-Manchu mustache.

I finish my set, sit up with my palms on my knees, and wait.

"Don't worry about the count tomorrow night."

The count, when usually I play guard-ape.

"We got it covered." He smiles. "Take a little vacation. Grab a shower and a movie. Don't worry about anything."

He knows I won't be upset about this, and I'm not, but I have a little fun with him. "You going to guard the count?"

"Yeah, right, funny guy. Fiero."

"Fiero. You think he's tough enough?"

"Sure, he'll cut it. You see what he did to that Lottiger dude?" He makes a twisting motion with his hands, like unscrewing the lid on a tight jar.

"What if someone my size shows up?"

He smiles. "Hell, I guess we'd be out of luck, then. You worry too much, Croft."

Don't try selling Cadillacs anytime soon, Bozo.

He leaves, and that is all. I won't guard the count. And since Bread hasn't been asking me for anything else, I don't see anything coming on the horizon, either.

I sit there, dazed. Just rip him off a little, that's all it took.

I lay back and lift the barbell off the forks.

Of course I don't believe it's that simple, but if it ever had a chance of working, now would be the time. Bread doesn't strictly need me anymore. He has enough hard guys and enough hacks he doesn't need a castle neck popper for anything more than show, and even if he does, he's got Fiero. And because of our little cover story, he isn't forced to act. Some other case started robbing him, everybody would know it was a straight-up shakedown. Not so with me. And if he feels like he wants to handle it...his usual method is to butcher his way through his problems, but I can't be handled that way. I realize this is where I've been wanting him: not being able to act and not really having to.

I finish my set and sit up, cupping my knees. My eyes don't focus on anything. Pretending this has a prayer of working, the only question is how much I should steal before I let the situation drift.

A castle named Faber is passing by and drops a fresh towel on my leg, and I run it across my forehead and over my ears.

To really fine tune it, I'm thinking a couple hundred more.

2

I quit stealing and go back to minding my own business once I hit the thousand mark. It's like tearing a shirt just enough so it can't be worn. Then I don't approach Bread's gang, and they don't approach me. A week drags by. Then Bread avoids me right into November. Business continues as usual. Hacks bring in his drugs, and he pays them well and takes care of some of their other business besides. They have their own lists of names, and the gang on top has always played a part in keeping order. I can see the wheels turning.

From one point of view, there's a sense to it. I wouldn't make the difference I used to, not with Fiero in the gang and more weapons coming into the prison each week. It's a matter of time before a big castle like me doesn't add a lot on the margin. Bread wants me gone, anyway, and gone's where I'll be.

I drift back toward my old routine, skeptical but enjoying the smoother time, like pulling the wrinkles out of a sheet with one tug. I've played this game before, waiting for a bad man to try and take his revenge...or not. I've known one or two who could take a hot coal from a fire and tend it for years in a cold room, keeping it alive by blowing on it when no one else is around; then, when everyone else has forgotten it, dousing it with gasoline. I've known others just as bad who couldn't spare the time for that. I've said it before: it depends on who Bread turns out to be.

With a smirk I listen to a bank robber named Sizemore tell me that now it looks like someone *else* is stealing from Bread. Someone else tough. Sizemore sees I'm enjoying the story and gets jazzed about it, shuffling his feet and adding details that may or may not be true. Nearly everyone in prison does some hot-dogging – the lack of common respect that comes with living in pigeon holes makes them too desperate not to. I assume it's nothing serious and don't think much about it at the time.

I'm on my way back from the weight pile on a cold Tuesday in November when I spot them coming in through the tunnel into C Block. Five of them, came in just a few seconds after me, moving parallel to me on the ground floor. We see each other at the same moment, and there's no doubt who they're here for. Two of them are Chris E and Parker. The others I've seen with Bread's gang but don't know by name. I keep walking. Bread's gang is tougher than it used to be. Killing Vanderventer attracted some of worst decks to his cause, guys like Randy Lafferty and Hacksaw Ricky Chavez. They're looking up at me on Tier 2 as I move toward my cell, but they're also looking in every direction, seeing who's around, witnesses. The dozen or so cons they pass get out of their way.

We keep moving at the same speed. I debate whether go inside my cell or walk right past it.

They're armed. They'd be crazy not to be. They're crazy anyway.

I reach my cell when they are close to the center stairs.

I duck inside.

It isn't a matter of how to stay alive but of how to avoid cuts or punctures that could would make me weaker the next time. Something I heard that's never left me is the way Vanderventer's gang took out a castle the year before I got here. One guy walking past in a crowd cut him a deep slice to the back of his arm, just above the elbow where the tendon is. Nothing life threatening. Later, a hand reaches out of another crowd and plants a shiv in the back of his knee. The castle gets wise but can't avoid crowds everywhere he goes. He gets the third guy, but not until after the guy slashes his other arm. A few days more of this, and a group of them corner him and take him without much trouble. No fear of reprisal, either. Castles aren't a gang.

I sit down calmly on my mattress, and as I wait, I grip its edge. I can stand it in front of me and run them right into the railing and probably over it. I doubt they've got a wolfpack like Vanderventer did, anyway. Still, I'm surprised. This is sudden and actually kind of ludicrous. They have a chance, the five of them, maybe, but I wouldn't give them odds. I experience no physical fear; just fear of myself. I can feel the cobwebby sunlight falling on one shoulder through the little cell window. I hear someone coming up the metal stairs. One man. The dim afternoon light makes an eye-straining stew of weak shadows while I listen.

Then I'm looking at Parker, who stops on my front porch. Not the one to send on something tough, even if one guy had a shot. He'd been in my old deck and pretty serious about staying tough and doing his time, but since then he's gotten skinny and has a hollow, violent look around his eyes. Today he looks worse than usual.

To reach me, he'll have to step inside. I wonder whether he is supposed to be some sort of human sacrifice to get me sent down for the big M. He looks almost nervous enough. I let go of the mattress and stand up.

Parker looks over his shoulder and seems to gather himself and plant his feet, then says, "The big guy wantsa see you."

I step up to him. I have ten inches and more than a hundred pounds on him. A smirk that I feel in the muscles of my face does not quite surface. I say, "The big guy."

"Just wantsa talk, man," he says.

I take my time answering. I don't let the smallness of the man in front of me lull me into thinking I'm safe, but I also don't let shadows grow in my mind. I'd stolen money from a savage drug kingpin in Seamax Penitentiary, and now he wants to meet with me. Probably someplace quiet. I don't bother to ask. Let them think that anywhere I can follow them, I'm certain of my fate. And theirs.

Parker walks in front of me, the other four behind, but at a distance. I ignore them. We go down the stairs on the west end of the cell block and into the tunnel. That would be the first reasonable place to stick someone. With half the lights always burned out, it's dark. From the hesitation in the footsteps around me, they seem to think I entertain the idea, myself. The smell of sweat and adrenaline that comes off them only adds to the same scent already embedded in the old walls of the tunnel: the smell of generations of men burning up like candles, from the inside out.

Only when we're through the tunnel do I say, "Where we going."

"Hog shop."

At the end of the tunnel, Parker turns into the main SO corridor alongside the chow hall. I can smell the gooey food already cooking for lunch, the steamy mashed potatoes that they'll manage to turn ice cold by the time chow is on. The corridor is empty and silent. Convicts wear soft-soled shoes, so echoes only come from voices. Lights are out during the day, adding to the constant *dimness*. I get out of here, I'm going someplace and turn on all the lights.

As we get close to the hog shop, the narrower corridors, the tighter corners, I slow to a more deliberate pace, and Bread's guys have to slow with me. Sticking a deck is a matter of will. Taking down a case, even a smaller one, takes more will plus a real plan...and probably the element of surprise. I pay attention to small sounds. Five guys could suddenly become nine or ten, and then I might have a significant problem. I deliberately crowd Parker. I screw up his timing make him practice his footwork.

We reach the little hack cafeteria without incident. Parker waits for me, and I invite him to go inside first. Into the room where they'd smashed Bingo literally to bits with a chair. He goes in, and I follow.

Bread is inside, leaning against a wall. Parker and some convict cooks leave the room, and we're alone.

"Sit down," Bread says, gesturing to a bench.

Neither of us sits down.

"I want to say this to you respectfully."

I wonder if the man knows what respect is. His own impulse to control others and expand his power is so rabid that it leaves very little room for anything else. He can show other superficial emotions, and he isn't empty like a sociopath, but he is an actor like one. I sense there are others around, not in the room but very close, just in case.

I wait for a threat or a platitude. Anything we can say to each other feels too obvious to me and not worth saying.

Then Bread says, "You have to take care of Troy."

I just stand there. It takes an active effort not to let my face rearrange itself. "Troy."

"Has to be you. Fiero doesn't want anything to do with him, and I can see why."

I feel like we are standing on a record that's taken a bad skip.

"The shakedowns have been hurting business. He doesn't give a damn about his deck, so it won't do any good to take retribution on them for what he did. We need to send a message: it doesn't matter how tough you are."

I finish being surprised long enough to think about what he'd said. Troy. Big case, maybe the third biggest in Seamax, if you count the Rook. Works for no one, does exactly what he wants, especially since Rook went away. The exact order of strength doesn't matter so much because castles don't fuck with each other every chance they get like the decks. They say we live in the suburbs. I've heard grumbles about Troy in the past and assumed it was nothing serious. Every organization's little soldier ants are going to brush up against a castle having a bad day now and then.

Then I'm suddenly certain it's some kind of double talk and Bread's just calling me by another name, and that's his way of discussing things.

"I've tried reasoning with him. He doesn't want to talk. Today he broke Pratt's arm and took off with a week's worth of product."

It's not double talk.

To think all this time someone's been giving Bread's gang a worse time than me, and I didn't have any idea.

"It has to stop." Bread moves closer to me and stands almost beside me rather than facing me, like we're business partners talking in an elevator. "He's costing us a lot of money."

"Us?"

"It's your name. It's our money."

"Yeah?"

"You want people to respect you for your brains, speak in full sentences."

"Say that again."

"Just being practical, Croft. It's your name out there. Troy and everybody else believe he's stealing from *you*. You going to let that slide?"

That old yarn. It's been awhile since he's needed it, and the story feels worn out and threadbare to me. Bread presses it home a little more. "Come on. You and I know you're not afraid of Troy. But what's everybody going to think?"

Bread won't leave it to chance. He'll send out his bible salesmen to spread the good word: the money is mine, and Troy is stealing from me. Any number of cons in here are dumb enough to believe I've suddenly gone soft for no reason after never flinching for a day, before. A deep fat fryer behind the serving counter lets go of some bubbles. I feel a twitch in my neck.

"I've already got it worked out. You take care of this problem, you won't have any trouble with the hacks. You won't have any trouble at all."

Loaded statement. Is it a threat and an offer of truce at the same time? Is Bread even capable of such a statement? And that's assuming the whole thing isn't just a two-way trap that will eliminate Troy and me and the same time. I make my mind stop racing. I turn away from him and tilt my head back like I'm letting a cooling rain fall on me, slow my breathing. "I'll think about it."

When I turn back to him, red has climbed up Bread's neck. That furious, murderous, always-frustrated flush that he is too small to unleash on the world all at once, like he wants to. But he surprises me. He takes a pair of bibles out of his shirt and flips them onto the table. "I get it," he says, and stalks out of the room.

After I've stood there a minute, what is left ringing in my ears isn't anything between us, but what he is out to prove. That it doesn't matter anymore how tough you are. Am I the one to deliver that message?

I leave the hog shop to go back to my cell. I don't know whether I want to go and break records in the weight pile or go to sleep for the rest of the day.

As I go, I decide the whole thing feels cheap and convenient. Something bad had happened and Bread had just called me up an hour later like I was an office boy, told me what he wanted done and tossed a couple of bibles at me. Used to be a deck had to hide a razor in his cheek or spend hours filing a toothbrush handle against concrete. Now the men around Bread – some of them my old deck – carry ice picks and real knives behind their belts because they rarely get patted down. They've let me know in ways they think are subtle that big muscle is getting cheap. It doesn't have the effect they want. It would on a neck-popper, I suppose. I'm a crook.

When I get back to tier 2 and see the edge of my cell, I know something is wrong. There is a litter of papers on my front porch like a trail leading inside. Then I can see the sheet pulled off the corner of the bed. The mattress askew. I get closer and see that the papers on my front porch and littered across a few feet of the tier are pages from my sketchbook. I get to the cell. The mattress is pulled partway off the bunk, slashed several ways and left like a dead body. The bed frame is bent, the nightstand crashed on its face, the sink pipes pulled apart. A pool of water has fanned across most of the cell, and more of my papers float it in. The sink itself has been rotated on its fixtures and left nearly sideways. My shelves are empty, everything I own brushed onto the floor. A few books and a dozen magazines drink up water. My pillow lies in a corner with a shoeprint on it.

It's a few moments before I move. A great numb feeling has come over me. I pick up the nightstand and look inside the hollow space where the drawer was before someone had pulled it out and stepped on it, cracking it. The contents, a few coins and toiletries and a cheap watch, are everywhere. The sketches I'd done of buildings, cars, streetcorners are strewn around the toilet like autumn leaves (the ones of the fuses and machines are rolled up inside one of the legs of my bed). Nothing is missing, that I can tell, but they'd been looking for something. And maybe they were in a hurry, but the destruction is so severe I can't believe there wasn't some deliberate mayhem.

I never have much more on the outside than I've had in prison, but what I have, I take care of. My watches keep good time; my pencils are sharp. For a long minute I just stand here, my mind frozen. Then my eyes begin to jerk back and forth, scanning around for something more to destroy. But that's part of prison. Everything around you is either too flimsy to provide satisfaction, or indestructible. It has been a while since I've had a real and immediate sense of *prison*.

I step to my cell door and look out. I see a few people, but they all study on not seeing me. A porter slow-dances with a mop on the other side of the tier. I'll hang him over the railing until he tells me who it was. I'll stop at each cell along the tier, and whoever is home will tell me a story.

Except I already know the story.

He got me out of the way while they searched my cell for the money. The anger about Troy, that might have been real another time and place, but just now he'd been killing time with it. Maybe. Maybe Bread's so maniacal, he thought he could get me out of the way and toss my cell to have a real conversation with me about something important. Who does that?

The porter with the mop is moving away as fast as he can without looking like it.

I walk to the railing in front of my cell and wrap my fingers around it, look up and down the length and height of the block, inhaling deeply through my nose. I reach into my pocket and take out the money that Bread just gave me. Two bibles. I'm allowed to have the money he gave me, but he'd tried to take back what I'd gotten on my own. They hadn't found it, of course, but that hardly matters. The logic of it is so wheedling, so intense and specific.

I hear someone coming – something about my state of mind reduces my peripheral vision – and look sharply to my left.

Standing there are two blacks from Willie's deck. The one in front is Lyman Williams, a sort of lieutenant. His knees and elbows are slightly turned in from a sinewy musculature that's like ropes and wires wound too tight, with knots at the calf and shoulder. The man with him is bigger and hangs back like a scolded child brought by along his father to apologize to someone. "My man Grendel," Lyman says, cocking his head toward the other man, "Saw it across the tier."

I grind my jaw. "I'm supposed to think it was guards who did this."

"It was," Grendel says. He has a mouthful of metal teeth.

"Sorry," says Lyman. "It ain't right."

I don't answer. Space has a weird curve to it almost like I'm about to pass out. I imagine it's the way a bull sees.

"It was Ratel and Libretta," says Grendel, "Case you wondered."

It gives me pause. Bread had used guards because his own guys probably wouldn't take the risk. Maybe he got me out of the way because he thought I would have fought with the hacks – stupid lug that I am – and he had just enough use left for me that it wasn't in his interest having me in the hole. Yet. It only makes me madder that I'm standing here trying to figure him out. He's like a scratch in the cornea of my eye.

"They's something else," says Lyman. "I know what he must be tellin you."

"What?"

Not 'what' like 'what do you mean?' 'What' like 'where'd you come from?' I feel confused and headachy.

"It ain't true. Troy know it ain't your money. A lot of people do, now. They respect the idea, it's smart, but they know you just a brand name on that shit. It ain't you. Not really. You got no fight with Troy."

I hadn't known for sure whether the word was out on Bread's real scheme, but right now I don't care. "Don't tell me who my fight is with."

"This just infumation. Fiero the one people afraid of, now. First they thought it would be you coming if they didn't pay what they owed or took something they shouldn't of took, but they's always a few crazy junkies gonna do anything for a fix. It's the rest of the gang and Fiero came down on them. That's how it's been goin. Two and two added up. Don't let this breadloaf motherfucker run your emotions."

"Where's Willie?"

"Infirmary."

"I think you better leave."

They walk away without another word, neutral. I begin to feel like this is somehow my own fault, being so disinterested, trusting to that invisible line that's supposed to separate me from the decks. If castles are guilty of anything, it's that we sometimes live on the moon.

I stand there another minute screwing my head on straight. More than anything, I want to remember who I am. Am I really here, standing in front of this trashed and pathetic prison cell, losing my head over it? In another world, I'm the kind the FBI likes because I get them interviewed on tv. They love to talk about how dangerous my kind of personality is, the kind of rare criminal who can gather intelligence, make a plan, and then follow through with military precision. And, they'd say, I have an excellent disguise: my gorilla physique.

Lucky for me, most people don't believe conspiracy theories like that. The world doesn't tolerate those kinds of combinations. No one is allowed to have too much. If you are big, you have to be dumb. Smart, weak. Attractive, helpless.

My cell looks like a place where a bum might sleep. This mess is mine. I can't go back into the cell and be surrounded by it. Instead, I turn away and look out at this small world I live in.

It isn't just today. It isn't just this place. Every day of my life someone tries convincing me that I don't exist. My fear is that one day the gorilla physique will stop being a disguise, and that crook with the crack timing will become someone I used to be until I couldn't cheat reality anymore. The small men around me will breathe a collective sigh of relief, and they'll all like me better, then. An old, rotten anger starts washing over me. I hate the race gangs and the politics because they don't account for the real Us and Them. They only mask things. It's the weak, toothless, squalling people who will pull down everything of value and then crawl back into their hovels when there's nothing left to envy. They're like the dogs that can't survive in any sane environment, bred to kill better dogs and then die from being stupid. They won't be happy till there's nothing. Fuck equality.

I begin to walk.

As I go, I wrinkle my nose at the cloying, burnt odor of contraband heaters and cookers made with split electrical cords. I go out of the cell block. I stomp off like a troll from under a bridge to avenge the wreck of my prison cell, and the feeling is alien and upsetting. I don't belong to myself, and the feeling creates a fear and weakness in me while I walk. Memories break in perversely to drain my strength even more. There is a mining exchange-turned-hotel where I once stayed outside Phoenix. Hardwood floors and a clawfoot tub with brass shower head, lacy curtains, toilet that worked on a pullchain. Michaela had the next room, taking baths and drinking champagne from the bottle and enjoying her time away from the German. She insisted on carrying my bags with a smugness that said Americans didn't know how to treat their employers. Nights I'd take a mild shower and sit at the lobby bar eating peeled clementines with a cup of hot Sumatra, the clementines smoothing out the coffee acid so much it was like buttermilk in my mouth. The images and sounds are suddenly so insistent that I have to blink my eyes or I won't be able to see what's right in front of me, to whit, grey walls and floors, mildewed cracks and rust spots that look like burn marks.

To keep what focus I've got, I try to think about what I've done right in this place: I have built nothing. I have no ties, no debts, nothing of value. All of my memories here I would trade for one cup of Blue Mountain coffee on the outside. All I've done is spend countless hours thickening up every muscle in my already huge body. That's proper. It's right.

I turn left into the SO. They say you get used to the smell of the corridors – a bouquet of bleach, sweat, and hate – within a week, but sometimes, like now, it says hello to me again like we've only just met. I can remember other places, that's safe, but not the specifics. If I let the details in, I can smell the prison again.

I enter D Block on the second tier. All convicts of any tenure have a thinly restrained violence to them, and right now I feel it like steel shavings in my veins. Chow is on, so there aren't many people around. I see only one hack on the whole block: Phister only nods at me as I approach Bread's cell, because I'm part of the gang. As I approach the bars of the closed cell, I somehow know that Bread's not there – maybe giving me time to cool down, like he can run out the clock.

The stupidity and obviousness of Bread's schemes has never caused anyone here to balk him or slowed down his advance. I see that now. Each person figures Bread may not be able to fool *them*, but he'll fool the world, and isn't that worth something? The cell door is closed. Blood pushes into my chest and arms, and my hands ache to close around something tense and alive and overpower its struggles – a real, lusty ache.

I rattle the bars.

Nothing happens, so I rattle them a lot harder, making a racket. Chris D pokes his head around from the count room.

"What are you doing here?" he says.

His two pinky fingers are broken, which must make him count awkwardly, like a crab. I say, "Open this door."

"Why?"

"Open it."

"I can't," he whines.

He still doesn't come out of the doorway, into plain view. I can see the top half of his body and his tender hands.

"If you make me open this door myself."

His eyes widen, and I see him appraise me: can I really do it?

Then he comes to the door and reaches for the bolt, his eyes turned up at me to make sure I don't grab his arm.

I wait for him to open the door partway then shove it, knocking him into Bread's bed. I storm inside and yell at him, "Get down on the floor! Now!"

He withers to the floor in an instant and wraps his arms around his head, his body curling on itself. Bread's things are set up around me like Coke bottles on a fence, all targets for my anger, but I don't trash his cell. It doesn't seriously occur to me to do that, any more than it occurs to me to eat garbage. That would be going one-for-one with a disturbed deck. Even when you're not yourself, you never want to forget who doesn't stand up to your height. You don't want to lend them any inches.

Instead of trashing the cell, I just knock a few things around to make noise and keep Chris scared, and I move into the count room. Inside is about half what there would be during a count, several thousand dollars in neat stacks. I look around, stomp back into Bread's cell and pull the pillowcase off of one his pillows and grab a pile of folded shirts. I go back into the count room and stuff the money into the pillowcase - all of it - and drop the shirts in, shake the whole thing up.

Behind me, Chris D has gotten to his feet. His joints look frozen, as if the fear that had crumpled him to the floor is still fighting for possession of him. His face is twisted. "What are you doing?" he says.

"I told you to get on the floor!"

He doesn't seem to hear. He shrieks at me: *"You're crazy! He'll kill you, man! He'll fucking kill you!"*

One of Bread's goons on the tier hears the shouting and comes inside the cell looking angry. "What the f-" He gets a look at me and slips out again like he'd walked into the ladies' room by mistake.

Chris' eyes are the eyes of a lunatic. He is terrified, hypnotized by what he is seeing and the consequences of it. Maybe he's imagining himself in my shoes, right now. But he's not me.

"You don't know him!"

I'm shoving the last of the money into my shirt and pants, not bothering to make it neat, but now I whirl on him. *"Do you know me?"*

His mouth flaps, and like a blow my shout makes him fall back against the wall. I watch him become hysterical. His eyebrows arch like those of a comic book villain, the eyes reddening and filling with fluid. But he seems to be looking inside. *"Oh, no!"* he screams. *"No!"* He would give anything to be able to attack me now, but raw instinct won't allow it; he is unfocused and screeching like a man falling down a long well.

"Shut up!" I roar.

But he can't seem to stop himself. It's convulsive. *"Don't do it! Don't do it!"*

I can only ignore him as I finish. Then he seems to ask a coherent question.

"What's it *for*?" he screeches.

"Damage bill."

He laughs then, and his eyes roll like two marbles. "*What* damage bill?"

"Ask your boss."

After I hide the money in the old workshop, I sit on the edge of my bed, the wreck of my cell around my feet, thinking about what I've done. I can't say whether it was impulsiveness or something I really wanted to do. (Impulsiveness strikes me as a bad experience: it's always seemed like diarrhea of the mind.) Either way, it will be war, now. Implications come and recede like ocean waves. For an instant, a powerful feeling of stupidity and regret tortures me. It's like a pinch between my shoulder blades that makes me stand up suddenly.

For some reason, I think of the two small bundles of look-the-other-way money that Bread had slipped me when no one else was there to see it. Maybe if he'd bothered to mention to me what he was planning, but he's arrogant even when he's being magnanimous.

I pop the joint of my right wrist and elbow.

War? Who am I kidding? I'll just go to the hole, and who knows when I'll ever get out. My only chance is that Bread starts thinking he's Vanderventer and comes for me some other way. But that's the prisoner in me talking. In reality, the smart way to handle this is the way anyone on the outside would: by making a phone call. Call for that ride like I should have, months ago. I turn in my cell and chuckle exactly once, to myself, the kind of sound I'd make if someone poked a stiff finger into my gut. It's comical, what's happened. Letting them get to me like that. Over a few scraps of paper and a cell like a tenement bathroom. Already I can't believe any of it — that I'd stolen the money, that I'd let someone make me angry enough to steal it. Is this how the rest of them start focusing on life's unfairness, how they couldn't help themselves and they deserve another chance, time and again?

I'll make that call for my ride, and then I'll just have to last until dark or maybe tomorrow morning.

I start walking up the tier, thinking of getting to a phone, not really sure that's where I'm headed. Once I'm in the SO, something that feels almost like an inner ear problem starts tilting me down one corridor or the other, and I realize with a subtle fascination that I'm not the one driving. When I think about picking up the phone, a feeling of unspeakable dullness comes over me, like I'll go to sleep on the spot if I so much as take the handset out of the cradle on the wall near the visiting area. My feet carry me along like a pair of huskies. On the outside, I'd as soon trust an instinct like this, think it would justify itself and I would be glad I'd let it play out. But that was also a guy who hadn't gotten mad enough to puke over his prison cell getting tossed and then stolen the pride of a gangster who could make him disappear.

As I pass the weight pile, I turn inside. For a minute I just stand there, watching other guys work. It occurs to me that the weight pile is brighter than the rest of the prison, more serious, better. I see the sandy-haired young case who features in a lot of Bread's fights. He's doing curls by himself, and he is bruised and blackeyed something worse than he'd have gotten in the ring — he's been stomped. Old school castles like carneys about as much as the decks like perverts. I feel like I'm not really here. Just to move my body, I start messing around, doing some unserious lifting with dumbbells.

When I can either drift out or stay and do a serious workout, I stay, though I don't work too hard because I don't want rubbery arms if they come for me. I enjoy the effort and the atmosphere of hard work. I eventually stop feeling like I'm watching my actions from behind a one-way mirror. I'm still there around the time the sun starts going down, and Eddie Vanderventer, the Champ's brother, comes in and starts working his triceps. That's a strange note. He looks pale and carries himself like someone proven but ordinary, a regular con, keeps to himself. Only a couple of guys tap their buddies on the arm to say, Check this out. I fool around some more, doing wrist curls and working smaller muscle groups.

Before I know it, it's time for lights-out. I never made the call. I expect to toss and turn through the night but sleep like a baby till the sun comes up.

3

Maybe it's the good night's sleep, but by the next morning I feel a lot more confident. I get up and start my routine with gusto. At breakfast, I barely raise my head from my bowl of slimy oatmeal with raisins and the peanut butter that I scooped out of half a dozen plastic single-serve cups. Then I go for a short but intense workout in the weight pile and am stronger than yesterday.

I'm on my way to the commissary for a new sketchbook and putty eraser, momentarily alone in the lower AB corridor, when Fiero turns the corner and is suddenly walking toward me. No one else is around. I listen behind me and keep walking, blood moving into my shoulders. The average convict probably can't plant a shiv deep enough to accomplish anything. Fiero can.

He's short for a castle but has shoulders that make him almost as wide as he is tall. His arms are long and full, bigger than you'd find on a deck iron freak. He looks like a porcupine from not shaving for a few days, and his lips look red inside the dark facial hair.

My pulse doesn't quicken as we draw near, but my heart beats harder with a healthy drum.

But Mr. Scary Enforcer never looks at me, just passes me by. Then I chuckle to myself, under my breath. Just a chance encounter that made him more uncomfortable than me. How would that be for a running theme - them more uncomfortable than me?

It's been almost twenty-four hours, and I'm surprised word of my robbery still hasn't gotten out. (What convicts lack in Snitching to the Man, they make up for in blabbing to everybody else under the sun.) No one mentions it. At chow, in the yard, nobody has a thing to say about it. Bread's got the gang good and muzzled. What I do get from the convicts are a lot of odd, appraising looks, like I'm going to be in a cattle show.

The explanation comes to stand near me in the weight pile. I'm on a situp bench bending my body with bundles of surgical tubing over my shoulders for the added resistance. A friend of Blister's says, "What's up, Croft? That's a shit lot of situps, man. You could crack walnuts in there. You remember walnuts?"

He's awfully friendly. Then I notice that he's wavering a bit, has a slight heat shimmer to him. Drunk, probably. He seems to think I should know who he is. I wait for him to make a point – probably about my stealing the money.

"Just wanted to tell you, standing up is the right thing. You got a lot of guys at your back. Just let us know when you're gonna do it, man. Fuck that big bullfrog."

"What are you talking about?"

He smiles. "Yeah, right."

A couple of blacks are looking at us across the weight pile. Lyman is pushing one of his friends onto a weight bench to keep him from staring. Another black deck, short with deep vertical hate lines in his brow and bright yellow baby shoes, stares and doesn't try to hide it. The Skin Brother next to me looks back at them and smiles. He keeps smiling as his gaze slides over to a group of big white convicts standing with their arms crossed on their chests.

"Bullfrog?" I say.

"The big nigger."

"I don't have time for this."

"Hell you say. Fucking Troy said he's going to kill you, man. What's the beef?"

Troy. Going to kill me. I put on my poker face while I spend a few seconds catching up with myself. Then I say, "The beef is maybe somebody else has a problem with this guy, and he's trying to put me in the middle."

I said it before I really knew what I was going to say, but it'll do. And it's most likely true.

He just stands there, the wingtips of his red eagles poking out of his shirtsleeves. He looks excited, eager.

"Something we haven't talked about?" I say.

"I'll say there is."

I sigh. "Where's Blake?"

"You don't want to talk about it with a deck, that's cool. Got your back. Blake will come say hello."

Addicts that run out of money for heroin go for cough medicine with codeine to lessen the withdrawal. The heroin they get from Bread. At this deck I think: Keep peddling that cough medicine. He returns to his squad of iron freaks, takes off his shirt, spreads his arms, and airplanes his red eagle around the weight pile while the small black with the high yellow baby shoes stares holes in him.

I cut my workout short because I'm attracting attention, but it doesn't stop at the weight pile. Over the next couple of hours, I get treated to a disturbing stew of rumors about Troy. Not only is he going to kill me. Apparently, I'm going to kill him.

I think about it at chow as I clean out a pair of pudding cups. The way it's suddenly everywhere means somebody with influence wants it this way, like maybe someone who told me I had to take care of Troy for him. All he'd have to do is let it slip to the Skins, and they'd do the rest. It's almost reassuring. If Bread is this determined to have me go head to head with Troy, that means I'm not going off to the hole just yet for ripping him off. It's unbelievable, but he's still stuck on what he asked me to do before he tossed my cell and I cleaned out his count room. I've never been on this end of it before, but maybe the saying is right and it's better to be lucky than smart. I don't think so, but it's been said.

As the day goes on, I start getting these meaningful little nods from near-strangers, and a few watch-your-backs. On the yard, a trustee gardener tries selling me a trowel sharpened into a serrated knife blade. I don't know Troy much and don't know how seriously he'll take the rumors, so that's something to find out. Bread, still dragging my name through garbage - at some point he stole my shadow, and he just can't let it go. Troy and me. Either way it comes out, Bread wraps up a problem. I remember passing Fiero in the corridor and how I thought he was scared. But maybe he'd known something. Maybe something else was supposed to happen to me, and why fight with a dead man?

Back in C Block, I see Lyman Williams giving me a half guarded, half confused look from across the tier. We look away from each other at the same time. I go into my cell wishing it was Monday, the start of the work week when everyone would be too occupied and tired for all the drama. They can't resist something like this. The two biggest castles left in genpop gunning for each other? The World Series for a deck convict. Barnum and Bailey. It's on the air, like a faint smell of popcorn and cotton candy. I wouldn't mind talking to Willie around now, but U.S. Marshals have taken him to a hospital upstate for tests. Maybe the Big C. I begin to re-arrange the books and magazines I'd set on top of some of the more rumpled, sodden sketches I'm trying to save since the ransacking of my cell, then stop and wonder what I'm doing.

Next day I'm eating cold, overcooked broccoli for lunch at my usual table when Blake, who sits almost opposite me, stares hard over my shoulder. I turn my head and see Grendel, second man in Willie's deck, standing behind me. Grendel seems like he has at least half a brain. If he's come to talk to me here, there's something behind it. I turn to him.

"Croft," he says. "Don't mean to bother you, but-" he leans down close. "You gotta check your cell, man. Before there's a sweep."

"What is it?"

"Just somethin I heard."

Before I can ask him anything else, his discomfort over talking here takes him away.

"What'd that boy want?"

That's Casper, a few seats down. Not a Skin, but a friend of the Family.

"He wasn't asking favors," I say. When I see him about to speak again, I say, "I give you one question, and you just asked it."

I decide to wait a few minutes so it won't be too obvious what Grendel told me, in case somebody who knows about it is watching. I wonder what can be in my cell, and who'd been bold enough put it there. After a minute or so, I look up and see Troy eyeing me from across the room. His spoon has paused halfway to his mouth. Staring isn't something it's normally wise or polite to do, and it's hard to tell at a distance what the exact look is on his face.

I look back at my food. When I look for him again, Troy is gone.

I head to my cell, where I take some unwanted pills from my mattress and flush them. Then I'm only searching for a minute before I find it against the wall beneath the bed. Sissy shank, made from a toothbrush handle and a sharpened sliver of metal. Whoever'd hidden it must have been in a hurry. The hacks who toss the cells would've been downright insulted.

I hold it in my hand. Way too small to be used on me or by me, a deck weapon for other decks. But it's a major violation to have anything like it. I put it in my pocket and check the rest of my cell, just in case. A lot of cons have nothing hanging in the balance. I do. Red felt pool tables. The taste of a good cigar after a meal cooked with truffle oil. Refuge from the shabbiness that's overspreading the world. It's out there, right now, and it doesn't stand still just because I'm in here.

I stand in the middle of the cell. Bread, trying to create a situation only he can fix, for leverage. If it was about the money, I'd be in the hole already. So it's about Troy. It isn't a distraction or a setup - he's really trying to pressure me into killing Troy, like a guy who learned to be a criminal from dime novels.

I check the elbow pipe under my sink for drugs or weapons.

Bread isn't the kind of problem I ever imagined having. I remember a phone call I got from a certain New York detective. He'd caught up with me years ago and knew me but not my identity, just got me on the telephone as I was blowing town and said he knew I liked to stay out of the papers, but one of these days he was going to make me famous. I remember his tone, sort of admiring but also tortured by the fact that he'd been too slow to deliver it in person with a set of bracelets.

I look around the cell and out at the cell block, feel the slight bulge of the sissy shank in my pocket. What a buggy situation to be in. And it might get a whole lot buggier, soon.

I hear the officious shouting of the hacks coming onto the tier in force just as the swing shift comes on duty. They call everybody out, and I move to the rail and put my hands on it as they start to toss cells. I'd disposed of the shank in the furniture factory and am clean. It gives me a cool feeling to know that Bread won't get what he wants and that it will never be explained. He'd wanted something done and given his orders, and they had simply evaporated into thin air, his intentions without weight or consequence. I'm doubly glad for that as I listen to my cell getting turned over for the second time in a month.

The search is less severe than the first one, but it's still poking a bruise. Going back inside feels like being served a steak that someone has already cut into.

Later, I'm outside watching a basketball game slowly degrade into a four way brawl between the black and white players on two teams. A guy stands there with the ball under one arm, shouting. Someone taps it out of his grasp, and the play picks up again. There's a lot of body blocking, fingers in the eyes, impractical lunges for the basket on pure adrenaline.

My eyes fix on a pair of high yellow baby shoes, attached to a guy I recognize from the weight pile. He seems to be directing one side of the action. Lyman and Grendel are playing on the other team. Grendel scores a layup every other minute because of his height. Surprisingly, Eddie Vanderventer is in the mix. He runs hard and doesn't back down, but gives no attitude. Just a guy. He's smart to lay low.

The teams would work better if they were a black team and a white team – less in-fighting, but then that game would probably turn into a straight brawl. Dirty looks go around like there's skunk on the air, shoulders fail to turn for someone passing close. The racial tension has the decks buzzing like angry bees.

This is exactly what I don't respect: the melodrama of prison life. Take a 'jacket'. It's a folder. Just a folder where the prison bureaucracy keeps information about a convict. Listen to convicts talk about a jacket, then tell me they wouldn't rather be Inside than out. Hear them talk about the Big Yard, about The Max. If they had to speak plain English for a day, half of them would drop dead from boredom, and the other half would die of shame. Maybe that explains it, but I don't think so. Some guys are born looking to play a grand role on a tiny stage and accomplish it wherever they go. No amount of separation between the reality and the role is too obvious for them.

As the hostility rises, a few guys get confused about the game and start playing football. The shortstack with the high yellow babyshoes has stopped playing completely and stands mid court, checking me out. A couple of times the teams begin to tear along racial lines, come back together, and there's a half-decent play for the hoop. When the bursts of shoving begin, guys start looking in my direction: white looking for support, black to make sure I'm still sitting down. I get up to leave.

That's when a trio of red eagles comes over from a dominoes table and signals the white players off the court. The players hesitate a moment, then lower their heads and walk off like captives toward the rusty bleachers where I'm sitting, the Skins coming with them. Before I can leave, they land all around me like a flock of pigeons. One of the Skins, a guy I only know by sight, grabs my hand and shakes it aggressively, my arm limp. I sit back down. Being near me seems to give them a position of altitude, where it's safe to call down insults on anyone below. I'll wait a few minutes to be polite, then leave.

For a moment, the bright sun feels like it's going through a magnifying glass on the back of my neck. Then the door of the SO shuts behind me.

People believe their troubles come from wherever they're told they come from, as long as it's not themselves. It's a neat politician's shtick. But one thing you never do is try bringing liberal notions of race within prison walls. You will be perceived as a combination of naive, untrustworthy, pandering and, some will say, a liability to everyone who looks like you.

I get up in the morning and hit the weight pile and go to work. I've been keeping an eye out for Troy, but we don't see each other often. That gives things a chance to get worse without us doing anything.

Lunch in the chow hall, I notice people looking at me in a new way. They'd always sized me up when I passed just because I was so big, but now they keep me in their vision like they might miss something. In the weight pile, they're more aware of me, watching my weights, I imagine, so they can compare them with Troy's.

When I stop by my cell before heading back to the factory, I see a notorious yard book named Leon watching me across the tier from my cell, one foot up on the railing. He smiles at me, showing his bright gold incisor, when he sees me looking back at him. He's there another minute before he looks to his right and Blake is standing there, two feet away. The smile drops off Leon's face so fast it looks like the impact of seeing Blake has knocked out all of his lower front teeth. There are a lot of sorry specimens in prison with comically inbred features: missing teeth, missing chins, awkward figures. Blake's a tank even for a case. Leon scurries.

Blake comes over, a broad, generous grin on his face. I assume he'll try to shake my hand once he gets close. I raise mine up a little. He walks right past it, throws his arms around my shoulders and hugs me. He holds on a bit, slapping me on the back the way that they do. When he lets go, he says, "Heard you backed up the play by some friends of ours out at the basketball court, brother."

"You could say that."

I notice for the first time that he has the full-sized red eagle across his upper back, now. The wingtips show like two trails of blood coming out of his shirtsleeves. "That's how we stay strong, man."

"Or you could say I got put in a spot."

Blake's face drops and he looks genuinely confused. "Really?"

"Little bit."

"You want me to talk to someone? These guys aren't supposed to go around starting up whatever they feel like."

"Forget it."

"Still, I'm not surprised you stood up. It's who you are, I know that. Shit, it ought to be you telling some of these other guys about standing up. How you feeling? You need anything?"

"Skins take a contract on the Rook?"

"What?"

I look at him to see if he's faking ignorance, but he really doesn't seem to remember what I'm talking about. I let it fall away as if it'd never been said, but inwardly I wonder if I'd really have done it. I have the money, but I have a feeling Bread would just find out about the contract and kibosh it. He's trying to get more leverage, not lose what he already has.

Blake has more to say. He moves his head back and forth a little bit like a snake until he has my eyes. "You know what's got to be done, right? What everybody knows?"

"What's everybody know?"

"Brother, this thing's way out in the open. Way past turning the other cheek. We have to stand together."

I just look at him.

"It's going to be you or him. It's what there is, brother. It's the reality."

I can only tolerate so much reality from a convict who probably can't get a driver's license on the outside. I'm starting to feel something hot and red climbing from the base of my neck to my jaw, then my ears, then my scalp.

"Croft-"

"We both know where this is really coming from, Blake."

"What?"

"The guy Troy's been ripping off. It's not you standing here."

He shifts his stance suddenly and points one finger at the air. "Hey, you know who we are. You know what we do.

What we protect people from. You hear about the days of the KM Blacks and Mil Cuchillos?"

"You're awfully close to pointing that finger at me, right now."

"That's not what I'm doing. We're on the same side. What's gotten into you?"

"I'm dealing with it. I have to go."

I start walking away, back toward Industries.

"You'll do the right thing, Croft. I know you will. There's a lot of eyes on this. There's only one way this can go, or a lot of shit hits."

I think, When I want to know what Bread wants, I'll ask him.

As I get close to the corridor into the SO, Blake is still standing in front of my cell where I'd left him. For a hair of a second I almost turn on my heel in a red and visceral haze. In my mind's eye, I see myself walking back to Blake, slapping him open handed, and when he swings at me clipping him on both sides of his face and then slamming his head into the railing before sending him over in a heap with an extra shove. I see it all in a flicker and feel my blood stand up by itself, but I keep walking away. I move quicker, in fact. With violent images like that comes a certain paranoia, and I don't want to wonder later if he'd somehow sensed the run of my thoughts.

4

A couple of unpleasant days pass. It's reasonable for Bread to assume that even I need to work my way around to handling someone as bad as Troy, and I let him assume it. I don't argue. I never tell anyone that I have no intention of doing what they want. Saltier that way, and it leaves some chance for things to cool off on their own or ignite around some other issue, leaving this one forgotten.

The second night after the robbery, I have a lot of strange dreams I can't remember, and while I dream them over several hours, I have the feeling of being slowly cooked. Shortly before dawn I dream of being enraged and screaming at the top of my lungs. That is the dream: screaming and screaming, though the sound that comes out is barely at a conversational volume. I wake with my jaw wide open and wonder if I'd made any real noise. This has never happened to me before. I sit up in the dark and let myself calm down while I wonder what poison is catching up with me. Is it the last few months, or the last three years? It's a hell of a thing, finding out that some part of you is so offended, it can scream you awake. I know I'll offend it some more when the sun is up and I have to ignore it like a stepchild. I'm just amazed at the intensity of it.

Count is called, I go to breakfast. The sickness of the night has burned away like a ground mist. The sense of expectation from the convicts touches me as soon as I leave my cell, but I sense that it could start to fade if something doesn't happen soon. That means Bread will try something else to gain leverage over me, try and make me fight his fight. That's alright. I catch a magic act whenever I'm in Vegas, and sometimes I can figure out how the tricks are done. Those magicians are a lot more talented than Bread. The man's wires are always showing. This is the guy that tries to manipulate me.

After work, I head to the commissary for apple juice and vitamins. I'm on my way back through the second level of the SO when I hear something strange. At first I think it's a basketball game on tv, decks shouting at the screen. Must be a lot of money on it, the way they're howling. Then it reaches such a pitch, I'm not sure there's that kind of money in the prison. I have to slow down to listen better because the rec room doors are closed. Those doors are rarely closed during the day.

Once I get a little closer, I realize the sound has nothing to do with the television. The noise is totally wild, as if the hacks have filled the room waist deep with water and released a couple of six-foot sharks in there. The way the sound seems to change when I realize it isn't excitement but bedlam tightens the hair all over my head. The closed doors are muting it, which is why everyone hasn't come running out of the weight pile to see what's happening. I don't look through the small windows in the double doors. I pass on by. That's an instinct refined in prison – you walk on past. As I'm passing, something slams into the doors with a THUD, rocking them outward but not opening them – they've been barred shut, somehow. I stop for a moment, like I'd heard a twig snap in the woods. Then I start moving again. I'm only a few steps away when the doors crash open and a dozen decks come running out like a soccer team shoving and tripping over each other, their eyes blind with fear. I turn sideways to deflect the brunt of the stampede, but they break around me at the last second. The shock I see in their faces makes some of them do things that are slightly superhuman, leapfrogging each other or knocking aside someone twice their size. One skinny con is knocked headlong and slides seven or eight feet on his belly like a fish, springs to his feet again mid-slide.

I stop again. What the hell just happened inside that room?

Whatever it is, it isn't over. There's a crashing sound. Loud, quick breathing, suddenly choked off. Wood splintering. Silence for a moment, then a high, yowling scream followed by scuffling sounds and a clap like someone slamming a wet side of beef down on a concrete floor. I feel my body hairs standing up. It's a monster movie in there.

I follow my instincts and start walking again, not wanting to be caught up in an investigation. I don't get far before a single hack comes into the corridor from the A Block end and moves toward the rec at a trot. Some newjack. I slow and keep moving. Then I watch from a distance as the newjack goes inside the rec, alone. I feel my scalp tighten some more in anticipation. He wouldn't have gone in if he'd heard what I had or been here to see that blank-faced stampede come out the door. A moment passes. The muffled thudding noises don't stop. I hear a hand radio blaring but can't make out what the hack is saying. I hear the loud blurt of the radio's panic button a few seconds later.

Something changes in the noise of the prison. At first it's almost below the level of perception, but it gradually changes into hard-soled shoes echoing in corridors and clanging on catwalks. The echoes hide their numbers. Some come from the direction of admin, others up through the belly of the SO, still more from the cell blocks. The first of them come into view a handful of seconds later, really moving, saps drawn. I keep my face neutral and lean into the wall. I can hear their walkie talkies blaring. They shove back a couple of clueless convicts who walk into the corridor on the cell block side. One of them tells me not to fucking move as he runs past.

From inside the room come angry, horrified shouts and the sound of furniture breaking.

I slip away.

Twenty minutes later, I stand at the back of a crowd at the end of the corridor and watch them wheeling covered gurneys toward the front of the prison, the dead men's noses poking at four shrouds, red blood blooming in the fabric.

I hear the convicts asking each other what happened. I don't see any of the guys who came bursting out of the room twenty minutes ago, and nobody in this crowd knows anything. One guy raises his voice: "...but it could happen to the rest of us, too." He bellows toward the guards, "Hey, what happened to those guys? Did you do that?"

The guards tell him to shut up.

Someone else uses his stage voice, says, "I smelled gas in there, earlier. Place is falling apart. Gonna get us killed."

A guard who knows him points a baton at his chest. "Pipe down, Rolley."

When the bodies are gone, the paranoid crowd starts to disperse. I see the set, hateful look on a big black deck's face just as he bangs into my upper arm to show he's not afraid. Just turns himself aside like he ran into a doorjamb, but a thick white arm pokes out of the crowd and shoves him hard. When he turns to face the one who pushed him there are three guys shoulder to shoulder in his face. They smile at him, and he backs off. Then I feel more than see a group of white convicts with thick arms and short-cropped hair surge up around me like tugboats, and what am I going to say?

Maybe the heat around me and Troy isn't dying down just as quick as I'd hoped. I'm not much on wishful thinking.

Then there's a lockdown for the rest of the day, so I don't hear much. The hacks drub everyone back into their cells to pace and jeer. Everyone knows something happened, so there's a fevered atmosphere. When none of the gossip sounds legitimate, the cons turn to jokes and taunts to vent their energy and keep the hacks on edge. I hear it without listening to any particular voice. If the lockdown doesn't end soon, some cons will take chemical furloughs, breaking out private stashes of heroin, pruno, inhalers, cough medicine, and psych medication. Some will wait stoically or just sit and stare into space. There are guys in prison who, no matter how bad the boredom gets, won't read. They'll bellyache and consume themselves with their thoughts for hours, for days, they'll go stir, but they won't crack a book. Not for anything.

I wish Willie was next door, but he's still at the hospital. I pace. What I'd heard had been shocking, but with no facts to accompany it, it isn't all that interesting. It's quarter to six. The days are shortening, but it won't be dark for almost two more hours. Every once in a while the closeness of my cell makes me a little breathless until I get used to it again.

As I eat meatloaf and collard greens out of one of the Styrofoam clamshells the trustees are handing out, I think: I'm out of the hole as long as Troy is still around and Bread thinks there's a chance I'll have to kill him. Maybe I've got a better thing going than I know. Problem is, it can't last. Darkness finds me frowning out through the bars of my cell. There's a reason I don't like games. I don't like cards, dominoes, won't waste my time on a game of chess. The winner of most games is the one with nothing else worth thinking about. It's the more trivial person, the one with less sense of his own mortality. Not the smarter one.

The cells open at 6:00 the next morning, so that's it for the lockdown. The rec room is locked, but people are stopping in the corridor to look through the turret windows. The hacks have soaped the windows in anticipation of this, but the white swirls leave slivers and half-dollar sized holes where convicts can see the blood and wreckage. I have a peek myself: it looks like there's been a rodeo inside and the bull did most of the riding.

When I go into the weight pile, Willie is there. He's working his shoulders, which are round as bowling balls. Lyman is talking to him but leaves when he sees me coming. I wait for Willie to finish his set, but he takes his time, gets up, stretches before looking at me, and then something in his eyes can't seem to come to rest until he looks away again for a minute at Lyman and Brett, another guy in his deck. "Croft," he says.

"That's a hell of a greeting."

"Well, I'm old. Some days older than others." Then he does seem to focus on me. "Glad you okay."

"What about you?"

"Get out of my business. Heard about a ruckus, yesterday."

"You probably know more than I do."

He does tend to know things sooner than most, probably thanks to Lyman. He says, "Couple of fish looking for a gang and two guys from Rook's deck that went over to Bread. They cornered Troy in there and he took them apart."

So that's what I'd heard. My mind puts the idea together with the sounds. Quite an image. It must have been too late when the hunters realized their prey was going to get the better of them. The last one or two wouldn't have fought – they'd have run away, if they could have. I remember the sound of that last hard, wet, bony slap. Then my eyes float to one side. If Bread is going after Troy himself, now, that means whatever grace I have on account of Troy is probably coming to an end. Soon we'll be back to the fact that I ripped Bread off big time. It isn't the wholly unpleasant thought it should be.

"Troy in the hole?"

"Infirmary. He was going in when I was coming out." Willie picks up the barbell he's been using. "They'll be an investigation, but nobody saw nothin. Self defense. Troy be out soon. Nother day." He focuses on the air in front of him, teeth showing as he presses the barbell over his head again and again. The film over his eyes is thicker than a few months ago. He will probably be blind in a couple of years. And then he'll probably still be in here, pumping iron.

Guys around the weight pile are checking us out, black convicts and white, convicts who don't know we're neighbors and never had a reason to pay attention until the last couple of weeks. I don't see Yellow Baby Shoes around. I've had the feeling he'll say something to me soon.

Willie sets down the barbell again and stares at me.

"You got something in your teeth?" I say.

"Li'l surprised to see you. Thought you might run off."

"Yeah?"

"Might not of been the worst idea, either."

"Is that advice?"

"I don't give no avice. Got out of that business."

"Advice no good?"

"It was too good. I started thinkin, what these bastuds do to deserve such good avice?"

Then all the humor seems to leave him again, like a visiting spirit, and there is something grim and broody left behind. "I been hearin about Troy. I been hearin...."

He interrupts himself and seems to grind his teeth, flexing his jaw. "That boy. That boy."

As if Troy is an unruly nephew who needs a whipping. Then he turns the look on me. "The two of you."

That's when Joel, a castle friend of Blake's who lives right across the tier from me, stops by to gossip on his way out. Like everyone else, he's charged up by what happened, like he's just eaten sugar cereal. He has a killer's naturally blank face that is even more blank when he's excited. He says, "God-*dam*. Did you see that room?"

I feel something tighten behind my shoulderblade and turn my head each way to try and loosen it again. It's like taking off a wet leather shirt, and I groan. Black and white convicts around the room are watching us. Joel isn't a Skin, but like a few others he's a friend of the Family. Blaine Mitchell and Lou Stibb are edging their way closer to support Willie, if anything should happen. They're not sure about me, which is generally how I like it.

Joel's eyes are wide and his body animated. He can't resist the attraction of a true badass, even if it is big black Troy. "He took out four guys, man. And when I say took them out, I mean took them out of the fucking world." Then he seems to remember something. "But you could have done even worse, I know that. And those guys that went after him-" he lowers his voice. "Ballsy motherfuckers to try it, man. You gotta admit." He laughs. "Sometimes even I don't know what's happening to this place."

He leaves without acknowledging Willie's presence.

Willie seems to think he's gone to fat in the hospital, and I leave him to his workout. I start doing curls, thinking. I'd stolen from Bread, but I was the only way to get rid of Troy without losing face by setting the hacks on him. Yesterday proved that. The hacks just drag him off, it will be at a long term cost in respect. At the same time, Bread won't forget what I've done. Even if Troy comes after me and I do end up taking him out, evens won't be good enough for Bread. No way.

I switch and curl with the other arm. The shape of the muscle is slightly different on this side, shorter and higher. Always has been. I stand in front of the scratched metal surface used as a mirror and flex.

After yesterday, maybe Troy will end up killing Bread.

Or Bread will lose all patience and set the hacks on us both.

Maybe Troy will come for me, and we'll just see what happens.

Yeah, I'm glad I got that all figured out.

Later that day, a guy in Troy's deck gets shanked outside his cell and goes to the infirmary, where he develops complications and dies. Another one gets so demolished physically, I have people looking at *me* sideways (old trick of Bread's). For his part, Troy shakes down one of Bread's dealers and leaves him with a concussion and pupils like eightballs. It turns into a migraine so bad the hacks drag him from his cell balling and clutching his head in the middle of the night.

Bread is hiring more muscle. Within three days of the disaster in the rec room, he's brought in a new castle named Ruiz from Rochaloch. I find out about that when a hard-line castle named Cross complains to me about it, says they don't honor the code in California prisons. The guards aren't crazy about it, either, but maybe they should have thought about that before signing the transfer paperwork. Bread's also hired the sandy-haired young case who fights in the laundry room gladiator pit. The kid goes to work full time as a collector. One for one, neither of the new hires is a match for Troy, which maybe sends my own stock up again – also the heat. Nick Karoulas and Chris D pay me a visit in the yard and offer me two grand to take care of Troy in the next few days. I don't let myself laugh. I ripped them off for over three thousand dollars, and they're throwing more money at me.

Karoulas says, "Honestly, you'll just wind up having to take him on, anyway. Might as well take the initiative and get paid."

I tell them I'll take their money, figuring Troy might take the choice out of my hands any minute, and Bread no doubt plans to screw me in the end, anyway. Then I actually feel a pang of something like jealousy that it isn't the other way around: that someone else is winding up Bread instead of me, and he isn't crawling to someone who loathes him and saying, Please take care of Croft.

"When are you going to do it?" says Nick.

"You'll know when it gets done," I say. For a few minutes I can't keep the smirk from my face. Then I study a scrim of dead leaves along the bottom of the fence and the yellowing grass beyond until the hacks say to roll it up. I march off the yard without regret. Another season is going by senselessly, in a cycle that's never seemed worth paying any attention to. Prisons aside, I like a brick and mortar place that stays open year round. When I have to have trees, I'll take evergreens.

November rain keeps a lot of guys in from the yard the third week of the month, and the air is like the air on a submarine. Blankets and pillows feel damp to the touch, and people's clothes don't hang right. All the time I can feel a heat on me, like the heat from a spotlight, making my skin itch. I nod back at the Skins and their lackeys when they go out of their way to acknowledge me. In public, I ignore the blacks as if we are separated by a glass wall. I play along.

Because most guys don't want to go to the rainy, muddy yard, the prison is more crowded, quarters close. Even though our routines don't bring me and Troy together too often, I still can't avoid him completely. I still see him at chow, at a distance, and in the line at the metal detector after work. He is very aware of me, and of Bread's gang. The first thing I do when I enter a room or a corridor is look for his large ebony form.

Lyman stands with me in a secluded corner of the yard on a cold, sunny day when the air tastes like rust. Lyman is the main man in Willie's deck, yet he never speaks in front of Willie. Not to me. He'll find me alone and sometimes tell me things he's heard, usually beating around the bush so it's not like he's helping me.

I have another favor to ask, today. I say, "Know anybody who talks to Troy?"

I figure maybe I can spread the situation out a little by starting some kind of conversation, but I'll have to trust the messenger. Too friendly and I'll look scared, which would be like throwing jet fuel on a fire. Too harsh and Troy will look scared if he doesn't fight. And anything at all might convince Bread that I plan on doing nothing, if it gets back to him. I'm playing for days.

Lyman looks away from me for a minute, counseling with himself. "I don't know as you need to worry about Troy. You could stay away from him, leave him alone. It's nothin but a lot of hype and bullshit around the two of you."

I'm looking at a hack who is pretending to stroll the muddy yard forty feet away from us and keeps stealing glances in our direction. New operations lieutenant on the swing shift, quiet type mostly. Keeping an eye on Lyman. He stands out against a sea of grey uniforms. Every once in a while you'll see one hack surrounded by hundreds of convicts on the yard, and it's an image you have to think about.

"Stearne," says Lyman. "Don't worry about him."

"Lieutenant, that's impressive."

"Typical guard is divorced and far from home. It's a system for making burned out drunks. This guy got a pretty wife and a pretty little house and's on the way up, and he don't want nobody's money but the Bureau's and mine. What's that tell you? You ought to listen to me."

"That's why I'm here."

He thinks another minute. Not thinking so much as making up his mind to say something. Lyman's guys Brett and Blaine stand a little further away than Stearne, hands in pockets and kicking divots in the dirt, Brett with his signature Q-tip behind one ear.

"If you din't want to get stuck fighting with Troy for some made up reason and go to the hole, easiest way would be to tell someone in public that you got nothing to do with Bread's gang. You still settle any personal scores, but you ain't with them. Everybody would understand that. They know you don't like to be ganged up in the first place."

"Just like that."

"Might be easier than you think. You steal from him?"

I laugh without expecting to, which actually unnerves me a little.

"It don't matter for this."

Doing what Lyman suggests would push Bread into a corner and make him use his trump card, DO Stepner. And after he used it on Troy, he might as well use it on me. I tell Lyman that.

He gives me a queer look for a minute. Then he looks off and just says, "Shit."

I say, "I never knew it got this thick, Inside."

"It don't. You ought to be dead or locked down three different ways. You want to talk to Troy, or not?"

I need to decide, now. My stomach seems to harden, the way that it does, lately.

"Not yet."

Things are still too hot with the convicts watching my every move, and Troy's. It's a good idea for when things cool off a bit, if we make it that far.

Blake believes whatever hype is going around the prison on a given week. He's one of those diehard cons who keeps time in terms of prison history that nobody in the streets knows about. He'd say his kid hasn't seen him since Carry Oakes started the riot in Himesburg; he stopped trying to get his sentence reduced around the time Ship Oleman finally got busted and showed up at Seamax holding his shoes. I keep a calendar on my wall. Blake doesn't see a need for one. He's all prison. The last time he spotted for me in the weight pile, months ago, he kept telling me he's not as strong as me each time we changed up the weights and seemed nervous as a schoolgirl. Now he's got the red eagles, but the apple never falls that far.

He sits nearly across from me at the lunch table, which has made him hard to avoid. It's been a week since Troy killed four men who attacked him in the rec room. The last few days, Blake's just stared into his food, probably to avoid an uncomfortable conversation with me. Today that changes. A con with red eagles whispers something into his ear in passing, and at first Blake doesn't seem to react. It's a table of castles, and there's not a lot of the herky-jerky behavior that goes on at a deck table. It's also ingrained in a castle convict not to move too fast, raise his voice because it really grabs attention. A few minutes after the Skin Brother whispered to him, I look up and find Blake staring at me through the tops of his eyes.

I figure it's a fluke, catching him looking at me like that, but when I check again he's still doing it. His eyes are deep brown with a suggestion of red, and they're troubled. Before I can ask him if he's got something in his teeth, he says, "Can we go somewhere?"

He gets up, and I put down my fork with a cold chunk of rubbery pork chop stuck to the end of it. Then I follow Blake out of the chow hall and into the bright haze of the yard.

Whenever you go with someone to an uncertain fate, never ask where you're going or what it's about. They're expecting you to ask, maybe even beg to be told, and when you don't the balance shifts back a little in your favor. Your confident silence makes them curious, then worried, and they begin to think you know something they don't. That's if it's a short trip, like this one.

We don't go far. A door leading out to the yard comes out near the dock, which is caged inside a fence so convicts don't try and hitch a ride out in a delivery truck. The fence is unlocked now, and Blake leads me inside it and around the loading platform to a blind corner.

Blister and a handful of other deck Skins are waiting there, below the platform. They look both angry and scared, but they don't speak.

Blake walks into their midst and then turns toward me.

I fold my arms across my chest, showing them that it isn't going to be me who speaks first. They want to know something, they better ask or we'll be standing out here a long time.

Blake waves a hand at the prison and says, "They're out of patience. This thing can't wait anymore. It's right in all our faces, man."

One of the men with Blister raises his voice and says, "They're getting away with it, they're-"

Blake turns on him. "Quiet."

Then, to me. "Any way you want to handle it, do it soon. The Brothers are all out of patience."

I feel myself darkening. "They're out of patience with who?"

Blake blinks. "What?"

"They're out of patience with Troy, or they're out of patience with me?"

Blake shakes his head, negating he isn't sure what. "No, with the situation."

"Sounds like you've got a real problem. What's it got to do with me?"

"Come on, Croft. It's better this way. One guy takes him out. Takes them all down a little. It's good for everyone."

One of the deck peckerheads raises his voice again. "He doesn't care. He's got no pride."

Blake's head whips around. "Shut. Up."

It starts to rain a tiny bit, the kind where the air spits and the ground seems to turn a darker shade without getting wet.

Blake says, "I know Troy's a crazy son of a bitch, but crazy isn't always tough, man."

It's easy to give this free advice to me. Blake's a bad case, but Troy could probably put him through the floor.

It's been my policy to keep quiet and not try to explain the truth to anyone, but now it gets out, anyway. I say, "I haven't heard Troy say anything. It's somebody else pulling strings."

Then he looks like I whipped a rat tail across his eyes.

I'd intended to make a real suggestion about what was actually happening, but Blake goes stiff. My statement is a violation. Only a castle could forget the cardinal rule: whether it's right or wrong, smart or stupid, you don't back down. Ever. You don't make excuses. If you look like you might back down, those who are most like you will want to know your plan, and they will have something to say about it. They will lose face, not just you. And you do not stand up to these people like enemies. You do not burn these bridges. Not when you're Inside.

One of the decks says, "What was that he said? You're kidding me, right?"

I see a fury wake up in Blake. His face and body move slowly as if he's partly turned to stone, and for a few seconds he is a castle first and they are a bunch of stupid decks. "Get out of here."

"Hell we will."

Blister stands by himself and doesn't get involved.

"You will or I'm going to see what you look like as women. And if this guy-" cocking a thumb at me, "-decides to turn you into Siamese twins, I'm not gonna stop him."

They go a little white and look to Blister, who doesn't acknowledge them. Then the four of them scurry over the concrete platform so they won't have to pass between Blake and I. Blister steps a little closer but still keeps quiet, as if he'd agreed to let Blake do the talking but wants his presence known.

Blake says, softer now, "They've got a point though, brother. It's not just what we want. It's your name, your reputation. Troy's stealing from you, man. It might not be right out of your pants pocket, but it's still you. Doesn't that get to you?"

I smile at him. It's my contempt for the lie, and the idea that now I'm supposed to believe it like everyone else.

"Is something funny?"

"Just had a little déjà vu. You sound like someone else. All this my name, my money. You're not this gullible, are you, Blake? Or maybe you are."

Something is happening, in me, now. Building. The first faint spiderweb cracks form in my self control.

"I'm saying-"

"And another thing. If I find out somebody's been helping to set me up, he's going to get what Troy would have got. I promise you that."

"Don't talk like that."

"Why not?"

"If that's your attitude, you'll be *out there*. You'll be alone, and I don't know what can happen, then."

I feel prickly heat rising up my neck. This is final talk. We are coming to absolutes.

I say, "Tell Bread I said hello."

"This is *us*, man. This is light and dark, right and wrong."

"Lie to my face again."

"What did you say?"

Something finally breaks loose in my head. The slow acid of the situation has just about cut through my brake lines. Bread, getting me in more hot water, and now I'm his agent against myself. "Am I getting through, now? Use your head. If you can't handle Troy, how are going to handle me?"

"Ok," says Blister. "I've heard enough."

"Wait a minute," says Blake. "Just wait."

He steps closer to me, an intimate distance, and tilts his head so he is speaking into the side of my neck and no one can hear but me. His voice is full of honesty and feeling. "You can just forget about all of it, man. Forget the whole thing. Just come inside, man. Come inside. It's been good for me, it'll be good for you. You'll have backup Inside and out. There'll be jobs, respect. Family. Just come inside. We'll get you clear of Rook. Forget Troy. You won't even have to worry about Bread."

Blake really believes what he's saying, and I think he genuinely wants to help me in a way that he wouldn't help anyone else. It has a calming effect. But the Skins are blood in, blood out. If you get out – ever – you're dead.

I don't want to have this conversation a third time, so I rest a hand on Blake's shoulder until he looks me in the eyes. "No."

He just stares. At first he flashes colors of anger, remorse, pity, but then something happens. It looks like dawn breaking over his face. His features smooth out until he looks like a younger man. He seems to shrink down and be looking up at me as if I'm standing on the side of a mountain. Finally he stands up straight and shakes my hand, not giving me a choice about it. "I'm glad we talked," he says.

What the hell. "Me, too."

"I'm really glad. Good luck, man."

He walks away tall, like he's feeling tougher than he had on the way out here, his bad doubts erased and almost like he's gained some new faith in the world. Blister walks alongside him and doesn't try to talk. When they're almost out of the dock cage, Blister turns on his heel and with a serious expression comes back to me and shakes my hand, too.

"You got my personal respect," he says. "I know Blake's right about you."

There's an empty light in his eyes, like he's memorizing my face.

"So, what now?"

"I don't even know. We got no more parameters. Stay strong. Stay loose."

"Grow eyes in the back of my head?"

He shrugs as he walks away, a gesture without sympathy. "Couldn't hurt."

I stand there a minute and blink away their hocus pocus about honor and brotherhood. They make their money reselling inmates' wristwatches, shaking down fish and exit-taxing guys during their last week, extorting protection money from weaker inmates or anybody with a wealthy family. They go through the prison's files with help from bad hacks and split the take. It's small-time even on the Inside. Murder for hire ought to be serious business, but in prison that can pay as little as a few hundred bucks. Narcotics at least can pull in a few thousand a month for the heavies.

Still, I go back inside the prison feeling exactly like Blister said: like I have no more parameters. I'm strangely numb, as if I'm seeing myself from the outside. My own angry remarks are a little mystifying. All risk, no percentage.

When I go back to work, I want to think but feel like I'm looking for the secret doorway that will let me back inside my own head. It's somewhere under a flap of scalp, behind a chunk of skull. I want to pay attention to my surroundings – if you want to experience prison, go someplace where humans aren't at the top of the food chain and take a stroll through some tall grass. I want to pay attention, but I feel like I can't see quite straight. I want to worry, because there are those who worry and those who fear. Apparently it never gets this thick for a convict, and I should already be dead or locked down three different ways.

I eat a light dinner and am still feeling distracted. I bite my lip like a son of a bitch, so hard I experience the texture of a chewy piece of steak between my teeth, feel the resistance of the meat and the salty puncture, and have to fight the sudden violent urge to put my fist through the table. I can see the blood on a tasteless soda biscuit each time I bite into it. I leave chow, take a last stroll around the yard and go to the pile.

I go into the large room where the weights clank and clang, and start winding my way toward the chest press. I'm thinking of what Blister had said at the end, more the way he'd said it, the kiss goodbye with a little bit of stink on it. I work my way toward the middle of the room in this state of distraction, past the light freeweights and jump rope area near the door and into an area of mixed rusty Nautilus machines and heavy barbells, cracking my knuckles. Guys lift weights all the time when they don't feel safe.

I hunt around my feet for the weights I need until I sense something vaguely unpleasant to my left, like an area cleared of humanity by a smell. Ten feet away, a carney who fights in Bread's gladiator pit warms up by himself, swimming with his shoulders in front of an upright bench. Like other kinds of prison untouchables, he seems to look slightly inward so there is little chance of catching anyone's eye. His presence seems to negate every possible interaction because he is big and strong but among castles someplace between a pederast and a punk. Because he's fought, he can now be sold and traded, even transferred to other prisons against his will for bigger fights, or his sentence extended. It's an evil fate on the Inside, losing the respect and protection of your own kind. Given my situation, I might have had more sympathy. Despite my disdain for the convict code, the rule against arena fighting is one that has always made sense to me.

I begin pumping the whole stack on the chest press one arm at a time. My mind is cycling, and I try to breathe through it. I'm still aware of the carney on my left, and I had come in distracted anyway. That is the reason I look up with an ugly shock at a huge lump of ebony towering over the blacks around him. Troy is barely ten feet from me, closer than we've been in weeks, cleaning a heavily loaded barbell from waist to shoulders, really ripping off the reps. His back is to me, but a lot of other people are looking right at me like I'd wandered into Il Vino in my underwear. I must have wandered in here like a guy blinded by a flash camera.

Maybe I'd assumed I was safe because Troy wasn't normally here in the evenings. Or was he? Somehow I can't remember. His torso has more lumps in it than a platter of giant manicotti. The skin at the back of his neck becomes stacked rolls when he tilts his head back at the top of the rep. A lot of other guys have stopped their own workouts to watch. And listen. He begins to bellow each time he lifts the massive barbell, so big it looks like it belongs in some giant piece of industrial machinery, not a man's hands.

If I hadn't come so far into the room, I would've pretended to be casual and gone back out again. But I'm looking out now across a prairie dog village of yard rats, iron freaks, other assorted decks, and gang members all poking up from their own workouts to look at me and Troy. What else can I do? I take a few breaths and start pumping with the other arm. I can barely feel it.

Troy pauses with the barbell at his waist and seems to feel the room. He turns his head to one shoulder, his back to me, listening along his body. He knows I'm here. I think he'll turn and either puff himself up and confront me, or do something small to defuse the situation, like give me a nod. But he can't ignore me. I've seen to that by wandering in here the way I did.

What Troy does is tighten his grip on the barbell and hoist it extra hard to his shoulders with a loud bellow. He lowers it blowing air through his lips and then shouts it up again, ridiculously loud.

So maybe I'd rather work with a freeweight tonight. I move away from the old Nautilus machine and toward the open area of the floor with its racked weights and barbells, heavy dumbbells, ropes, chains, car parts and battered paint cans full of rusted bolts for extra weight. I don't like his bellowing. Or like an effete acquaintance once said, I don't hate it, but I despise it. A loose crowd that hasn't exactly been following me shifts direction as I move toward a barbell beside a large weight rack. A pair of bald white men appear beside it. Neither wears the eagles. "What you want?" one of them says.

"Two hundred," I say.

It isn't much weight, but I've been tense lately and don't want to pop a shoulder. So I bend to it with my knees once the spring clip has been secured on each end and hoist it to my waist, then arch my back and set it on my chest. Then I pitch it up over my head. The first rep feels kind of heavy, but as I warm up it becomes very light.

There's a shout followed by a terrible crash as Troy lets the weights drop at the end of his set. The hack at the little grammar school desk by the door makes a sound of complaint and is ignored by everyone. He's watching me like I'm a porno film.

I place the barbell on the ground gently and smoothly. More white guys appear around my weights. I don't tell them to get lost because they are in the way of a handful of Skins who want to get closer. A posse of blacks stands around Troy. Blaine Mitchell and Lou Stibb, Luke and Trey from Willie's deck and a few others from Troy's make sure nobody crosses the color line that has formed across the middle of the room, dividing the barbell area. "Three hundred," I say.

After initially hoisting it to my waist, I clean and press the barbell barely pumping my legs. Just a smooth motion from the waist and shoulders. It's very heavy, but my form is still good. Soon I feel twice my normal size from the bulge of muscle in my arms and shoulders. Men are looking back and forth between me and Troy like we're a tennis match. Troy has stalked to a new exercise, attached weights to the end of a chain. He wraps the chain around both hands and hangs its length behind his head and lifts straight up using only his arms, pumping from the elbows. We each face roughly in the other's direction without being dead-on.

I hold the bar in front of me and change my grip from overhand to under by letting go of the barbell for a split second. No one else has spoken above a whisper the last few minutes, but now one guy claps his hands and yells a yeeeahh like a buzzsaw. Others join in. I begin to curl three hundred pounds to my forehead. A strict curl with this much, on a barbell, would have put me to the test, but with the shoulder involvement and slight swing of my hips, I can rip off a few. I can watch the intricate shape of my bulging bicep, the swelling veins in my forearms, and the striations of my front shoulder muscle, looking left then right. Clean breathing, no bellows.

The shouts and some whistles get more enthusiastic, but I'm getting absorbed in the movement and stay just a hair short of the point where black holes thread the edges of my vision. Across from me, Troy bellows out each rep as if proud of his volume, and new lumps keep popping out of his body. The chains rattle. His own guys stand around him talking his weights up in a rising chant and then celebrate the finished rep with a lot of 'babies' and 'dogs' and you-the-mans.

The decks have always had numbers sheets for which castle is going to come out on top in a fight. Guys from different decks get so whipped up over a crack about their castle—a guy who doesn't give a crap about them and might not even know their names—that they do something which gets them solitary or wind up in the infirmary. Their heads are so full of the destructive possibilities of a knockdown-dragout between castles that they don't notice most of the real violence goes on among themselves.

I'm between sets and walking in circles, rolling my shoulders to keep them loose. Guys on both sides press the color line, testing it.

Finally one of the whites talks to someone on the other side, "You looking at something, friend?"

"Not much." Dry and to the point. At this, Yellow Baby Shoes pushes his way to the front and angry-eyes the white guy who'd asked the question, his stance saying, Next time, ask me. A group of Troy's decks stays close behind him, waiting on his next move. So, Baby Shoes is Troy's lieutenant.

The hack at the little grammar school desk inside the door looks like something has crawled down his shorts. He's slowly getting up, his hand on his radio.

Troy drops the chains and starts taking deep breaths and circling his arms. He still hasn't looked directly at me. He notices the standoff that's building and pays no attention. The swell of his neck and shoulder muscles makes his ears appear small, like buds; one of them is slightly misshapen, like an alleycat's ear. His eyes stay blank and focused at the same time, and he prowls around for his next exercise. The line of whites tenses as his bulk approaches their side of the room. Troy finds what he wants dangerously close to the center of the room, an arm's length from a lot of white flesh and red eagles. He chooses a barbell with a lot of weight on it. He starts adding more.

And adding more, and adding more. Him and his guys clean out half the racks. Everyone in the room has something to say about it, from groans and laughter to remarks that he is crazy or The Man. Troy works at it like a bricklayer, the ultimate intensity in his face and body. Then, when he has built something impossibly heavy and actually sort of gruesome to look at, he stands in front of it, arches his back, looking up at the lights. Someone comments that it's over seven hundred pounds. The room goes quiet. Then Troy bends and wraps his hands around the bar.

Nothing else moves.

At first, it doesn't look like the bar is going to budge. Troy's body tenses, and that is all that happens. The decks have the same look on their faces that's always there when something happens that fascinates them but in which they can never participate. Then there is a light clinking of the forty-five pound plates as the barbell leaves the floor. They hear it before they see it. Troy lifts something that looks like a piston from a hydroelectric dam to his waist, pushing with his bulging thighs. He pauses there a few seconds, inhales, tenses, and shocks everyone – not quite everyone – by dropping his body and hoisting the barbell to his shoulders with one quick jerk. The tenseness of his huge muscles seems to ripple through the floor like a passing truck. Then he drops again and straightens his arms over his head, then stands upright. He turns his head then to look around the room, meeting a lot of eyes.

A few guys from Rook's old deck stand off to one side, afraid without being impressed. I'm impressed. Not much, but impressed – if he'd been trained in the technique, he could've lifted more. Troy even earns himself a few low whistles from the white side and a few nods of the head. The Skins turn their heads as if disavowing it.

Troy drops the barbell back to his waist and lets it fall to floor with a crash like a crane letting go on a construction site. It looks like few guys' knees almost buckle.

Troy breaths a few more times and walks away without taking the weight off the barbell, takes it easy with some dumbbells while looking in my general direction.

I let him clear out. Then all eyes are on me. Some of them watch me with an intensity I've rarely ever seen, anywhere. The Skins look at me as if it's my chance to fulfill some atavistic vision of glory for them all, and I'd better not fail. Some of the blacks watch like arrows are about to be shot into them.

Personally, I don't have any real doubts, just want to be careful I don't throw out my back or bust a knee. And this is as close as I ever want to get and closer than that to entertaining the decks. I indulge in only one flourish: instead of loading up my own, I go to the same barbell Troy used. The color line bulges as it did for him. The tension ratchets even tighter. Then I do it slow, smooth, and professional. I loosen my jaw and pull my shoulders back, and then I bend and wrap my hands around the bar. Then the tension catches in my thighs and lower back, and for a second it seems impossible. The compression of my lips blocks any air from escaping. Before anything moves, the bar is bent like a smile. Then the light clinking of the plates comes when they leave the floor. It's hard. I don't want to say it's not hard. But once I get going, I get that barbell with all that weight up over my head a couple of seconds faster than Troy had, and I hold it there a few seconds longer. Some men celebrate. Others avert their eyes. Others watch as if it meant nothing and nobody could prove it meant anything. Then I drop the barbell to my waist and let it crash to the floor.

I walk away to do some wrist curls and take it easy. There are some catcalls and a bunch of hands touching my back.

I watch Troy. He'd finished what he was doing, and now he swipes at the side of his nose with a thumb, still looking at the ground with that focus. He's walking back toward the barbell again. I feel my stomach tighten. Convicts who were walking away stop and turn.

Troy has almost gotten there when there is a shout from the doorway. Lieutenant Lipkin is there with half a dozen guards. They look wired and scared. "What in the *Christ* is going on up here? What was that noise?" He looks at the desk guard and looks like he wants to hit him. The guard looks like he's just waking up from a dream. The lieutenant looks back at the room. "What is this?"

The battle lines start breaking up on their own, with a couple of exceptions. A couple of the Skins decide to angry-eye the hacks, and that makes the lieutenant pop again. "What the *fuck* are you looking at, convict?"

I keep on curling my left wrist. Troy starts taking some of plates off the barbell, as if that was his intention all along. I'm sure he'd been about to add more when the hacks showed up. And maybe we could have settled it that way, put it to bed. Maybe.

The next day is Sunday, and Industries is closed. That thundering numb feeling is gone and all I want to do is sleep, so I make myself walk a few laps of the yard and shoot hoops for an hour. I go to confession and slip the monthly twenty to the chaplain to keep writing how I'm saved in my record. The day wastes away in a stew of bad thoughts, and the weights feel heavy in the afternoon. I'm very thirsty all day but have no real appetite, and no real plan. I wonder, is this how it happens? Is this the same hog chute that's swallowed up a lot of otherwise capable people? They take one wrong step to the left and find themselves running up the down escalator?

I'm in my cell by nine o'clock and in bed by nine thirty. Long, thin day; I'd felt the weight of my bones. Now I start to wake up as soon as I start thinking about sleep. Imaginary bats roost in every corner and the lights only seem to filter the darkness instead of pushing it back, making the eyes strain. My heart rate is slightly elevated like I've taken a bad step on a set of stairs. I see a bright amorphous throb on the back of my eyelids. There are a lot of things you do on the outside to keep balanced that you can't do on the Inside. Tonight I'd have had a late steak and a belt of Scotch. Things being what they are, I'll sleep badly. I've always been mildly disgusted with people who accept sleeping badly. It's a problem of undisciplined minds.

Around nine forty-five, fifteen minutes before lockdown, I hear someone outside my cell. I slit an eye and wind up looking at a bright yellow pair of baby shoes. That bright yellow color on the Inside is presumptuous, aggressive, indiscreet. As I trail my gator eye upward, I see the small black deck with the wide nose and the ears like a bat. Troy's lieutenant, and a mouthpiece I still don't have a name for. I gauge the distance between us, whether I can grab him through the bars and break his spine before he can light whatever he seems to be hiding behind his back and throw it. It occurs to me, as it has for some time in the back of my mind, that if I really needed to and didn't mind breaking a collarbone, I might hit the bars so hard the door would sheer through the hinges and go right out.

"Croft," says Yellow Baby Shoes.

Knows I'm awake. Came to talk, or wants to get the last word before he thinks he's going to do me in with a gas balloon. Bad way to go. When I don't respond right away, he says, "Yo. Raw."

I sit up, slowly. I think I can feel Willie listening in the next cell.

"I came to set the record straight. Few hours ago, Lyman come around saying Croft don't know the word is out about the hustle. Said Bread's people telling you everybody thinks it's your name on the money. But it ain't. Dumbest rat in the yard knows it now. When he told Troy you didn't know it was all in the open, Troy felt like he had to do something. Make it right."

What's he going to do, give Bread the money back?

Baby Shoes kneels down and takes a stack of bibles from his shirt, sets it just inside the bars of my cell and slides it forward. "This is a cut of what he took. He wasn't aware of this shit, man." He stands up again. "I want to ask you myself, where you been living? You ain't on the hook for no retribution. Nobody lookin down on you, least of all Troy. He know you got Rook problems and you doin what you got to do. And another thing. This ain't me and it ain't Troy. Rumor is this breadloaf motherfucker is tryin to organize the whole prison. No more decks, no more castles. Everybody's going to respect one organization or become a target. You okay with that?" He lets that sink in for a minute. Then says, "Why don't we just wrap this thing up as a little business deal, no hard feelings."

He waits when I don't answer right away, then says, "We good?"

"What's your name."

"Noah. We good?"

I wonder, How come I never had a deck that was worth a shit?

I see Lyman smoking in the yard with a crowd of other unhappy convicts. They'd been showing a movie in the library, and the projector had snapped the celluloid. Another burn. Now they're circling out here, talking and smoking while they wait to see whether it will be fixed.

A bored hack paces the yard with the grumbling movie crowd, and he tilts his head over the men between us when I approach Lyman. I've been studying him a little. He's one of those hacks whose name you never know or care about, who never buddies up with the other guards. The kind that won't last a year and doesn't seem to want to touch anyone or anything like it's all coated in the same slime. The kind that either never says anything or shouts too much. Sometimes I want to look at something because I tend overlook it. Maybe that's the crook in me.

Lyman looks at me twice. "You sleeping hard or hardly sleeping?"

"One, then the other."

"You still walkin around." He knows a little bit about what had happened between me and Bread, and a lot about what can happen anytime between me and Troy.

"Somebody's still got a use for me."

"That's a good thing."

"Not if you know him."

Lyman smokes his hand-rolled cigarette like it's a pipe, puffing it between drags and watching the flame like it might go out, making a process of it.

"I heard you run into Troy in the pile."

"It beats Mexican Train." I wait a beat. "Noah came to see me."

He turns his head a few degrees to show he's listening.

"He said Troy didn't realize I was a fool and threw some money at me."

"Is it settled?"

"You tell me."

He throws down his butt. "Talkin to you is like getting my palm read. I never met somebody who couldn't say nothin for sure about anything."

"I don't do guesses. And I don't celebrate early."

Lyman grows suddenly serious and almost angry. "Well, I hate it. I'm a stupid convict. You still talk like you on the outside. You got that mind nobody in here's got. You'd get out of here tomorrow and take down a bank, stash a little here, little there, and not spend a dime for three months. What you talkin to me for?"

"Because I'm not outside. I'm in here, and I need to walk a certain way."

He thinks for a minute with his lips pressed together. Then he starts shaking his head.

"Let me tell you somethin. You ain't walkin no way. Watchin you is like watchin some actor play a badass convict. Guys in here afraid a you cause they can't figure you out, think you might be crazy. The only guys think they know you are crazy, themselves. You ain't in here. But maybe you better *get* in here. You never heard this from me, but maybe you better choose sides. You ain't big enough to be alone. Not no more."

Men are starting to head back inside – the movie is probably back on. Lyman joins the procession, somehow a perfect fit for it all. So familiar, not looking around, like he could do it blindfolded. He's a part of this place and sees what they all see.

I look across the yard, the flinty taste of irony in my mouth. Turns out I'm not tough at all, I'm nuts. And now everyone, right on down to a handful of black decks who might not want to see me get killed, are telling me to join the Skins or get right with Bread.

Bread. He might be the one thing in this joint that I see better than they do.

Once there was this dictator who held a sham vote. Even though he won by a landslide, he wasn't satisfied. His advisor told him that only one percent of the people hadn't voted for him and asked what more he could possibly want. The dictator turned to him and said: their names.

5

Over the next couple of days, I hear two kinds of stories. The first kind is about the contest in the weight pile, and they're distorted mirror images of the truth: I had attributed my strength to my race. Or the hacks had stopped Troy from going all the way, signaling to him that he was going down if he won. The second kind is about the slaughter in the rec. Troy's name is growing. You do not fuck with Troy. It doesn't matter that a lot of people could have guessed the outcome of such a battle. What matters is that he'd done it. He's a proven stud. Isn't even being investigated, since nobody attacks four men with pigstickers, and it isn't a crime to defend yourself. Bread obviously isn't pushing the issue with the DO, which means he's set on getting it handled another way. Our contest provided a temporary satisfaction to both sides, since (to hear them tell it) everybody won and nobody lost, but it also locked the spotlight on me even tighter.

Every corner I turn, it's like getting shocked by static electricity. I could really use a break from it. A day off, after everything, to rest a raw nerve. But this is prison. There is no rest.

I see Troy with his deck in the weight pile. Most of them hang around him, changing his weights. Noah stands off a ways, leaning against an old Nautilus, and looks like he's sucking on a lemon. He may have offered something like a truce, night before last, but the race gangs still have their minds made up. And it feels significant to me that Troy didn't come, himself. I might send a smart-talking deck too, if I knew I was a bad liar.

I don't get lost in the movements while I exercise. I have to keep track of where everybody is. Right now I can't tell whether Troy is purposely staying away from me or if he's where he wants to be on the far side of the room. There are two extra hacks with the one at the little gradeschool desk inside the doorway. I steal a few glances at Troy. I've heard he has a new tat that's a necklace of teardrops, one for each of the supposed twelve people he's killed in his life, including the four in rec. It's supposed to have a hollow thirteenth teardrop in the middle of the chain that's bigger than the others, just an outline for someone he hasn't killed yet. So they say.

I've been out of work less than an hour on the last day of November when I hear men shouting through corridors and the echo of soft-shoed convicts running through the tunnel from the SO. Men on the block are coming out of their cells.

I watch the word trickle through the tiers, filling the place up like water. Joel, a friend of Blake's, is the castle who lives in the cell directly opposite mine. I see a carrot-topped guy from his small deck skid to a stop outside his cell to tell him something. Then Joel comes out and checks with a couple of people in the cells next to his, sees me watching and comes straight over with an excited look on his face, like he's just heard a guard has broken his neck falling off a ladder.

"Another squad chased down Troy in storage A," he said. "Five guys. One of em a case. He's going down for sure, this time. But hell, sometimes you got to get it on."

Joel is one of those castles who forgets what he is, sometimes, starts talking deck. He forgets his size and his buddies with the red eagles. He keeps checking over his right shoulder for no reason. "Doesn't have a scratch on him."

I feel wires tightening around my ribcage and take a deep breath to loosen them up again. "When did this happen?"

"Couple of guys just happened to be passing by. They heard something down in storage and went into the stairs to listen. Said a couple seconds later Troy came bombing out of there and blew past them like a truck. It just happened. Two minutes ago."

"What?" The wires tighten double. I push back one shoulder and then the other like I'm fighting with a squid.

A quiet suddenly grips C Block from the inside out, like the air has been sucked out. I look around for the cause and don't see anything right away.

Then I see Troy. He's just come into the block, below. He's glistening with red blood on his neck, hair, chest, face, legs. His eyes are wide, like he's just gotten religion, and I can see from here that the pupils are dilated like he's high. Troy is walking normally, just a little slow like he's in a mild daze. Decks hug the walls to keep far out of his way.

In the middle of the cell house floor, he stops. Troy looks around. He looks up. His eyes pass right over me, the electric whites unlike any other white. Then he raises his trembling fists and roars like a silverback, cheeks shaking and back muscles flaring. The primeval sound pumps adrenaline into my system. The decks hold still as deer. Blake looks at me across the tier.

Later, I would find out that it hadn't been just any squad that had chased down Troy down in Storage A. It included four of Blister's hard-core friends, all contract killers and feared men, multiple murderers wrapped with corded muscle like spooled wire. The fifth man was a case. All of them armed. When they had him cornered, Troy had turned to fight. Now storage A looks like Bread's squad had stumbled on an angry Kodiak bear.

Troy's eyes scour the cell block for a challenge. I can hear him breathing and see his chest moving in and out. A drop of blood moves down his nose and gets blown off in a fine spray. Some of the guys who should be meeting his glare look only at me. They consider Troy an animal and have nothing to say to him; me they see fit to judge.

Troy walks out of the block again, dazed-looking and a little mechanical, as if he's been bolted together like a Frankenstein, muscles pumped, glistening with quarts of blood. His shoulders are bunched and his arms don't move when he walks. Maybe he doesn't know exactly why he's come here, just an instinct to return to his cell on Tier 1. The block is still silent. Troy is gone. Blood from one shoe left behind a faint, sticky trail of footprints.

Less than a minute later, like specters coming through the tunnel where Troy had come from are Bread, seven or eight deck gang members, Fiero, and Ruiz. They look like a little chorus with biggest boys in back. With the exception of Bread, they look secretly happy that they haven't caught up with Troy, yet. Bread in front, they move down the block toward Troy's cell on the ground level. Nobody's home.

Then Bread stalks partway across the block like he's going on after Troy alone. But like Troy, he stops in the middle of everything. He looks directly up at me, nowhere else. Lines of crimson under the skin give his face and neck a blotched appearance. "Did you see him?" he yells, like I still work for him. "*Did you see him?*"

The accusation rings on the block.

I look back at him for part of a minute, then deliberately turn and move back inside my cell.

An hour goes by after the attack, then two. I find out the castle Troy killed is the kid who used to fight for the prize purse, Jack something. I'd thought of him as Jack Shit, but then I'd seen him fight a couple of times, and he was nothing to sneeze at. I would have thought even *alone* he'd have kept Troy tied up for a minute or two, at least long enough for the rest of the crew to put something long and metal into the soft part of his neck. For some smaller castles, four of Blister's stone killers might not even need the help.

The atmosphere in the cell block becomes dangerous. There's been an improbable and bloody victory, close enough to smell. The convicts' blood is up. If the hacks try a lockdown right now, it will definitely get ugly. Good thing not all of them are stupid. I can tell they want a lockdown and think it's the right thing, but we stand for a count and then go to chow, instead. Troy isn't there. Neither is Bread.

I keep to myself and eat too fast. Blake won't look in my direction, and his Skin Brothers are constantly coming to the table to whisper. A shot of hot milk jets back up my throat before I swallow it down. Things are hot and haywire. It's going to happen soon. I'll be dragged into the mix any random minute now. Is Troy violent and insane enough to come straight for me? He's been around long enough to know he has no future anymore, after everything he's done, so he's capable of anything.

I swallow more milk with the tip of my tongue against my incisors like it's a shot of whiskey. When I see that Blake can barely eat and is just sitting there not looking at me and flexing his jaw, I put down my spoon and stare at the side of his face. He's not going to sit there like that in front of everyone at the table without looking me in the eye. I keep staring until it's clear that I'm challenging him and he's doing nothing. Some of the others at the table aren't thrilled with all the visits from whispering decks. Blake sighs and loosens his jaw, and he blinks something away.

I wonder whether Troy's deck will get involved in the fight. Might make a difference because because Bread and the Skins won't trying anything so straightforward again. Before my time, a group of Vanderventer's people covered their naked bodies with soap and took a lone castle in the dark with razor blades and stiffened wires. It didn't go quite right, but the castle died and half of Vanderventer's guys still walked away. Normal times, no one would try it. If I wanted to pretend it was normal times, I'd have to dig up last year's calendar.

A little after eight o'clock, I'm brought out of my cell by a ruckus for the second time today. I feel a sudden irritation that is part weariness. The convicts are yelling insults; the guards are yelling orders. Then I do what I've heard the hacks griping about every time there's a lockdown: the first thing a convict does when they call a lockdown is come out of his cell, if he's in it. I go out to rubberneck.

From my front porch I can see a wave of men retreating from an advance of navy blue uniforms with black buttons, coming out of the tunnels onto each tier. The hacks are bullying the C Block convicts back into their cells. The convicts are doing all of a hundred different things they do to confuse it and slow it down. They move in every direction, ask pointless questions. The deck convicts are loudest, but they aren't the only voices. Castles also spend enough of their lives confined that being put back into their cages in the middle of the evening bottoms them out and makes them mean, especially when they can't see the reason in front of them. It's been hours since anything's happened. If one of them decided to take a stand, not me, not the guards, nobody has any idea what would happen then.

I'm pretty sure I know what the lockdown is for. A few veteran convicts also know the score. They stay out on the tiers as long as they can to show solidarity with the convicts, but calm and quiet, their eyes looking for Troy.

Bread has finally had enough. Even as the thought occurs to me, it gives me a dark and almost hopeless feeling. I look at the advancing lines of guards. A convict ordered this.

I back into my cell and close the door as the tide of shuffling grey and blue reaches me. The decks aren't exactly fighting, but they are forcing the guards to push them along like cattle and arguing all the way about rights and appointments and what someone else has promised them – some because they believe it, others because it will add to the din and make things harder for the guards. The atmosphere has already been electric, like the prison has built up a great charge of static, and this kind of disruption is dangerous now. Guys already locked in their cells are still shouting. They don't have to be free to riot. They can throw things, light fires, cause floods.

It becomes difficult to see once I'm inside my cell. Everything below the tier 2 catwalk is cut from view except the far ends of the building, and I can see very little above me. Directly across the tier is Joel's cell. He's at the bars and looking toward the tunnel. I feel a surprising wrench of the muscles next to my heart as some feeling catches me like a hook. I want to see. I want to move. I want out. I have to fight it down to keep control. When the hacks reach the end of the row and have everyone in their cells, the electronic locks engage. The noise of the convicts doesn't change.

They always call a lockdown on the cellblock when they're going to rhino someone. The convicts get too excited. Maybe it feels too much like a stand-up battle. If the hacks just wait a while after locking the block down, it might be alright.

They don't wait.

The noise is steady for a minute, then seems to coil down for a leap. There's time for me to realize I haven't seen anything like this, yet - a moment when the convicts are wired and the system decides to go right at them. I know someone spots the rhino coming out of the tunnel when a single loud shout rings through the cell block: *"Fuck you pigs!"*

It sets off bedlam.

They scream as the rhino comes into view below on the west end of the block. I don't know who it is in front, covered in thick grey body armor behind the big Plexiglas shield, baton in the hand that isn't holding the shield. Probably Berry, he's the biggest hack. Three more big ones follow behind him, each with his hands on the shoulders of the man in front of him, all in helmets and padded armor. Behind them comes a phalanx of hacks in regular uniform, with the long black batons instead of the small thumb-like saps, all ready to crouch behind the rhino and then rush up along the sides of it once their convict is down.

There seem to be several reasons why most convicts don't respect even the toughest hacks, but I don't understand most of them. Whether or not I agree, there's one I do get. People who've done serious business in the streets and been locked up through no choice of their own see themselves as entrepreneurs and risk-taking businessmen. Hacks are government employees who've chosen situations that are limited, unimaginative, financially low risk, and have everything taken care of for them. They may have dangerous jobs, but so do factory workers. Hacks in turn see convicted criminals at their most helpless and absurd. The mutual contempt flies like monkey shit.

A piece of wadded up paper falls from the tier above me as the rhino approaches, below. The weather changes: it begins snowing garbage. It comes down in a white curtain, and I can hear it ticking against the concrete floor, below. A rising bedlam of screams and curses fills the cell block like a solid thing. Convicts hate the rhino.

Troy's cell is just beyond the point where the second-tier catwalk cuts off my view to the right. Another two cells in that direction, and I would able to see. But I will not see, just know what is happening, like a radio show. If the rhino is here in the first place, I know the hacks ordered Troy out of his cell to be taken someplace, probably the hole, and he refused. For that, everyone will respect him as much as they hate the rhino.

It gets its name from the thick grey body armor and the fact that, because of the way the hacks stand together in line, it appears to have *length*, like a large four-footed creature. Garbage snows down. The noise is so huge now that I can't tell anymore where the rhino is by the cells it's passing.

Echoes cross each other and reverberate to make false high-pitched sounds I can feel in my teeth and eyes.

I didn't think this ever happened on C Block.

Absolute control doesn't exist in prisons, as far as I know. There's a lot of agreement involved. Consent. Guards are always outnumbered and vulnerable. There are no firearms inside the prison. There's always the threat of a riot. A sticking. Tough rules are set on the one hand, and then the budget gets cut. The cons have to believe they'd be no better off with someone else if something were to happen to the hacks they've got. Castles add stability. They will always be castles. It's a life sentence. And like the other convicts with life sentences, they like things smooth and quiet.

But not today.

After everything that's happened, the sight of the rhino – the hammer of institutional hack power going to cell-extract the new Robin Hood of strong individuals – is too much.

Before they'd been eclipsed by the catwalk of the tier, I'd seen the hacks looking sort of bewildered at all the commotion – in C Block. Clear up to the cathedral ceiling, it rings.

Then the extraction begins. I can see Joel and the other convicts straining at the bars of their cells across tier 2, trying to wedge their heads through far enough to see, eyes all looking down and left while I look down and right. The chaos of noise starts to take on a pulsing, rhythmic quality. The garbage slows. The pulse rises through the noise until it becomes a clear chant. A foot stomp pounds along with it.

"Troy! Troy! Troy!"

Louder, louder, louder.

I look around as if I can see the whole of the great sound. Inside the cell block, a hundred and fifty men sound like a thousand. I can smell an accelerant, probably kerosene.

Seconds later a burning roll of toilet paper flies down past the bars of my cell, unrolling like ticker tape.

"Troy! Troy! Troy! Troy!"

The rhino is probably outside the cell looking in, Berry or whatever big hack is in front asking Troy one last time if he'll come out, hoping he'll say no so they can rush him and show us all who's boss.

And of course he'll say no. Because You Do Not Back Down Ever.

The noise rises and twists like steel under strain. And then…then it changes.

The rhino always wins. That is the theme. There is no one so mighty he can absorb the charge of several large armored hacks in chain and the rush of infantry that comes in on the flanks, fifteen hard men pushing against a wall of armor in a tiny cell. Except maybe one.

The chant rises in intensity. The stomp grows so heavy it must hurt their feet. They yell Troy's name a few more times, and then when I'm guessing the rhino must have crushed into Troy's cell, the noise piques. The foot stomp vibrates the air. I can see the convicts going crazy across the tier and know it's happening all around me.

Then, gradually, another name rises up through the chant and becomes it.

"Troy! Troy! Rook! Troy! Rook! Rook! Rook!"

Wanting them to know that even when they take Troy, it isn't the last word in the power of the convicts.

They're screaming it, and it's four times louder because they're in perfect harmony: *"ROOK! ROOK! ROOK! ROOK!"*

A minute later, I realize something with a small shock: my throat hurts. In the totality of the noise and vibration, I haven't realized something incredible: I'm shouting at the top of my lungs. It convulses my body in a vomit of ugly pent-up emotion: rage, savage hate, uncontrollable lust. A small rational particle of my mind somewhere panics within its rationality, saying *My God, I'm in prison and I'm a prisoner like everyone else! Like everyone else!*

And still I convulse. I can't hear myself, just feel my chest and stomach compressing and my mouth opening and the soreness in my throat. *"ROOK! ROOK! ROOK! ROOK! ROOK!"*

I'm shaking the bars of my cell, not because I'm trying to bend them but because I've abandoned myself to the shouting and need them to hold me in place while my body jerks like it would under an electric current.

I feel that I want the Rook to be here, and I want to be cheering him on. My feeling is identical to the feeling of every other convict on the block, scary and wonderful in the total harmony of its insanity. To my immediate right I can see Willie's temple and eyebrow sticking between two bars of his cage, and I can see that he is screaming too.

It is widely believed that Rook might be able to kill the rhino. When it appeared today, he was instantly elevated to heroic status. I'd heard of this happening in the hole before, where the rhino tends to show up often. Rook is a part of us the system can not subdue, can not break this way. Of course, that was then. And when he'd gone willingly to segregation the last time, Rook probably thought he'd be let out soon. Maybe this is on our minds, too.

I know the instant that they've extracted Troy from his cell — successfully — when a section of screaming convicts with a clear view of the cell breaks from the chant to shout jeers and curses. Everyone knows what the sound means as well as I do, and across the tier I can see the ugly hate-masks of their faces as they kick at the bars and try to spit past the catwalk to the floor below.

Little by little, the harmony of the chant begins to fall apart. The hacks reappear out of the east end of the catwalk that blocks my line of sight, moving toward the tunnel. They're carrying Troy between them, in chains. But they also look like they're retreating from a hostile force, and they look bewildered by the abuse they have experienced. They aren't used to this kind of eruption happening in C Block. But then, they don't usually bring the rhino in here. It feels like an agreement has been broken.

And they had better hope that is not the case.

They disappear into the tunnel, and the shouting goes on, chasing after them.

After the last of the shouting dies off, the cell block is quiet because the convicts don't want to extend a lockdown that was just for Troy's cell extraction. Ten minutes pass, and it's just shy of eight thirty. We ought to have another hour and a half until we're locked down for the night, and everybody wants to be out, moving and talking. That's probably why the doors don't open. It's part precaution, part punishment, would be my guess.

As for me, I'm very quiet. I've given myself things to consider. But when the talk starts up this time, the decks aren't alone in it. They start catcalling at the guards on the galleries the way they do, but here and there I hear a deeper castle voice, crooning.

A shrill deck shouts: "This is bullshit!"

Then a smooth, deep voice says, "Why don't you open the door? I ain't gonna hurt you." There's mockery in it, and an enjoyment of the fear it causes.

After a few minutes, I hear a hack break down and ask, "You shitheads walk around like this is your private mansion, you think you're being treated unfairly?" He sounds scared.

"Oh, yeah? Where's the Rook, man? Where is he?"

I can see the shift sergeant standing in the doorway of the little office on the first tier, neglecting his paperwork so he can watch and listen.

A deck yells, "Fuck them, man!"

Some of the guards and convicts who know each other a little from conversations on the yard, they call each other by name: "You're really pushing me now, Rivetti."

"I'm pushing you? Who's locked up when he wasn't doing anything wrong?"

It goes like that, off and on, until ten minutes to ten. The shift sergeant on the block tells his hacks not to respond to the inmates, who keep crooning to them. But just before ten, when the convicts realize they've lost, a voice rings out on the tier: "Rook! Rook! Rook! Rook!"

And it gets picked up by several others like a radio station until the whole cell house is shouting again. Not me. This time. But the chant is going clear up to the high ceiling again. I can see the sergeant on his radio in the office doorway. He's getting heated with someone on the other end because – I'd guess – they can't believe it's jumped off in C Block. Twice in the same night.

And the convicts might have shouted themselves out again in a few minutes, except maybe a handful of rowdies, but guards make the wrong read. That, or they feel like they can't let it go. More hacks show up in the block carrying long riot batons. Decks and castles alike start banging on the bars, and the hacks whack the bars with their batons so that both sides are trying to hit them harder, louder. I hear one of the hacks say he doesn't fucking believe this.

I sit on my bed, eyes shrunk like there's a sandy wind, looking into a corner of the wall. I know I won't participate this time, yet I can't deny what happened – even though I try.

At some point I notice it's after ten and all the lights are still burning. An buzzing-angry hack wacks past my cell saying, "What about you? You don't have anything to say?"

I don't turn my head, and he moves on.

The hacks are trying to show force without going too far. Hoping a lot of shouting and hand waving will do the trick and the castles will just let them fight it out with the decks like always. But something's seriously wrong. The castles are in it. They're thinking of Troy and shouting for the Rook as loud as anyone. If the guards insist on shutting it down, they'll have to bring the rhino back.

That happens with the atmosphere the way it is tonight, it will probably be war. That means the prison will be unsecure and no one will be safe if they let us out. A lot of guys will be scattered – transferred to other maxes or to Mount Washington for twenty-three-hour-a-day lockdown. Maybe it's for the best. As long as I'm not one of them, that is. Nobody comes out of Mount Washington the man he was going in. It happens in a short time. Since the guards will use the disturbance as a chance to get rid of anyone they think is trouble, I may well be on the list. The marshalls won't worry about my size. I'll be pumped with so much Thorazine, they'll just try not to get any drool on their uniforms.

And after that, it will always be war at Seamax.

I wait.

The small hours come, and the trouble slows down but doesn't stop completely. They pull a couple of decks out of their cells. When one of them doesn't cuff up, they just rush him and don't bother with the rhino. The castles are left alone even though some of them still make noise – that means there's an officer somewhere with his thinking cap on. A few hours ago, that might have made a bigger difference. Now it's easy to tell things have changed. If it's not war, something's still broken. I feel it too, like the heat of a spotlight on my skin every time a hack goes by. There's a new anger and disrespect between us.

The lights keep right on burning. I hear guys whispering about doing something about it if the cell doors don't open in the morning, about how they're being punished for what someone else did.

At some point before sunrise I undress and climb under my sheets just in case I can get some shuteye, and I actually do fall asleep for an hour or two. When I wake up again, there's no way to know what time it feels like it ought to be because of the bright lights all night. It could be three thirty or eight o'clock. When I check my little battery-powered clock, it's quarter to six. There are still extra guards on the tiers, and Lieutenant Lipkin is leaning on his baton on the center walkway between the tiers. At six o'clock precisely, he shouts the order to line up. Then the cell doors open.

We go to breakfast without incident, but everyone can tell it isn't the same.

When there's hate in the air like this, it always lands on someone.

That was November 31st. December 6th is a pearl grey December day, a day when the clouds are pressing down on the earth and all the wafer-thin pillows and bedding in Seamax feel colder than the air. The kind of day that sends the nice people running for prescription drugs. I like cold weather and snow. Any rodent on two legs can live someplace that's warm year round. You go into a place that's open after dinner on a cold, snowy Wednesday night, you can leave your money on the table while you go to the john.

I'm talking in my cell with Willie and trying to understand my behavior on the day they'd extracted Troy.

For a week I've been haunted by the memory of having screamed and pounded with the rest of them in a hellish mental oblivion. And the idea that some dyed-in-the-wool convict has crept into my blood, put thoughts in my head, occasionally taken control of my actions...that has been bugging me for months. I haven't wanted to talk – or even think – about it until now. That hardcore convict that had possessed me is tricky: he'd leaped forth that evening a week ago, but now that I want to ask who he is and where he came from, he's not around.

It's late afternoon, but some of the lights have been changed in C block and replaced with brighter ones, so it's hard to tell the time of day. Willie leans against the wall with his feet in front of him and his hands sandwiched between the wall and the small of his back.

"You done what you done," he says. "Same as me and everybody else in the cell block done."

"I've got no love for the Rook."

"But you hate the system."

I have the feeling this isn't a very interesting conversation for Willie, but he's humoring me. I think he thinks I'm searching for a problem.

"You a convict with four years down. You always hate the system. Cops goan smell it on you, outside. You a part of the us and them, now."

Like complaining about a headache and being told you've got a brain tumor. "I don't know about that."

The jumping, the screaming. I'm just your typical sports fan.

"Won't really know till you get out."

A castle named Casper, another of the Friends of Blake, is coming across the flyway to my side of the tier. This is a strange thing. Blake's friends and other members of the Skins rarely approach me when I'm speaking with Willie. But Casper has a look on his face like it's Christmas morning, and he comes bouncing right on over. "Did you hear?"

All he does about Willie is wrinkle the outside corner of an eye at him, trying to shut him out of his vision. There's no love lost. Casper is big and blank. All Blake's friends look a little like Blake.

He says, "Troy jumped a bunch of guys on the dock and got away with a ton of cash."

"Troy's in the hole," Willie says to no one in particular.

When Casper doesn't acknowledge the statement, I repeat it. "Troy's in the hole."

"Not anymore. He got out this morning. There was a delivery truck from town and a few guys doing a buy. Troy jumped out like the fuckin boogeyman. The guys in the truck were so scared they clipped the gate on the way out, and I hear the gun bull threatened to shoot them if they didn't stop and write out a check."

Casper is pleased and offended at once. Troy is black, but all cons love a good caper.

"You believe it?" He laughs and shakes his head. "Couple of hours he's out of solitary, and *bam!*"

I watch something about Willie become old and wilted in front of me.

I don't say anything. Bread has been able to keep Rook in a box for months, so how is Troy out after a week?

Casper says, "It ain't over for that boy yet. It ain't over yet."

Like a big ballgame headed for extra innings.

I have a bad feeling now, but not because I'm worried about myself. I'm finding it harder and harder to believe there will be a problem between me and Troy. It's taken too long, and by now anybody can see the real issue is between him and Bread.

Casper leaves, but he doesn't get far before stopping for another conversation about the latest action.

Willie slumps against the wall and shifts his big feet. He's shaking his head at the empty space in front of him. "Troy ain't that bad," he says.

He has more. I wait.

"He just a young guy. Born wit too much. World been gettin even with him ever since." Again he's quiet a minute. I don't see his eyes, but I get the feeling that some alien presence is filling him up. Then Willie looks straight at me, and his rheumy eyes are spooky, like he doesn't quite know me. I think he just sees a large form, a big person like himself or Troy. He stands up and approaches me, and I feel the faded presence of a violent man who is a stranger to reason. His stance is unsteady, and there is a sudden miasma of bad breath and body odor I'd have sworn wasn't there a moment before. Willie's voice comes out deep and his words slow, the way a drunk talks when he's about to say something of great dark alcoholic significance: "You listen to me. Some little mouth tries to take something from you, you kill his ass. You hear me?"

He'd begun shuffling in my direction while he spoke. Now he seems to regain some self-consciousness and retreats to his own cell. He moves like a sleepwalker, throat sticky and dragging one leg in a remembered limp. I drop the hand I'd been using to scratch my jaw – just to have one of my hands up – and decide to leave him alone for a while. I just met someone. Maybe a younger felon who woke up to find himself in an old man's body. There's no more sound from his cell.

I look out on the tier. Willie's never wrong. He's never wrong because he never talks about things he doesn't know about. I could spend hours thinking about what he'd said and what was meant by it, if he even knew – that I should have killed Bread when he'd told me to, months before? – but I have enough to think about, and that old standby can wait.

A little voice argues against that, says there's nothing to think about, just a phone call to make. I turn my head, like it's an echo coming from one direction.

There is a festive air in the prison as night falls and people realize their entertainment has been extended. There is also a breathlessness as they wait for the other shoe to drop. If it doesn't, of course, that's just as good. Maybe better. What if it turns out that the buck stops at Troy? The gangs, the hacks, nobody can break him? The possibility makes people itchy, riled. Maybe nothing is the way they've come to believe, and it is still possible for individual strength to be the last word. I can feel them dreaming about it: that maybe we have somehow harked back to a misty Valhalla where the pure warrior drinks the blood of clever little men, distant rulers, pale institutions. Even people who've lost money on the deal Troy hijacked seem to experience a kind of wistfulness about that.

I think Troy must be in some kind of terminal overdrive, so much that a week in the hole has had no effect on him. I had also assumed it was Bread who'd gotten him rhinoed and sent to solitary, but if it *had* been Bread, Troy would've enjoyed a much longer stay there. I put the question to Willie, and Lyman has an answer for me within the hour.

He doesn't know why Troy went to solitary, other than the fact that he'd become an obvious source of trouble. But it was Bread who'd had him sprung.

6

The tiny Seamax library has seen its share of trouble, but not my kind of trouble. Between Troy and the Skins, there aren't many readers; not much chance of an accidental encounter. I'm slumping in an armchair with my shoulders around my ears, paging through an old Fortune magazine. I need the rest – even though I've been packing away more than usual, I still feel like I'm drinking myself for fuel. I've always been watchful, but no one is meant to be on high alert all the time.

I look at the pictures in the magazine, but it's hard to read more than a few lines at a time. There's the low light to thank for that, but more of it is the readiness in my body. If I had to summarize prison lately, I'd say it's a place of Never and of Any Second. There are any number of things that will never happen here, and a number that can happen in an instant and often do. Troy's been out of the hole for thirty-six hours, and it feels like the prison is holding its breath.

Someone crowds up the doorway. I raise one eyebrow.

Bread and a bunch of his gang members.

They don't look ready to fight, but I'm still surprised at how I don't react, inside or out. All I do is slowly shift in my chair so that my feet are flat on the floor. Decks don't always know how to even think about coming after a big case. They might come in with blades not realizing that to a castle shelves, tables, sinks, and doors are all handy weapons. For their part, Bread and his guys could have done a much better job creeping up if they wanted trouble, and this isn't the tough set, anyway. Mainly guys from my old deck: the Chrises, Dodd and Parker, Pratt.

Bread stands at ease in the doorway. The cheeks that flush when he's angry look smooth. He's clean shaven, and I can smell fabric softener on his clothes. "Mind if we come in?" he says.

"It's not my library."

As they shuffle in, Bread's guys are strangely quiet, respectful, like dogs that have just been shouted down. Bread chooses a chair across from mine and looks into my face. I look back at him through the tops of my eyes the way I've looked at a lot of people over the years: this piece of paper I'm holding up under my face means I'm trying to read.

Bread misunderstands the look, holds up his palms. "Peace."

I look at him and wait. His guys, fanned out behind his chair, relax when I don't do anything sudden. Bread says, "We got off on a bad foot."

It's the Troy situation, putting pressure on him. Bad timing on his part, then, sending his hacks into my house right when Troy started taking bites out of him. He studies me a minute with his breadloaf-shaped forehead. "What's it going to cost me to get on your good side?"

I smirk a little. It's in my nature to provoke someone who's wasting my time.

Bread isn't deterred – there's a shocker. "Someone's coming to see us in a few days. A businessman from the city. We're going to wind up in business together, but he wants to come check us out, anyway. I'd like it if we had someone there who could shake him up a bit. Someone he'd have to believe was the baddest. Word is he's old fashioned that way."

Why do I always feel like I'm on a record with this guy, and someone is picking up the needle and putting it down again someplace else in the song? Is it always like this with really driven people, or is it some defect in his criminal mind? I sort through his statement for a minute, picking out the faint praise and what a lot of guys might take as insults, but this is Bread. Sometimes I think he has as little control over how he says things as someone with Tourette's. Who knows, maybe it's a compliment he's paying me. I'm a businessman selling an expensive dog-and-pony show to the marks.

Bread chews his lip for a moment. Then he sits up straight and takes a small stack of bibles out of his shirt. "Cash up front. One job. All you have to do is show up and make it look good."

He flips the cash on the little magazine table between us. I figure he'll get around to Troy in a minute.

"He'll be here on Saturday. You'll get the day off work. If the deal gets made, there'll be more money."

He isn't exactly telling me, and he isn't exactly asking.

I just sit there. How long have I been losing sleep, wishing I'd made different decisions, gone with the grain a little more? Until he'd had my cell ransacked, I might have jumped at the kind of soft deal Bread is offering now, no matter how much I detested him. Now I feel like I've walked onto a used car lot and finally found a sensible automobile, but the price is suspiciously low. Unlike the guy on that car lot, I *know* something is wrong with it. It would be great not to have to worry about Bread and his ties anymore, but getting back on his team now would mean going after Troy. It would have to.

I don't reject the deal outright because I think I'm kind of blown away. An animal like Bread does a one-eighty and bends over backwards trying to appeal to your sensibilities, the rooms spins a little. I can sort of see why the guys in his inner circle find it exciting working for him. Soon he'll be as dangerous as Vanderventer ever was, and here he's rolling out a red carpet to a guy who ripped him off – twice. Practically speaking, it's a nothing deal between two guys who don't trust each other. Otherwise, it's a bit fantastic.

The mark on the car lot hems and haws, doesn't want to drift too far from that suspiciously low-priced car. He sweats around his collar and asks a lot of questions, knowing that none of them is the *right* question.

"If I say no, I go to the hole."

"No. You don't want to do it, you'll take PC." His voice grows a little cold and commanding for the first time since he came in.

I feel my eyebrows snap together like a mouse trap. Protective Custody. I feel like I must have just spilled something down the front of my shirt. Tell the hacks this deck sitting across from me is going to hurt me. Comical. But hadn't that always been Bread? The joke that just kept coming true because it didn't know it was a joke? I watch his face for anything like comedy and don't find it. Why PC? Because too many guys know he told me to handle Troy and

I accepted his money for it? Somebody found out I'd robbed him?

"I'll take PC?"

"You'll take PC."

Doing that to escape a deck gang would be one of the most humiliating things ever to happen to any castle, that I know of. And it would finally make Bread supernatural, if the whole prison didn't die laughing, first. A tense and sort of queasy feeling comes over me, an echo of other things that had seemed either too good or too awful to be true, in the past, and had been true nonetheless.

Bread says, "Of course, I don't want that. I want to work together. Under terms more favorable to you, like they should have been in the first place."

I want to explore the nuance of my taking PC. I want to ask what in the world makes him think that would ever happen, but then I realize my eyes are blinking and I feel vaguely fuzzy headed. Who would be asking that? Me, or The Convict inside who screamed Rook's name until his throat was raw? Which of us would want to turn a rational conversation into one about his image in prison and a convict's opinion of him?

Neither of us needs to discuss what happens if I choose Door Number Three: the Rook can speak for that.

I put the magazine down on an end table.

Wouldn't cost me anything except a bad taste in my mouth, taking his deal and burying the hatchet: at this point, I'd just be trading bitter for sour. If it's real. There is the possibility that it's a trick, that we're around that corner now and there can never be any kind of deal. In that case, my taking PC would be far more satisfying for him. And there is no reason he can't get to me there, too. Tamper with my food, or just pay someone to throw a Molotov through the bars of my cell.

I have no idea whether or not he knows I'm able to calculate all this.

"Suppose I said yes."

We grin at each other, a sudden lapse of pretense. There's that inkling of pleasure at the intimate knowledge of shared distrust.

Then Bread spreads his arms, generously. "I want to put things on the right track, Croft. Maybe I didn't understand what you were worth, before. You tried letting me know in the only way you could."

Again the back-handed flattery. More grinning. Suddenly the only voice opposed is The Convict, whispering to me that Bread had told me I'd have to become a living joke for him if I refused, and that PC has no privileges and isn't much better than the hole. A Block. Think about it.

"I know you don't drink. You don't use any of my fine products. Let me get you a girl."

I don't respond.

"Next weekend. Little privacy. Little action. To celebrate."

He needs to seal the deal. His guys smile. He slaps the arm of his chair. "That's it. That's what I want to do. Won't hurt for people to know it, either. Let them see you living well. The way it ought to be."

What he doesn't know about living well could fill an airport hangar.

The others are still standing in a semicircle behind him and grinning with their mouths, but I feel them staring hard as if they've been told to watch very closely.

Now that he's laid it all out, I say, "What about Troy?"

"Don't worry about him."

It takes force of effort not to let my brow rumple like aluminum foil. We just watch each other for a moment. Then Bread repeats: "Don't worry about Troy."

I take a deep breath that's almost a sigh. I'm feeling a little cross-eyed, which is not something I'm used to.

If he's ever going to believe I'm serious, Bread – like any gangster – will need me to accept a gift. Especially with our history. The larger the gift and the more public, the better. That way, if someone double-crosses, everyone will know his word is no good. The enterprising criminal world runs on relationships.

I feel my diaphragm give a flutter and then, just for an instant, experience a fantastic, screaming level of indecision. Then I say, "Dark hair. Dark eyes."

On some level, I can't believe what's happening.

Behind Bread, Parker knuckles Pratt on the shoulder. They look at each other, then at Bread, as if saying among themselves, He's done it again.

Bread stares at me for a minute, then says, "Done."

And suddenly that's that.

"There's just one other thing," he says.

Here it comes. I have to take out Troy. I have to pay back what I took. I'm not paying back a penny. At the thought, The Convict in me re-opens his reptilian eyes.

"You need to stop fucking with Fiero. I understand, he's not you. Everybody knows that. There's only one Percy Croft. But you messing with him in public, makes it hard for him to collect. Time to let business be business, my friend."

He just can't get past my looks, the way he talks to me. I'll always be an ape to him unless the misconception hurts him so much that he becomes a different man entirely.

I don't respond, but it's answer enough. Bread sits motionlessly staring at me for a handful of seconds, then winks at me and hops out of the chair. Then they're all leaving quietly, the way they came in, only now it's like someone told a joke in church and they have to wait till they're outside to bust their guts laughing.

I'm left sitting here, overflowing a tiny chair.

I wonder, Why hire on the one guy capable of taking on Troy – offer him a sweeter deal, with perks – and not try assigning him the job? Again I can't believe it could be so simple, and then I remember who I'm dealing with. Bread pissed on the Rook and killed Vanderventer, hardly stumbled. He's already thinking about next week, next month.

I know that's what I'm supposed to think.

Still, maybe he does give me the creeps a little, the way he walks on water in the bleak, violent places of the world. And so tone deaf, so assuming. If it's a species of genius, it's one I've never seen, and it isn't genius enough for the outside. On the other hand, he's come to talk to me like this once before, when Vanderventer had only hours live.

I walk down the lumpy concrete of the bleach-smelling corridors, out to the yard. If I'm being honest, I'm too relieved to care about the details. I want to believe it. No more Rook problem. No more Bread problem. Job here, job there. Money up front.

So I'm not sure why, as I walk, I experience a kind of claustrophobia. Something twitches in my neck, and I feel a little out of breath. I try to ignore it. These things are probably harder for Bread than they are for me. His need to dominate those around him gives him pain. I can do the same, dominate people and scare them, even hard men, but I don't have to. I'm constitutionally capable of leaving them alone.

Later it will be one detail of our talk that keeps my mind working when the lights go out. At the conclusion of every truce or deal – every one of them – the two parties shake hands or make some kind of physical contact. Neither Bread nor I had offered to shake, and we never did. And we never would.

The weights are shuttling up and down, faster and faster. It's been an odd day that's seemed to fly by. An hour ago, I hadn't been able to believe it was already dinnertime. The barbell, alternately smiling and frowning, nearly leaves my palms at the top of the rep. I can feel the convicts watching. The weight's not heavy enough, I'm ripping them out too fast and the plates are knocking around. I've been feeling better about the deal every hour. Sure, Bread would try to destroy me, but he didn't need a deal to do that – which means it's down the road a ways. Plenty of time to handle other things. I search the corrugated ceiling and caged lightbulbs for angles I may be missing, and they don't appear. Then Willie's face is above me. His big hands wrap around the bar, and it grows heavy. I pump it up and down and try to guess the poundage he's adding to it. A hundred pounds? He presses harder, and still I push him up.

I'd told him about the deal earlier, except for the part about taking PC if I refused. His lack of response had been so total that I had wondered whether he'd heard me.

Now he talks. "Gonna make you a slave, Raw," he says. "Gonna put you with a woman, now."

I'm starting to gas out from the rapid movements, but my chest isn't done yet. Veins I've never seen before are popping like pythons in the hills. "So what?" I growl.

"He know a case like you don't never have anything regular. He know you big, shy, and lonely. Gonna put a spell on you, Raw, this woman. I bet she the dark hair, quiet kind, make every move just so. Decks can't let a big ole case like you live free. Not a big ole crook like you."

I unfocus my eyes as the weight grows very heavy. Lights and ducts in the ceiling blend together. I have been thinking about the woman, back of my mind, and not exactly looking forward to it. I'm so damn big, I've never known what a woman sees when she looks at me. I try to remember it's just going to be some working girl, but five minutes later I'll forget that part and it will become this warm ball of tangled sensations, like a sentence that's not in any particular language, stuck in my head. A surprising number of cases are funny about women, full of secret crushes and awkward fantasies.

I'm growling with effort, now, reddening, slowing. My throat is dry. Still the barbell goes up and down, Willie lightening up a little because he's gauging exactly how much I've got left. I'm slowly realizing how much I trust this old goon, and the sensation is new to me.

But he knows how to get my mind churning.

Willie's quiet while I sit up and rest between sets. When I lay back down, it's with even more weight. I want it and I'm feeling senselessly angry. Up. Down. Simplicity.

"Gonna turn your head, Raw, mess you up. You been Inside longer than you think."

Willie's worried about the woman, of all things. He's embarrassed for me because he sees Bread working a personal angle. It's possible. Bread's not a genius but more like a mechanic or a cop, thinking in lowest denominators. Maybe he wants them to see him reach out and poke me. See, boys, you give him one of these, and-

Take PC if I don't want his deal. The Convict has hold of the idea like a half-starved dog. To him, that presumption is the evil of the whole thing.

When I've got maybe two more reps in me, Willie is saying, "Five more, five more."

Bring a starving man some caviar when he's forgotten how to eat. Watch it dribble down his chin. Maybe I'll turn it down, after all. I start to rack the weight and Willie's face appears above me like a full moon. "What you doin with that? Three more."

My lips peel back from my teeth.

Prick's not smarter than me.

I do five more reps.

On the last one, I see a flash of movement out of the corner of my eye and hear men grunting with effort. I can't do anything other than carefully put the barbell back into the forks, or it'll come down on my neck. Then I sit up fast and see Willie standing over a barechested white deck who's sprawled on the floor. I can see the small red eagles on his shoulders. White decks are shouting a few feet away, and the hacks are rushing over from the grammar school desk by the door.

One of them tells the yelling convicts to shut the fuck up, and when they don't stand down, he shoves the closest one, hard. The convicts never look at the hacks, just past them at Willie. One of the hacks steps up to Willie, looks far up at him, and demands to know what happened. In his attitude there's a memory of the trouble in C Block.

"I must have turned around too fast," says Willie, "Caught him with an elbow."

Then the hack asks the man Willie'd clipped if he wants to make a complaint.

"No. No complaint. We'll settle this another way."

"Come again?"

"Nothing. Never mind."

I step into their midst, and everyone but Willie takes a step back. "There's no problem here. Just an accident."

The guards' eyes get a little hot, and they take a half step closer again. I ignore them and watch the Skins walk away, talking each other up. It's possible they were just coming to talk to me and caught Willie by surprise. He doesn't hear so great, these days. Or maybe they were using him to put me on the spot? I look at their backs, bulging with deck muscle, and think, We all have accidents.

It was Sunday I'd talked with Bread. Wednesday morning I'm sitting in the chow hall, not hungry, chewing over our deal. My mind wants to settle on one reality or another but trusts neither. The deal is real. The deal is a ploy. When I think about Bread telling me I'll have to take PC if I don't deal, my head fills with red pepper, and a minute later my gut turns hard.

I try to think about something else. I look around. Far at the end of the room, under the windows in a spot where the sun shines on the brightest summer days, an unfamiliar convict sits in Vanderventer's old place. Closer at hand, a case who fights in Bread's ring sits surrounded by decks who ignore him, shoveling a double portion of food into his mouth. Turns out, I'm like a guy in love. Everything I see reminds me of my situation.

I catch Blake's eye and slide an unopened milk carton to him. "Seen Troy?" I ask, trying to sound disinterested. I've made up my mind to have a conversation with Troy, about the weather, whatever, just to take his temperature. Something I should have done weeks ago. I want to put all the fires out, now that I've started.

"He's in the rec."

We pause between sentences, chewing our food. I wonder how Blake knows exactly where Troy is at this moment.

"Doing what?" I say.

"Being dead, I 'magine. Been there since this morning."

"What?"

Castles snort and shift their eyes.

"You didn't hear? All you have to do is go up there. Nobody's cleaned it up. He's hung up with wire."

I put down my spoon. "You see him?"

"Decks have been going in and out of there all day. They got his hands."

I stare at him.

"Don't know," he says. "Guess they found a way."

"What are they saying?"

"Trying to escape."

Joel sits near one end of the table. He laughs, without humor.

"Who?"

There's no answer.

Then Joel says, "He was in custody when it happened. It was payback. You all know what that means. Now and forever."

"No," says Cross. "He was out."

I just sit there a minute, frozen. Then I slide my tray away from me and stand up. Men talk to each other across the large room, creating a babble of voices. After a moment, I start walking. I go down the long corridor out of the chow hall, up the stairs. It feels like a long way. Once I'm outside the rec, it isn't like Blake said. No one is around. There's a trail of blood on the floor. Tacky and purplish, not the brown color of old blood. There are slide marks in it like a pair of dragging heels would make, and there are the edges of footprints, a lot of them. The newer ones are fainter and go in both directions.

I stand in the doorway.

The rec room looks normal, except for the continuing trail of blood. Beneath the metal mesh that lets in the sun on the south side is a larger pool. There are three empty coils of wire strung through the mesh: two about six feet apart, and a larger one between them, slightly higher. He'd been crucified.

I stand back again, in the light coming through the latticed mesh and glass, and look at all the space between the wire loops that had held Troy's wrists, the height of those that had held his neck. The size of the man that had been bound here was great. Did that make it a worse crime? I'd really had nothing in common with Troy, that I knew of. He'd been a part of the grey mass of men who'd been washed down into this place the way they would down a drain. But still I raise my arms from my sides, spanning them between the wires, standing on the light and bloody footprints in the rec room with no one there to see.

I wonder how they'd done it. Of course I do. Troy was as large and powerful a castle as most people ever see outside of a circus tent, and you didn't have to shave much off of me to get him. Not much at all. It's something to think about. But the prison routine keeps on grinding, and I have to grind along with it. After the rec room, I go to the furniture factory. I stop in the entrance and look across the production floor. It's a slightly different place than I remember, somehow, like they've changed out the lightbulbs. My gaze sweeps the place, and I think: Troy. How'd they do it? And was it convicts or hacks?

Wondering that makes me unprepared for what everyone else seems to be wondering. As I wander around holding up my clipboard like a Geiger counter, I feel them snatching glances at me. Watching me when they think I won't notice, studying my size and movements. There were extra guards in the chow hall at breakfast, and a lockdown wouldn't surprise me. The violent death of a big castle is a rare event, a disruption of commonly held beliefs and assumptions. It also means there is someone in the prison, some force, more dangerous and willing to prosecute its agenda than anyone had realized. From the cautious attention I'm getting now, a lot of guys seem to think that force is me.

For the rest of the morning, no one looks directly at me and no one tries talking to me. I'm unpredictable, capable of anything. Maybe my blood's still up.

As the day goes on, though, I start to think it's something else behind the looks. A few convicts are obviously convinced I did it. But then moving through the yard and standing in the chow line, a lot of white gang members who should have been jumping all over me with joy are either watching me beneath their brows or giving me the same slow nods as always. The Skins are cool toward me. During a time when the line stops moving for no reason, I fall to wondering again about exactly how they'd done it. They could have killed him with gas balloons or zip guns while he was locked in his cell and then carried him out.... That's what I'm thinking about when it hits me. The guys stealing glances like I'm the boss's wife, they're measuring me for my own coffin. The decks need to study on me to try and make themselves understand that I can be killed same as them, to wait for their eyes to stop deceiving them.

My irritation at them passes in a moment. I don't blame them. Instead of angry I feel quiet and aware, like I'm covered with fine whiskers.

There are extra guards in the chow hall again at lunch, and the watch lieutenant keeps making rounds, checking in. Tempers are short. There'd been something in the convicts' deluded lives while Troy was around, giving hell to the powers that be. His death was another burn, another ripoff. The conservative convicts that go best with the grey colors, they're right once again, but the rest don't have to like it.

I think best outside since I came to prison, so I go out into the early part of dusk to pace the yard. It's cold and clammy and the air is still, like being inside a dead person's mouth. Bread doesn't need me for Troy, and he had known that before he'd proposed our deal. In a way, that makes things look more promising. He wasn't trying to maneuver me into that confrontation. But more important is the other side of the coin, something that I and everyone else in Seamax suspects, now: that Bread has an effective castle-killer squad. The case he'd taken out wasn't the type that could have been mistaken for a deck iron freak, either. That's why Bread trusts the deal. He doesn't even need the Rook, anymore. I stop my pacing and look out at the water tower, its bulbous shape floating up above the fence. Bread doesn't need anyone, now. He's finally where he'd always thought he should be. And what had he said to me, Wednesday night? All I have to do is show up and make it look good. The business connection was 'old fashioned, that way'. I need to stop fucking with Fiero because it doesn't *look* good.

Standing on the yard right then, I realize there's a real possibility that it's over. I feel my shoulders drop. Bread's victorious. He's relaxed. Doesn't need me but has a straightforward use for me. He wants it smooth, so the new deal accounts for past experience, what I will and won't do. He already has his example in Troy, and Bread's not the type for some drawn out scheme for personal revenge. I'm a show horse now, a badguy wrestler. Now nobody's bigger than the game, and everybody's getting what he wants on the rising tide. That's been Bread's way all along.

Of course I don't trust this hypothetical picture I'm painting, but I'm not trying to take it to the bank just yet. As an old accomplice used to say, you can't take it to the bank, but it will go through window glass.

If it's true, then it's up to me to play my cards right, ride it out and not let irrational feelings make me lose sight. Eye on the ball – out, free and clear in a year. For that, there's something I'm going to need. In my mind's eye I take it out of a pocket and slap the dust off against my leg. Then I fist it back into shape and snug the grey hat down on my head. It doesn't fit great, just well enough.

I stand there looking across my eyes for a long minute.

Then I go inside. I have one little thing to do before the night is done.

Noah sits on his bunk in his cell with his head down and his fingers clasped between his knees. His small shoulderblades are sharp through the back of his shirt, and his bald black head looks heavy as a river stone. He has his own cell. There are three toothbrushes in a neat row on the edge of his sink and an extra roll of toilet paper and hand wipes in little foils. He sits on a thin leopard print blanket. I stand outside his open cell a minute without being acknowledged. Then I speak words every man in this house of ill repute is familiar with:

"It wasn't me."

When he doesn't answer, I add, "Just wanted you to know."

"I know."

"How do you know."

"I just do."

Then he turns his head away, and the conversation is over. I'd said what I came to say. I leave him alone. A month later he'll tell me that when he was sitting there that night, the cell door was left open because he'd wanted them to come for him next. In his inside hand he'd been holding the handle of an eight-inch metal shiv.

Willie's standing in inside his cell before last count, in the shadows. Maybe it's a trick of the light that makes it look like one of his eyes has rolled lifelessly to the side. His expression is neutral, but he's completely motionless. I go into my own cell, briefly wondering how anyone could find real tragedy in the death of a someone like Troy, who was basically a common thug. For a moment it's cloying, an irritation, and leaves me with my own motionless stare.

After lights out, my mind's eye roves around in the dark. My thoughts turn to how strangely easy it is to escape, at least in theory, and I wonder why the outside fence doesn't go deeper underground, as if the fact bothers me. There are spots along the fences well known to everyone where the earth is soft, but the prison bureaucracy seems to be like any other – word has to get to the right person, the one who gets things done, but there are high walls of jealousy, laziness, and insolence in the ranks that keep this from happening.

Someone coughs in the dark, a flinty sound. A hint of smoke that smells like burnt toast drifts into my cell, someone cooking with a filched stove coil and split electrical cord.

At one point I face the wall and open my eyes, see nothing at all. I imagine I'm in a box beneath the hole. It's pitch dark in there, except the light that comes in through the meal slot for a few seconds, but then the rumor is they don't bring chow every day, just when they feel like it. There is no commode, just an open cess pit in the middle of the floor that inevitably overflows. The iron walls are padded with ancient mattresses on the inside for when I break and try to kill myself by beating my brains against the wall. There are random hosings at any hour of day or night, not that I know the difference. My only company is a tin cup they fill with just a few ounces of water a day.

I turn and have to look at the dim night lights for a while before sleep covers me.

Saturday. Bread said I won't be expected at work.

Right after count, I follow a guard named Robey to Bread's double cell. For a few seconds there's that feeling of walking in my own footprints, still warm from another plod just like this one. A week ago I wouldn't have believed it. Working for Bread again. This must be what it feels like going back to a bar where I got beat up. Robey follows me inside – that's familiar of him. The cell looks the same, except for being crowded. Most of my old deck is there in and out of the cell. Nick and the Chrises, Parker and Frankson, Lee, and some of Bread's other tattooed thugs. Playing cards are prohibited in Seamax, but there look to be at least two decks scattered around the cell in little stacks and fans. Bread's guys don't look at me. It's awfully close quarters to share with a big case who doesn't like you. Attitudes about size and individual strength may change since Troy was hung up like a piece of meat and his hands taken for trophies, but the immediate physical reality is still hard to argue with.

Bread comes out of the count room looking red in the face. He strides in and knocks Parker aside moving past him, glowers at the others in the room. He's put on muscle from his time in the weight pile, though he's still not rippling like some of his soldiers. He gives orders in curt little sentences. It takes me a minute to realize, with distant amusement, that he's behaving the way he thinks a castle behaves. Like it's his physical toughness his gang respects. Casting his glances like a castle does. And not just any castle.

Nice to know he's gotten so big he can live in a fantasy world and not be corrected.

I keep acting like myself but almost feel like I'm the one faking it. As we're getting ready to go, I work myself into the blandest state of mind I can manage and get ready to earn the little stack of bibles I was given in advance. I put on my grey hat. Really snug it down onto my ears.

We move through the SO toward the neck, and cons and hacks alike clear the way as soon as we're in sight. The respect Bread got from oldschool cons was damaged when they thought he'd turned the hacks on Troy, but he's not seriously hurt by it. Prisons are run by gangs, and gangs are about money, which is where a lot of the yadda yadda about respect comes from. Sometimes the respect and the money get separated for a minute, accidentally, but they always drift back together. Principles happen somewhere in the middle, stitched together from toughness and profit like a kind of Frankenstein.

We tromp down the hall, and I remember other walks I've taken with guys behind me, expecting to meet somebody important. A lot of the time they'd be looking for a deal or a job, and I let them assume I was the bodyguard, escorting them, patting them down. Then we'd go into an empty room someplace, shades drawn, one chair not two, a bottle of something on a desk or table. They'd look around for the big man and, seeing no one, start to get a little nervous. Then I'd move behind the desk and sit in the chair and wait for them to realize who they were looking at. I've come a long way, since then.

We take a turn off the main visitors' area to the private interview room where convicts talk to their lawyers. It's like a shithouse with the plumbing ripped out. We pause outside the door and Bread says, "Croft. Robey. With me." The others wait in a narrow corridor between the visitors' area and the private room while we go inside. I have to hunch slightly to fit through the door – or maybe not, but it's too close to tell. The "businessman" is waiting. He's nicely dressed, his hat on the scuffed table in front of him, his charcoal suit coat gathered around him. He's older but has a full head of dark hair and big, smart eyes that know how to see a lot without looking like it. I can tell he's been Inside at some point, probably years ago. It's 6:05am, must be an early riser, drove here in the dark. A large blue stone shines on one ring finger. Him and Bread sit on opposite sides of the table. I stand behind Bread's shoulder. His hack Robey stands behind his other shoulder. Nice way to make a point.

Bread does most of the talking, mostly about how he's got the prison sealed up tight and he's a low risk. He's trying to increase his traffic, get a line of credit, occasional favors. From what he says, Troy must not have caused any serious cash flow problems. That's assuming he's telling the truth – the gangster sitting across the table does not seem to be someone you bluff.

The message I represent for the businessman: I've got *this* for protection, in here. They talk a while. I don't believe this guy thinks much of Bread except that he's ambitious. For some reason I think he's imagining lunch with Bread in a fancy restaurant, someplace like Lidelle's in New York, and in this guy's imagination, Bread doesn't know how to hold a fork.

It embarrasses me, being here like this. Bread doesn't appear to notice when his new business partner's eyes keep flicking up to look at my face. This is partly because I'm so big, but I suspect it's also because I don't look right. I don't have a neck-popper's face: the slight pout of the lips, the heavy eyes, the slightly stupid, suspicious expression.

At least one person in the room has some vague notion of who I really am. Someone he wouldn't want standing behind him, even on his payroll. Although maybe I wouldn't be an embarrassment at Lidelle's.

It feels strange to be recognized. Some nerve bundle that had just started to quiet down stirs irritably inside me, causing a feeling of splinters in my brain, then slowly settles back again into the graveyard that's Seamax. Never go to prison.

I pass part of the day in a state of distraction before I reflect that overall, the gig wasn't terrible. Another one like it would not be terrible. I still have a shaky feeling about the new deal, because no gang ever worked this way. You don't quit a gang. You don't drop out or become a free agent. You don't step back or take time off like you do with a job or a girlfriend.

You don't forgive someone who has.

But it doesn't have to last forever.

I cross off days on my wall calendar of New York City brownstones. I wait.

During the day I experience a feeling almost like smugness, like I've finally done the smart thing even though it's unpalatable. This scenario, I reach my goal of getting out as fast and smooth as possible – a return to my senses, and the guy who'd been standing in my cell and screaming the Rook's name was just a bubble that's popped. That was a hundred years ago. Then I wake up at some hour of night that I know by texture, that I'm sick of, and feel like I don't know quite where I am. My bunk may as well have been washed out to sea.

Something's wrong, and it's not getting any better.

7

Time catches up with me. Another bland yet uneasy week has passed, like a week spent waiting for a plane in an airport. Then suddenly it's Sunday, time for my little conjugal visit. I'd wondered whether Bread had simply forgotten all about it (did I hope so?), but Chris E stopped by early this morning to remind me. I didn't sleep well and feel like my head is too junked up for something like this.

It's the first day of winter. My last here, with any luck. If someone had asked me a month ago, I'd have said it was up in the air whether I was ever getting out. But today, I get up, get counted and wait for chow as I watch the back of my mind, where things stir in a tidal murk. Something had been almost clear to me in the moments before I'd woken up. Something about Troy and the woman. I could say the combination is a good way to lay down rails for a person: kill somebody who could almost be their dark twin and then offer them something nobody would refuse. But that's not the understanding that came to me in my sleep and then slipped away.

I don't want the cold sausages and mash they're dishing out in the chow hall. I won't go to the weight pile. I can't back out of my little date without looking as strange as I feel, but I also can't enjoy it. Too much time has passed since last time to think it will go off right, and I've spent the last few years surrounded by deviants and sexual cannibals who punish child molesters by raping them.

I watch a couple of detective shows in the tv room until a game comes on and the sports crowd comes in, then go back to my cell to watch a square of weak sunlight move across the floor like a distant thought. I'm still thinking of the woman. Maybe I'm afraid of coming out of the experience with the knowledge that I've become somehow abnormal. Cons correspond with women on the outside and even get married without any physical contact, and are content with the relationships. Others are drool-eyed rapists. After a while, there's not much in between. That's when I think about something Willie told me that I haven't ever quite been able to shake: that I've been Inside longer than I think.

I look at the little clock on my nightstand. 2:00pm. It's time. If any part of me is really looking forward to this, it is currently out of contact.

I get up and stretch, then start to walk. For some reason I think about how they'd done Troy. I wonder whether it was quick or whether it was long and bloody, like a Spanish bullfight. On my way off the tier and through the SO, I think it seems like maybe word has got around a bit, like Bread had hinted at. I believe I catch a few looks. Might be my imagination. I walk faster.

There are no apartments because there are no conjugal visits at Seamax. The only decently furnished place is a trailer for hacks working split shifts, but it gets rented from time to time for other things. That's where she is waiting.

The little yard with the trailer in it is at the end of an L-shaped corridor that exits the north side of the SO. There's a tiny convict-tended garden there between A and B Blocks. The longer stem of the L is lined with boxes of textbooks and spare desks. The lights are off during the day, and there is just enough natural light coming in to make it look like an attic space. Eye strain is a defining part of prison life, so even on weekends, when I don't go to work, I'm careful not to read or sketch too much at a stretch. As I move down the hallway, the possibility of a trap briefly re-surfaces in my mind. I soften my footsteps so I can listen better.

Then I turn the corner and see them all there, lined up in the narrow hallway and flanking the door. For a second it looks like they're here to kill me. New strategy: broad daylight, no tricks, just lots of guys. Then it comes into focus. They're looking at me like I'm a fourteen-year-old they set up with his first handjob. Bread right next to the door, a cigarette behind his ear.

For a moment I can't move, I'm so surprised. "This a Broadway show?" I say.

"Thought you'd like a sendoff," says Bread, smiling and elbowing the guy next to him.

They all seem on the verge of giggling, their faces too tight and eyes too big and full of laughter and what is this shit?

"How you feeling today, big guy?" says Nick. "You eat your vitamins?"

"Don't break the bed," says Lee. "I hear they take it out of your convict account."

Bread laughs a little at the look on my face, says, "Just go right on in, she's expecting you."

The world splits in two. Out of one eye, I see a bunch of bored cons having a laugh over nothing to pass the time. Out the other, reptilian Convict eye, I see a venom-soaked landscape of clever barbs where every syllable is aimed like an arrow at some soft spot in my head. I don't know which it is because I don't really know what the decks are, inside.

Bread might not really have been laughing at me, only my reticence. It's a cool sort of laugh, I know that, but it strikes a chord. My angry eye picks his figure out of the poisoned world of deck derision, and I look straight at him. "Something funny?"

Bread's eyes go flat and his laugh turns to a mysterious smile. I've singled him out, and instantly it's just the two of us in the little hall. He leans back and his shoulders drop, and he says nothing. The cold curl of his smile grows deeper and seemingly more sure of itself the longer I stare at him. Then he's not just smiling but almost playful. I try to remember that I've smartened up and come to my senses about things, now.

For a moment, a cool shadow eclipses my anger. Something more authentic and closer to who I am outside the walls, a guy who lives with equal comfort in opera houses and dark alleys. I move through the hallway lined with human statues and stand in front of Bread. "Smart guy," I say. I set my face squarely in front of his, and for the briefest instant I think I see his eyes begin to lose their shape in an almost deathlike relaxation. I look around the corridor and take them all in. Then I look back at Bread, real close. "You think you're the smart one in the room?"

Bread looks me up and down then, and cracks up. The laughter is full and helpless, the idea of what I'd said naturally hilarious to him. He laughs only briefly but so hard the outsides of his eyes wrinkle up and he folds over a little at the waist, and a little wheeze comes from his lungs.

If I'd stopped a second to think, I would have thought of our new deal and what I'd already given up to it, and how short a time I really had to last. But I don't think. I punch the wall next to his head so suddenly that he doesn't have time to jump. Chunks of plaster rain onto Bread's shoulder. Men are peeking between their fingers as if a bomb went off.

Bread never flinches. His quiet smile is still there, and he looks like a self-possessed clown with plaster white cheeks and very red lips. Someone coughs. I almost jerk back when the dust clears and I get a better look at Bread. The man who got sent to solitary to take a piss on the Rook. If I've gotten away with doing things to him no one else would have gotten away with, it's been a two-way street. I counsel myself – I haven't killed him because I know none of this is real: my tough convict act, my attitudes about the old prison and respect. Bread had said he was standing in a cardboard cutout of me, before; what no one knew was that I was standing in a cardboard cutout of myself. I didn't really care about any of it. But lately I could sure fool myself. I harden up my face and try to push the smile off Bread's face with my eyes, but it's like trying to bend a spoon with my mind.

Bread's smile changes to something almost sympathetic and he motions me out the door with his chin, his eyes never leaving mine. *Let's see*, he seems to say, *what happens out there, big guy. Maybe then we'll see a thing or two.*

We've got a deal. A common sense deal I can't go back on without taking leave of myself completely. I make myself turn and walk out the door, and it's like driving a tractor with rust caked in all the levers and gears.

And it's like he knows everything that's going to happen, his smile frozen in my brain as I walk out into the white afternoon light. The pieces are set, knights, pawns…rooks. I cross the little courtyard to the trailer. I see my hand reach out and then listen to my awkward rapping at the small white door. My head's buzzing. My perspective floats up and I see a big guy standing at a tiny door not knowing what to do with his hands. In a different person – a different castle – this is where it would get easier to let someone else carry the weight. The Bread I'm supposed to see wants to give me money and favors and is asking very little in the end. So maybe my brains are my worst enemy because they show me another guy I'm not supposed to see in him and who doesn't want to be seen.

The door opens. I go up the steps into the trailer.

Twenty minutes later, I come out feeling small and rattled. A chorus of accusing voices prattles away in my mind. My fear is confirmed: the prison has made me a degenerate. As I move across the courtyard toward the door into the SO, my skin shrivels at the thought of them waiting in there, just the other side. I want to be angry, but I'm not. It would have been better if the girl had been some filthy, used-up whore I could have walked out on, but she hadn't. I'd barely had the strength to close my hands around her slender arms.

I walk across the courtyard. I slam open the door so its edge will crack the inside wall, heading off any comments they might have ready for me.

No one is there.

Motes cyclone in the sun from the swinging door.

I stand there. Maybe I was supposed to fall in love, and Bread would have had something new to hold over me. I feel very raw, but not from love. I head back inside the SO toward the cell houses. Moments from the trailer behind me play like brief snippets of film in my head, vivid as the effects of a drug. I want to be by myself, but that's hard to manage in prison. There are a lot of people and not a lot of space. And it's a small town in other ways, too.

People I pass in the SO, I feel them watching me. A couple of redheaded decks pass me in the corridor with a secret knowledge in their faces. A shadow down a side corridor whistles a salute at me. I walk faster. Sexual frustration pulses like acid in my wrists and chest. I feel sudden and dangerous even though my self-image at the moment is almost comical.

It must have been deliberate. Not just her beauty – and she was a beauty, not at all what you'd expect to show up for a roll in the hay with a strange convict. Her smallness. She wasn't a midget but couldn't have been more than five feet tall. I could look straight down at the top of her head and see the pale scalp at the part in her straight dark hair. Hands slender as a bird's. And it would be easy enough for Bread to claim that's what is in demand, these days. Very petite, and very beautiful. Or maybe I'm full of shit because I'm embarrassed. Maybe. In fact, I'm wired up to my hair.

As I walk, I realize there is no place to go. Not my tiny cell. The tiers will be crowded with eyes. The television room is packed with blacks howling at a football game. Suddenly I have no idea where I'm going. My back is peeling from the eyes I feel. My feet are carrying me toward the weight pile, up the stairs toward the southeast corner of the SO. It feels like a long way.

When I walk into the weight pile, there seems to be this interruption of what everyone is doing. Knowledge fills the faces of the men inside, and it's like they are shooting beams at me with their eyes. Maybe my final lesson is my impotence.

Someone steps to one side and then I see Bread. He's on the benchpress beneath the mesh windows on the far end of the room. He's working hard, sweating with too much weight on the bar, several spotters around him. With the help of his spotters, he racks the barbell and sits up. Weak as a joke, but actually getting sort of cut. Blood in his face and neck. And his gang around him doesn't look like a gang, it looks like a deck. Most of it is my old deck, as if he'd come along and been better at being me than I was. He looks around and seems to stare at me for several seconds before he recognizes me. Then he smiles. He wipes his face and neck, averting his smiling eyes, knowing I want something from him, some recognition of what I suspect. So he lays down again and starts benching with a man on each end of the bar, the three of them working together. He lies with his legs crossed carpenter-style above his waist, pushing, shouting on the last rep and clanging the bar back into place. Then he directs his spotters in the changing of the weight, standing with his back to me.

One of the men in his group thinks his back is turned to me enough and makes a masturbating motion with his fist, and the others do a bad job concealing their laughter.

The lights are suddenly too bright. The clanging noise of the weight pile is cymbals crashing around my head. For a dizzy moment, I wonder if everything I imagined Bread thinking and feeling about me were all just in my own head, that I'd never so much as distracted him. Maybe he'd laughed just like this after I robbed him. Maybe he'd seen it and said, 'Good, now he'll be more manageable for a while.'

I walk partway across the room and then half turn, hiding my face. My hand rests on a barbell that weighs thirty pounds with no plates on it and is six feet from end to end and could smash through six inches of concrete in the right hands.

Maybe I'm alive today only because Bread wants to do the same thing to me that deep down some part of me would like to do to him: to take away everything before he dies, and dies badly. That's something I'm beginning to understand.

I feel the surge move through my body like thunder, up my right thigh, through my midsection and right chest and shoulder and into the fingers of my hand around the barbell, the latticed grip digging into calluses a quarter inch thick like the rind of a cheese. I feel it happen, will taking physical form and standing up inside me like an electrified body getting up off a gurney.

In the end, it's the height of the rage itself that I don't trust. It's glandular, sudden, blank. At the last second I pop the clutch on it, let it spin and roar without connection. Instead of burying myself and Bread and his guys and probably a couple of hacks, I take a deep breath that doesn't relax me, is really more like breathing through a straw underwater, then turn and leave. That will buy me another hole in the stomach.

It seems like a long way down the tier to my cell, where I sit on the edge of my bunk and dig deep for the real anger I know must be there, but in the end I just feel exhausted.

I've been Inside longer than I thought.

A dream of punching through walls and flying plaster, boards, and cement wakes me before dawn, and a few minutes later the kitchen staff are unlocked, making it 4:30. The ink of night doesn't begin thinning out until over an hour later. I'd slept most of the night but feel like I'll be tired again before lunch. My mind is cycling. I'm figuring Bread again, like an addiction.

If you want to run a prison, the numbers and the drugs, you don't want the biggest case around for your castle. That case is going to be used to doing what he pleases, cock of walk. He's probably huge and stupid, and people are afraid of him because he's a child.

No, you want someone who's used to being more careful. If, like me, he's smart enough not to have gotten squashed so far, he's probably smart enough not to ruin your business. But you still need a pile of muscle. The optimal choice: the *second* biggest castle in the prison.

It occurs to me to mention this nugget of logical reasoning to Willie, so I reach for my little square of mirror on the basin, but I knock my toothbrush, comb, and soap into the sink and floor and feel a great pulse of urgent rage gush into my arms. I stop and pick up what I knocked down. I replace each item neatly. Then I get the little square piece of polished metal that's my mirror and carry it in a slightly shaking hand to the bars of my cell. The mirror reflects the bars of Willie's cell. I want to confess and have him tell me we'll work it out in the weight pile, torture it out.

So there's a definite sense of loss when I feel something about the silence and know that Willie is gone.

Just gone. I don't even know how I know his cell is empty. But I do.

I experience a brief numb sensation around the ears that's like being underwater. "Hey, Willie."

I wait a minute, my eyes moving around like a blind man's eyes. "Willie."

Someone else chimes in on the other side, a deep black voice, trying to help. "Yo, Willie, man."

I hold the square of mirror way out to try and see inside the far half of his cell. "Willie?"

But I already know what happened. Suddenly and absolutely. Not the details—I'll never know those—but I get the basic picture.

It doesn't take a genius to figure it out.

It's the day after Bread came to me with his new deal, about two weeks back. I get off the bench press and sit on the edge of the bench, my breath bad and body aching from fitful sleep. I've been doing a ton of weight, my form ugly, all the strength of my body in my right arm, the left buckling as it does when I'm at my limit. Then Willie slings one of the prison's stained towels over my shoulder, surprising me. He lays his long hand across the back of my neck and says, "Come on, Raw, let's sweat out the bad stuff." I heave myself up and go to the row machine.

We don't talk about anything. There's just his voice low in one ear, encouraging, then the other, mocking. "That all you got?" The cable connecting the grip to the weight stack could cut a man in half. "You best be jokin me. Lotta more, lotta more."

Soon I can't hear anything but the blood in my ears. Then I'm on the chinup bar hoisting myself plus the sandbags dangling from the chain hooked through my weightbelt. Willie says something in my ear and then stops pushing down on my shoulders. I keep going, teeth grinding, and I only seem to be getting stronger.

I lose the edge off my pump when I pry my fingers from the bar and see Bread across the pile, leaning in the doorway with his arms folded. He's not staring at me but at Willie, and Willie's staring right back. I realize this has been going on for a minute before I was aware of it.

I watch Willie. He's like a wall, full of the slave defiance of absolute blankness. Also in his face is a tough old man looking at a parasite. He's seven feet tall with hands big as dinner plates and looks like a monster from under some kid's bed.

Bread's wearing a poker face. He is not exactly staring, but his gaze doesn't waver.

This goes on for a handful of seconds while I feel something thickening between them. It makes me uneasy as I haven't been for some time, like witnessing an affair between people I thought I knew.

Then Willie puts a hand to my shoulder and guides me to the next purifying torment. I wonder whether I'll forget about Willie when I'm out, since in a way that might be freeing, being able to think of prison as nothing but a stain that would one day be faded and beyond memory.

Now I remember the way they looked at each other, like I wasn't even there.

I'm standing here trying to see inside of Willie's empty cell. He's been in that cell nearly every night and stood for count nearly every morning for sixteen years.

They must have come in the night. At least a half dozen guards with a sock soaked in chloroform, and maybe one or both of Bread's castles. They'd taken Willie like an army of ants. My breath catches in my throat for a dry moment.

It's what Willie always sees happening slowly to all castles, sped up.

In a prison cell, you can do nothing but stand up or sit down. Suddenly I'm very aware of my body. I think I can feel time collapsing into this singular perspective. I sit down. I stand up again. I turn inside my cell like a soldier on parade and begin feeling trapped again the way I suddenly did when they rhinoed Troy. For just a hair of an instant, like a single frame in a filmstrip, I feel the need to break through the bars of my cell, and the only reason I don't try do it is because I'm afraid I might not be able to, and then I'll know I'm really trapped. It's gone so quickly that I wonder if it wasn't just the result of standing up too fast. I shake my head clear.

The sun climbs higher and the prison begins to wake up. They call the count. The cells open, and cons begin stepping out onto the tier.

Willie was there when I fell asleep. This happened in the very next cell without waking me up. The sun is coming in through the high, narrow windows, and bars and footwalks appear to glow with their own nickel colored light. The rest is grey.

There's a glare on things in the prison, this morning. The wan sunlight is reflected back into my eyes like salt spray, and sometimes even in a dim corridor I'll find myself in a deep squint. I myself am like a man waiting to meet someone at a train station - and I'm not sure exactly who. I feel very little except impulses to do the things I normally do, to eat, to move. It is neither good nor bad, nor is it the first time in my life I've felt this way, although it is rare. Sometime today, or maybe tomorrow, someone is going to get off that train. Me. Which version of me it will be, that's the million-dollar question.

It's a hairy situation when you can't trust yourself. I'm half expecting the boil in my gut, the pulse behind my face – I'm half expecting anger and bitterness to come trotting back into my head like a proud bull racked with forward-pointing horns. There are enough of his fresh hoofprints in the dirt to prove it's partly his turf. And who knows what he'll do or when he'll get out of Seamax?

I take care not to move too fast, make up my bed crisply and have a careful shave, as if staying focused on the details will help remind me I'm not the bull. As I go to work, a tenseness creeps into the dull waiting. My neck tightens and my gut grumbles, and I sense that a headache isn't far off. The colors of the glaring light seem to reflect through my body like radiation, causing disorder on a cellular level. I QA the first half of the shift. A couple of times I stop and stand up straight to let something pass, inside me, like waiting on a curb for a car to go by. Doing a dance like this with myself is not something new to me. There are plenty of situations where you may need to push beyond some natural boundary - drive through the night; wait in a dark, close space for a night watchman to go on his rounds; talk with someone who's pointing a gun at your belly – but it's never safe. Doing this kind of dance with yourself is no different from doing it with someone else.

I'm finishing my lunch when it begins breaking up like a traffic jam. I'm sitting quietly and eating a ham and lettuce sandwich on white bread when I feel it. (The deck ahead of me in line had said, "If there's mayo on this sandwich I will come back here and fucking kill you.") My neck loosens and my shoulders begin to drop like they'd been stuck in that raised position with nothing more than warm glue. I hold still as if listening for a faint, irritating sound that may have finally stopped. A smile brushes against my mouth for a moment.

That didn't take long at all. I get up and throw away my trash, return my tray, and my walk is relaxed. My mind is back on the deal, the short time, the smart thing. I've remembered the truth...none of this is real.

I walk out of the chow hall toward the furniture factory.

It's less real each calendar day. As it was before the Rook, there's nothing that has to interfere with my routine. I know that soon, once the low anger quits stirring at the bottom of the well, I'll be relieved that Willie is gone. I refocus on the fact that there's not much more to my sentence and how I've got an even keel with Bread now, and I think: Priorities.

Priorities.

Of course I know how the dance goes. You've just relaxed. Adjusted. It's good. But the first time never sticks. All part of the dance.

I play the neck popper for guys who used to change my weights. I stand behind Nick Karoulas while he has unpleasant conversations, or I stand in front of Parker or Pratt like a nose tackle. Sometimes I still get frustrated and walk off, but it's treated as a kink of mine. "That's just Croft," Frankson says. The days go by without any serious disruption. The bile and acid never make it more than halfway up my throat. Christmas Eve rolls around. I hear Troy's body is going to be shipped home by relatives and buried someplace outside Philadelphia. His hands are still somewhere in the prison. I was foolish for having thought Bread might be laying a trap for me with his deal, but I had only thought so because I hadn't understood the real difference between me and Troy. He'd had to kill Troy to beat him.

If any of this were real, I might feel low about that. What is real is control. When I get out of here, I will have that. After a month, not having had it will seem like a strange dream. On the Inside, it's politics. I'd stolen from Bread. He had needed to hurt me for it, and he's done that. We've learned each other's limits and found those hard terms men come to in prison, the kind it's never quite possible to explain, elsewhere. Now it seems like whatever was so bad between us is finally over, and my wall calendar tells the whole story. I know that as I frown my way through the day, and when I wake up at 5am with my heart beating fast and watery. This is the way I want it. Whatever it took to get here, it's the right track. The only real thing. This is how I should've been thinking, all along. This is me.

8

The days come and go in a shadowed train. Sometimes they get stuck like a shirtsleeve on a nail and seem to tear long and slow.

There are so many holiday visitors the hacks give up on searching them carefully, and Santa brings a present for just about everyone. Stromm wears a Santa hat. New Years, a pedophile is lit on fire in his cell and burns up like a Roman candle. The first three days of the new year, there's the traditional seventy-two-hour lockdown so the hacks can catch up on paperwork, and I eat nine meals out of Styrofoam clams. It's a long stretch and a lot of time to think.

One thing you don't think about in my business is whether being a crook is worth it. Of course it is. The system is rigged. By the time you've done enough shift work to live the way they do in the commercials and magazines, your senses are so degraded that you're like a soldier on leave in Thailand. You can't do anything but blow it all. Crime can be self-preservation...you just wouldn't know it to look around, in here.

I get tired and almost sleep at night. A thin awareness remains. After a few days of this I'll sleep like a statue, and the cycle begins again. Comes to be I can feel the time, and that's not good. It's like an idiot that won't stop whispering to me. A subtle change can make the difference between someone who makes it and someone who gets out looking like he was experimented on by aliens. In my case, I've got so little time left to serve, it probably won't matter, anyway.

On a Monday mid-January, I fill up the doorway while a few of Bread's guys teach a lesson to a Mexican gang leader who transferred in and started stirring up trouble. Two short muscular Latinos covered in blue ink walk past a couple of times but disappear after I shake my head at them, real slow. Frankson, Dodd, and JoJo James come out of the Mexican's cell sucking air, and two of them walk off after a quick look around. Frankson sticks around to shake his swelling knuckles and swear at the broken heap inside the cell. When he works himself up enough, he goes back inside to kick the guy around some more. He comes out again and says to me, "I gotta get some ice on this hand and call my health plan. Hey Croft, you really never get high?"

It's a typical enough day.

I take a long shower after my shift in the furniture factory. My shoulders drop beneath the hot water; it's like stitches coming out. I enter the darkness behind my eyelids. I lean my head back and let the water cascade over my face. I slowly become lost in a cloud of heat, wallowing, keeping my eyes closed, breathing. Half an hour passes, I'm the last one left in the room, and that's what I'm still doing when they come.

I'm a castle but also enough of a con that I possess a sixth sense for movements of air and the sound of masses in a room, shadows I can't quite see. I'm facing the dirty tile wall beneath the showerhead when I sense the door coming open and the silk of cooler air on my calves. The echo of the room changes just a hair as figures move inside it, like someone shutting a velvet curtain in the dark. The few clean tiles reflect the light, and this reflection changes half a shade. Outside of a prison, these things would be below the level of perception. My eyes are slitted and my body is full of the tense energy of a man who lives with other men behind bars, nerve to nerve, skin to skin.

I sense them approach and then stop a few feet behind me. I know there's more than one.

I have a little time. There's no one, not even castles, in this prison who could walk right up on me without some hesitation. For a deck, the chances of killing me in a single stroke are small, even with an icepick or a real knife. They would know that. They would have to come inside and reset, take up positions. I try to remember who I saw guarding the door, outside. Stearne. Freshly striped lieutenant with a serious face, supposed to be on Lyman's roll. Doesn't mean he isn't on Bread's roll, too. Probably is.

I become more aware of the room, of the steam and the floor tiles that need re-grouting beneath my bare feet. I'm almost glad for this. Not afraid. Chance I'll turn around and they'll just run. Troy killed four at once and then five, including a case, before they took him down. I may do better. Blood moves in my chest and upper arms. My hands flex of their own accord; my neck grows as my jaw sets. It never enters my mind to wonder who they are; I let the cloud of possibilities float by, not grabbing onto it. I turn around, slowly, as if bored.

They're fully clothed, as I'd known they would be. They stand side by side between me and the way out. They don't flinch when I turn, and their faces are set like they've calculated exactly what they're up against, and this is their moment. Right away I can tell it's going to be uglier than I thought. Lyman and Noah stand there, Noah with his bat face, their shoes getting wet, looking at me.

Neither of them says anything for a long moment. Then Lyman says, "It ain't right."

I say, "Get out," then turn my face back into the shower stream, trying to relax again.

"It ain't," he repeats.

A vague pressure forms a mask around my eyes.

"You gonna let it go down like this? Not a word spoke? You and Willie was tight. You know who done it."

Noah says, "Only one motherfucker does anything round here, anymore."

"We gonna settle the score, Croft."

"You're not settling anything," I say.

"No?"

It's always a little odd discovering any real loyalty in a deck. There isn't much sense to it. From what I've seen, Troy had been like a drunk uncle to his deck. Willie treated his deck like friends on a good day, although I'd also watched him pass by them like he'd never seen them before.

"We gonna settle it, and you ought to help us."

"See him when we come in?" Noah chimes in, that lemon-sucking sourness in his voice. "He thought someone come to stick him."

"Anybody wants to stick me, they're welcome to try."

"That's right," Noah says. "You probly get shot trying to escape, like Troy."

"It ain't just us, man," says Lyman. "All Willie's boys. Some of Troy's. Some of Vanderventer's."

"You let white boys run with you now?"

"The enemy of my enemy," says Noah, "You big smart prick."

I turn enough to show them one of my eyes, and I see them resist the urge to step back.

"Which one of you masterminds is making the big plan?"

Lyman steps forward. "You. You are."

I laugh low in my throat.

"Would you take orders from anybody else?"

"I don't take them. I don't give them. Get lost." I turn away again.

There's a little cry in Lyman's voice. "It ain't *right*."

The pressure mask around my eyes hardens like the back of my face is full of calcium deposits and small tumors. "I'm going to give you five seconds."

Instead of leaving, Lyman steps closer. "You gettin out of here soon, that's good. But you goin out the wrong door. You just gonna forget all about this place and the people that helped you do your time?"

I round on him. "That's right. I'm gonna forget all about it, and all these stupid rat fucks in here, and all about you."

"And Willie."

"That's right. This place and everything that goes on here, it's not even real. It gets bought and sold every single day on the outside, a thousand times. It's not even a bad dream. It's *nothing*. You go on keeping score for nothing. Settle nothing. The only thing that's real is *out*."

Lyman stands there staring at me like I'm a ghost. His lip trembles, but still he starts to speak. "I'm not-"

My fist blasts through the tile wall of the shower room, scattering tile shards and a plume of dust that mixes with the water and washes away in a white paste. When I turn around again, they're gone. There is just Stearne, poking his blue-capped head inside.

If Lyman wants to claim I owe him favors, he's probably right. But he's wrong about everything else. Getting even for purely private reasons is small-minded. It's the way of all those convicts living out their lives in the hole or supermaxes like Mount Washington where they're lucky to get half an hour a day out of the cell, and where they slowly realize the insignificance of the piece of garbage they got even with. Getting even should be about keeping things smooth. Same reason I don't pulp the decks for insulting my intelligence. Who'd understand the message? And now I get these two, trying to put me on the hook. It surprised me, at first, but then, it's also surprisingly stupid.

My stomach feels a little off the rest of the day. It's touchy, lately. I cut myself shaving, next morning, and I have to stare at my hand until a little tremble goes out of it.

I find myself thinking about an odd case I'd known, years ago, Carp. Massive, bad complexion, friendly, shy. Had a couple of friends talked about what a nice guy he was, but out of their sight, everyone pushed him around. And the worse they got, the nicer he became, like he just hadn't proved himself gentle, yet. By the time I moved on, there was always this wince in his face and body, like the shadow of an upraised hand had just fallen over him. Sometimes he would just get tired suddenly and have to close his eyes in the middle of anything at all, even mid-sentence. Carp hadn't been slow, like some people had liked to say. He was a man of normal intelligence who'd made a mistake about human nature. You prove yourself with measurable quantities. That's all you can prove. That's the way it is.

A wet Seamax winter is underway. It's the kind of weather you don't think of as cold, at first. New transfers from the Dakotas and northern New England laugh at Seamax old timers when they talk about how cold they feel. But when spring comes, the new guys can't believe how long it takes to get the chill out of their bones.

My last winter of my last year. I have participated in no programs here, acquired nothing I want to keep, and have no friends. I'm clean. I examine myself in front of the polished metal in the weight pile and see again that even my skin is unchanged by this non-experience. I have no scars and no tattoos. I will return to the real world the way I left it.

I run in the yard on the coldest days when very few convicts go out. I take long showers and think I'll spend a day at a nice hotel when I get out, someplace I can get a sauna and a rubdown. The girls have to walk on my back to get at the deep muscles, and even then I'll have to have a stiff drink or two first to loosen things up. I have muscles high up in my back that feel like chunks of stale bread.

Nothing breaks the routine until the last Thursday in January.

I'd had another long shower before lockdown. My hair is still wet and the heat and steam are still coming off my body. I'm addicted to the pleasure of these showers, like so many others are on the Inside. All Bread's guys have a free pass to shower as often as they like. A cooker is slowly filling the cell block with the smell of burned macaroni and cheese. On top of the books on my shelf are a pair of pies I've been eating over the last couple of days, one pumpkin, one sweet potato, that Popeye's wife made me for Christmas, for helping him keep his job. A con offered me ten dollars for one bite, yesterday. This *small* world.

I'm sitting down to a bite in the dark like a kid with a girlie magazine and a flashlight when Nick Karoulas appears. He shows up outside my cell five minutes after lockdown, like some kind of ghost. Something's always up these days. Bread knows how to spin the wheel, but I'm not good enough to talk to personally, anymore. Nick stops an arm's length from the bars.

Used to be a nobody in a deck. He laughed when everybody else laughed and ducked when they ducked. He's blonde and has a hard face with a large bony skull but a soft, skinny body. Bread likes to shove him around – all in good fun – and try to punch him in the kidney, and Nick just shuffles awkwardly and tries to laugh. Anyone but Bread he would stab to death.

"Croft," he says.

I look at him. He's interrupting.

"Croft."

Something about his face or the way he's standing too far from my cell door. He doesn't want to be here. It goads me. My voice blends with the darkness. I say, "Did you know you can fit right through those bars?"

"What? No, I can't."

"Sure you can. I'll help."

He takes another step back although he was already out of reach.

"Croft, I came to tell you. You're gonna fight next Friday."

Bad joke. "What do you want."

"You're going to fight. Ruiz, man, you're going to fight him."

"I'm eating."

"I mean it. Bread says you're going to fight Ruiz. Ruiz gets a purse either way. You get a percentage."

I stand up and my plastic fork clatters to the floor. "I'm going to fight someone, alright."

"A percentage, man. Like it's not a pot, you own part of the action. Think about it, man. Like a score. And everyone makes out."

"Don't you talk to me about scores or money, you weasel."

Our conversation is slowly drilling through layers of my disbelief, the drill head getting closer to the hot magma on the other side. At this point, it hasn't quite broken through yet. Maybe it won't.

"It's not me, man. It's what he wanted me to tell you. I'm going, man. It's not me. I had nothing to do with it."

I move to the bars. "If I fight anyone, they're going six feet under."

Nick is moving away. "You have to, man. It's all set. Next Friday. There's a ton of money in it. Think about yours."

Not a convict anymore but a carney. Think about it, he says.

He starts leaving, waiting for me to protest. When I don't, it stops him. Nick knows my silence isn't agreement, that I have no intention of either responding or doing what he says. For a moment he stands there with his back to me, like he heard me mutter an insult under my breath. Then he comes stomping back, and he's red in the face.

"What did you think, you're some kind of free agent? You're a fucking day trader?"

I pull myself close to the bars of my cell. "If there's no deal, there's no deal."

"Wrong. You do what I do, what we all do. You do what you're told, or you know what happens."

Somewhere the Convict is making an ugly, raspy sound in my head – he's beginning to laugh.

"In a few hours, this door is going to open, Nick."

"No shit. You have just that long to get your head screwed on straight and not make things worse for yourself."

"They'll be worse, alright."

"It's no joke, Croft. You want to go in pieces, do exactly what you're thinking about. You fight next Friday. Welcome to the Max, motherfucker."

He starts walking away again, an angry righteousness in his walk. The Convict finds my shock hilarious.

The drill breaks through, and lava floods my skull. "Six feet under! Get back here!"

Nick turns to walk backwards, like he's going to blow a kiss.

My hands are wrapped around the bars. I try not to, but I yell, "Open this door!"

How predictable it suddenly seems. My own foolishness and how I'd gone along, swallowing my bile every day. I reach deep for the presence to calm myself and discover only broth and the fine grey silt you'd find at the bottom of a dead pond. It's taken all I've got just to keep going, to do the time this way. Maybe that's why I can't help but yell. "That's not the deal! Not the deal!"

Or do I mean to say – asks the Convict – that it's not fair?

From his dark corner in my head, The Convict is crooning. *Poor guy, is it unfair? A little unfair for you? Why don't you write a letter?* Something that was hanging loose on a single hinge for weeks suddenly breaks off and gets snatched out of the air by a murder of crows. The Convict laughs and wheezes and points his finger at me.

I can still see Nick walking backwards, sort of smiling now. "Sorry, man. I do my job. You do yours. Time to earn your keep, big boy."

He turns on his heel so his back is to me again, his arms swinging.

"It's going to be you, Nick, no one else! It's going to be you!"

I try to stop, but I'm running on the bitter yellow hatred of a creature that's just been killed, eyes lit poisonously, hissing at the pain in its own broken spine. That's what this anger is like. I hear people in the block stirring with the part of my hearing that isn't obstructed by the wail and pound of blood in my ears. A guard steps onto the tier. "What's going on?"

I pull on the bars, something I've never done before, really pull on them, and cakes of rust fall from the top of the housing. The lighter color against the darkness that was Nick's fading profile is gone, but I'm stuck against the bars like a fly, muscles jumping, eyes bulging, lips pulled tight over my teeth. A flashlight beam lands on me. Hard-soled shoes are stomping up the catwalk.

I hear myself yell, "Open this door!"

Convicts begin to whistle and shout in the dark.

"What the hell's the matter with you, boy? I'm not even going to count to one!"

"OPEN THIS DOOR!"

The Brains of the Operation
by Jason Palmer

"A brutal and unflinching prison-yard thriller, the follow-up gut punch to The Big Guy." -SPR

The flashlight comes closer until I can vaguely make out the guard behind it. My shouting brought him right over. He's one I've only seen a few times—clean and tight, with a mild voice he has to push out—the kind with an implacable temper. Eyes on me, he holds his handset upside down and barks into it: "One twenty-five."

The handset says, "Go ahead."

My hands grip the bars like they're electrified. Nick Karoulas keeps walking away and joins the darkness of the cell house. He's just informed me I'm going to be fighting in the carny circuit so Bread can run the gambling on it. Carny fighters are basically slaves. It's after lockdown, and he must have passed right by the guard, who didn't seem to see him.

"Need assistance at C two sixteen."

"C two six*teen*?"

"That's what I said."

He puts the light on my face and keeps his distance. Shoves the handset back onto his belt, says, "What the hell is your problem? Back up."

"Are you blind?"

"What?"

"Are you blind."

"I'm going to advise you to shut the fuck up."

Someone across the tier calls out, "Why don't *you* shut the fuck up?"

The guard whips around. "Quiet!"

Turns back to me. "You can shout all you want down in solitary."

My fingers relax, leaving stiff knuckles. I back into the darkness of my cell as if I can hide in it. Solitary—the Rook is in solitary, and I don't know how favors work in that part of the world, how a couple of cell doors get left open by accident. That's not what breaks through my immediate anger, though. The idea of solitary confinement—that sterile, silent nightmare with the solid cell doors—packs a nasty chill. Imagine the most senselessly wasteful, boring day of your life, multiply it times ten, and then multiply that times dozens or even hundreds of days. For guys on Birdman status, thousands. And wasted days are a worse poison for those with a better timepiece in their heads.

Even though I know this guard can't send me to solitary on his own authority, I still feel it.

At some point while he waits for backup, the guard clicks his flashlight off. I wonder whether he's decided to let things ride, but then I sense him waiting there, in the dark. Not for the last time, I wish Willie was still there, in the next cell. But Willie is gone. Bread saw to that. It's been two weeks since Lyman and Noah tried convincing me we should pay him back for it.

The door of the cell block opens a minute later, and more hard-soled shoes come walking across the lumpy concrete floor and clanging up the grated stairs.

"What's the problem?"

"About three hundred and twenty-five pounds of it, right here."

The light is back in my face.

"He started screaming to open the goddamn door."

The hacks are Marsten and another third-shift ghoul I don't know. Marsten steps close to the bars of my cell but talks over his shoulder to his pals: "You know, there's been a real shit smell coming from C Block lately."

"I'll say," says Flashlight.

In another cell, someone big makes his bedsprings creak.

"Maybe it's time they find out in here once and for all—"

The ghoul I don't know whispers something into Marsten's neck that makes him stop and reset. Then something happens that's a little eerie in the dark: I can see Marsten's pale face just well enough to see a grin curl the corners of his mouth as he looks at me. "Get your beauty rest, Champ," he says. "You're going to need it. Nobody's opening this goddamn door tonight."

They move off aways then, and I can hear Flashlight complaining to Marsten and Marsten not caring. He doesn't get paid to get excited on graveyards.

Champ. Going to need my rest. Guess I'm the last to know about the fight.

It makes sense for Nick to tell me right at lockdown because I'll have all night to calm down, and I'll be exhausted the next day, and that's exactly what happens. If I'd found out another time, I might have gone straight to Bread and turned him into a finger puppet, no matter who tried to stop me. But Bread has his long memory, and I have mine. He's going to pay, sooner or later, for putting me through a night when my brain felt like a boiling kettle of chili.

Men on the tiers heard the commotion last night, and they give me a wide berth as we stand count and shuffle off to chow in the light of a winter morning. I wonder how many of them know I'm supposed to turn carny and fight for their amusement. For some reason, I've spent a lot of my restless nights thinking about my rules: what I've made clear to everyone over the last four years. My prison version of privacy is the one thing I've built here. I can't tolerate the *idea* of Bread's fight, much less the fight itself. In the closeness of the night, it was suffocating.

In the chow hall, I look for two heads of blond hair at Bread's table, but him and Nick and the others in the circle are nowhere around. I can't tell whether I'm more disappointed or relieved. My spine feels like a lightning rod, and my head is floating on top of my neck like an angry balloon. For a while I've suspected that they have a hiding place; someplace only they have access to. I peer at their empty seats across a half dozen busy tables and wonder how Bread thinks he's going to make me fight at the time and place he wants me to. How's he think he's going to do it? My right eyelid twitches as I think about it. I'm sitting in a prison chow hall with a head like a pepper and a twitching eye.

At my table, I can tell they know, and I can feel them wondering whether it's true. Out of respect, they don't ask, but it's stuck in everyone's teeth. They'd know it's not my choice, but the same can be said of decks who end up putting on lipstick every morning after their shave. Then I'm pretty sure Blake tries to throw me a lifeline, in his way. He stops shuttling his spoon back and forth from his mouth and watches me. "What's the beef with Ruiz?"

Ruiz. Bread's second mail-order case, brought in to be a collector along with Fiero—and apparently to fight. I don't know what to say.

"It's something personal," Blake offers, giving me the right words to use.

The others at the table watch us and wait for a response.

"Sure," I say. It occurs to me to inform them that there isn't going to be a fight for any reason, but I also know I'm not seeing the whole picture yet. I keep quiet. The storm clouds roil in my brain. Telling me I'm going to fight means there are no more boundaries, and any understanding I thought Bread and I had is history, if it was ever real.

"It's not about the money," Blake says. There's just the faintest note of question, and perhaps even warning, in his voice.

Fighting one another for deck money and amusement is not done. But if I fight another castle in front of the decks because I've got a personal beef with him—and some people just happen to make money on it—that's shaky but not strictly against the code. But I don't have it in me to make excuses today, or even go along with one. I feel my eyes empty of all light. I go back to eating in my mechanical castle way, shoveling the food, just enough time to eat my large portion if I pack it in without tasting it. I feel that Blake trying to help me with an excuse makes me look even weaker, and I make it clear that it's not needed: I chew slowly, loudly, moving my jaw around like I'm grinding up bones, and I look neither at nor away from the castles at my table.

After chow, my gut feels like a graveyard. I head back to my cell, where bad ideas grip me for an hour at a time: I'm going to cripple Ruiz before he can make it to the ring. I'm going to kill Bread when he resurfaces. Maybe I'll ask around like I'm trying to find him, make him sweat. Then I remember I'm not supposed to be worried about some deck's frame of mind. I get up from my bunk and go to the tier 2 rail to look out. It will do me no good to try and guess Bread's strategy with everyone connected to the fight in hiding, but I wind up mulling things over anyway. This is the way prison goes.

Something will happen soon. I'll learn why I have no choice but to fight, and then I will or I won't. I wonder what I always do: doesn't anybody see how small-time it all is? For a smart crook or maybe a talented fraud, prison is like college. You want to graduate as soon as possible and start making the real money, and the people who are really successful at being there tend to flop on the outside. I wish myself luck explaining that to the decks. And I wait.

Turns out, I don't wait long.

Novels by Jason Palmer

THRASH

The Max novels

THE BIG GUY
THE BRAINS OF THE OPERATION
CROFT

Visit jasonpalmerfiction.com

NOBODY DOES IT ALONE. Special thanks to Allyson for staying hardcore and always pushing the envelope. The Stephensons and their open door were a light in the darkness. Without the Skipper, Gary Shepard, I couldn't have sailed through. I'm grateful for Josh Dees, a good partner on a bad beat. Without Tyler I might've just stayed home. Last but not least, thanks to Andy for rolling up his sleeves and getting in it.

A compulsive wanderer, Jason Palmer has lived in many US cities and traveled over much of North America, sometimes on the wrong side of the tracks, reading and writing constantly. He is the author of five novels, and his short works have been variously published, reprinted, and anthologized. He currently lives in Colorado Springs, Colorado.

Made in the USA
Middletown, DE
03 January 2023